BLOOD ON THE PLAINS

The boiling, churning waters tossed the keelboat around like a cork in a child's bath. With a sharp snap, Touch the Sky's pole became wedged between two boulders and broke. At the same moment, one of the Creoles manning the cordelles slipped on the sharp bank and tumbled down into the water, injuring his left leg.

Seeing that the Nose Talker was in no immediate danger of drowning, Touch the Sky leaped into the river, fought his way to the bank, and gripped the thick cordelle in the voyager's place.

"Heave!" Jackson shouted, fear replacing the surliness in his voice.

COMANCHE RAID

Again and again Black Elk brought his whip down, opening up lacerations all over Touch the Sky's body. Only when Black Elk's arm began to tire did the other warriors set upon him.

"Cry, Woman Face!" Wolf Who Hunts Smiling taunted Touch the Sky, breathing heavily from his exertions with the whip.

A moment later Wolf Who Hunts Smiling leaped back in rage when Touch the Sky hawked up a wad of phlegm and spat it in his face.

"Wolf Who Hunts Smiling!" Touch the Sky cried. "I warn you, best to kill me now, or I will turn your guts into worm fodder...."

Other *Cheyenne* Double Editions:
ARROW KEEPER/DEATH CHANT
RENEGADE JUSTICE/VISION QUEST

CHEYENNE

BLOOD ON THE PLAINS/ COMANCHE RAID

JUDD COLE

LEISURE BOOKS

NEW YORK CITY

A LEISURE BOOK®

January 1998

Published by

Dorchester Publishing Co., Inc.
276 Fifth Avenue
New York, NY 10001

ISBN 0-8439-4348-3

Printed in the United States of America.

BLOOD ON THE PLAINS

Prologue

Twenty winters before the Bluecoats fought against the Graycoats in the great war between white men, Running Antelope and his Northern Cheyenne band were massacred by pony soldiers at the Platte River. The lone survivor was Running Antelope's infant son. His Shaiyena name was lost forever. He grew up as Matthew Hanchon in the Wyoming Territory settlement of Bighorn Falls, adopted son of John and Sarah Hanchon.

The Hanchons loved him as their own and treated him well. But their love could not overcome the hatred many other settlers felt for Matthew. Tragedy struck in 1856, when Matthew turned 16 and fell in love with Kristen, daughter of wealthy rancher Hiram Steele. Matthew was viciously beaten by one of Steele's wranglers. Then Seth Carlson, a young cavalry officer with plans to marry Kristen, threatened to ruin the Hanchons' mercantile business unless Matthew cleared out for good.

But when he fled north to the Powder River and Cheyenne country, he was immediately captured by Yellow Bear's tribe and sentenced to death as a spy for the Long Knives.

But Arrow Keeper, the tribe's medicine man, had experienced a recent vision and recognized the birthmark buried past the youth's hairline: a mulberry-colored arrowhead, the mark of the warrior. According to Arrow Keeper's medicine vision, this tall youth was marked by destiny to lead his people in one great, final victory against their white enemy.

Arrow Keeper buried Matthew's white name and renamed the towering youth Touch the Sky. But Black Elk instantly hated the stranger—especially after Honey Eater, daughter of Chief Yellow Bear, made love talk with him. Black Elk's fiery-tempered cousin, Wolf Who Hunts Smiling, walked between Touch the Sky and the campfire—thus announcing his intention of killing the suspected spy.

Even after Touch the Sky and his white friend Corey Robinson cleverly saved the Cheyenne village from annihilation by Pawnee, he was not fully accepted by the tribe. Then whiskey traders invaded Indian country, led by the ruthless Henri Lagace.

Lagace kidnapped Honey Eater and threatened to kill her if the Cheyenne went on the warpath against him. A small war party, led by Black Elk, was sent into the heavily fortified white stronghold.

Touch the Sky was warned, in a medicine vision, that he must defy Black Elk's orders or Honey

Eater would die. He deserted the war party and infiltrated the white camp on his own. Honey Eater was freed and Touch the Sky killed Lagace. But much of his valor went unwitnessed, and many in the tribe remained unconvinced of his loyalty.

Their suspicions were heightened when he rushed back to the river-bend settlement of Bighorn Falls to help his white parents. Rancher Hiram Steele and Lt. Seth Carlson had first teamed up to drive the Hanchons out of the mercantile trade; now they had begun a bloody campaign to drive them from their new mustang spread.

Touch the Sky was torn in his loyalties. Chief Yellow Bear lay dying, and Honey Eater could not live alone if he crossed over to the Land of Ghosts—meaning she would have to accept Black Elk's bride-price and marry him if Yellow Bear died. But in the end Touch the Sky left, realizing his white parents' battle was his battle.

Assisted by his friend Little Horse, Touch the Sky defeated his parents' enemies. But seeing his parents and Kristen again left Touch the Sky feeling hopelessly trapped between two worlds, at home in neither. His tragic plight worsened when he returned to the Cheyenne camp. Not only had Yellow Bear died, forcing Honey Eater to marry Black Elk. But spies had watched Touch the Sky during his absence. They'd mistaken Touch the Sky's meetings with the sympathetic cavalry officer Tom Riley as proof the Cheyenne was a traitor to his people.

Arrow Keeper, acting chief since Yellow Bear's death, used his power to intervene and save the youth. Arrow Keeper still believed in the original vision which foretold Touch the Sky's greatness.

Now, he realized, the youth must seek the vision himself, and thus accept his destiny as a Cheyenne and resolve the agony of being the eternal outsider.

The old shaman sent Touch the Sky to sacred Medicine Lake for a vision quest. The journey became an epic struggle to survive Pawnee, starvation, flash floods, life-threatening wounds, a riled grizzly, and an assassination attempt ordered by Black Elk. But Touch the Sky finally experienced the key vision. Profoundly moved by the images and secrets of the Vision Way, he accepted once and for all his place as a Cheyenne.

When he came back to camp, Arrow Keeper announced that Touch the Sky had the gift of visions and would be trained in the shaman arts. Then Touch the Sky discovered to his joy that Honey Eater still loved only him despite her marriage to Black Elk. This strengthened his resolve. He still had many enemies, but he was home to stay. Anyone who wanted to drive him away now must either kill him or die in the attempt.

Chapter 1

"Now comes Catch the Hawk's band!" shouted the camp crier, racing up and down on his dappled gray pony between the lodges and tipis. "All hail our Shaiyena brothers!"

The tall youth named Touch the Sky joined the rest of those already gathered in a rousing cheer of welcome as the last of the ten far-flung Cheyenne bands rode into the temporary Tongue River Valley camp. Catch the Hawk's tribe, whose summer camp was on the Rosebud, broke into an answering chorus of whoops, shouts, and songs. The warriors had donned their single-horned crow-feather bonnets in honor of the chief-renewal ceremony.

"This is always the way it is when the Cheyenne people come together as one," explained Arrow Keeper proudly to Touch the Sky. The old medicine man's weather-lined face was divided by a wide smile. "The Cheyenne people live in widely scattered camps. Only during the chief-renewal or the Sun Dance ceremonies of the warm moons do they erect their lodges in one camp."

Touch the Sky watched, his keen black eyes wide with curiosity. He had a strong, hawk nose and wore his black hair in long, loose locks, except where it was cut short over his brow to keep his vision clear.

Already the newest arrivals were gathering by clans to set up their tipis. Besides the Cheyenne, the camp was swollen with visitors from other Plains tribes friendly to the Cheyenne: the Dakota, the Arapaho, the Cheyenne's Teton Sioux cousins.

"My blood is Cheyenne like yours, Father," said Touch the Sky, who had 18 winters behind him. "But so much is new to me. I fear I will make mistakes during the ceremonies."

Old Arrow Keeper nodded, pulling his red Hudson's Bay blanket tighter around his gaunt figure. The shaman had served as acting chief since the death of Chief Yellow Bear. Now the Council of Forty, known simply as the Headmen, had appointed Gray Thunder of the Wolverine Clan as their new chief. The chief-renewal was an occasion of grand feasting and dancing, of much gift-giving. The poor would profit handsomely, as it was an honored custom to give horses, robes, and other things of value to the needy.

"You will make some mistakes," Arrow Keeper said. "Mighty oaks do not spring up overnight. There is much to learn. It takes many winters to develop the proper spirit, to learn the skills of a tribe shaman.

"Think back to the time when you left your white parents and rode into our country alone. You made many mistakes as a warrior in training also. But today even your worst enemies within the tribe admit you are one of our best fighters."

These words heartened the youth. Arrow Keeper had recently announced that Touch the Sky was to be his shaman apprentice. With this decision, the elder had sent a clear message to Touch the Sky's many enemies within the tribe. Despite the claims of Black Elk, Wolf Who Hunts Smiling, and others, who still accused Touch the Sky of being a spy for the Bluecoats, Arrow Keeper believed in him. Though he had been raised by whites, Arrow Keeper was convinced he was straight-arrow Shaiyena.

Further conversation was difficult now as the cheering and shouting and singing swelled like a gathering avalanche. The cleared space in the middle of the huge makeshift camp was nearly a mile across. The lodges now numbered between five and six hundred, each facing east. The circle itself was a symbolic tipi with the open door to the rising sun.

Soon Touch the Sky would assist Arrow Keeper in conducting the huge Sun Dance, a celebration of the warm moons and the hunts to come as well as the annual tribute to the all-important horses. For this important occasion the tall youth had donned his best beaded leggings and clout. Several eagle-tail feathers adorned his war bonnet, one for each time he had counted coup against an enemy. He wore an elk-tooth necklace, and his face and body were painted with red-bank war paint. He would paint and dress again for the actual dance.

Arrow Keeper touched the youth's arm, then led him to his tipi. The shaman lifted the elkskin flap over the entrance. He stepped inside, then emerged again and handed something to Touch the Sky. The old man leaned close to his young friend's ear so he could be heard above the din.

"Here is a mountain-lion skin. I used to wear this in the parades. It is blessed with strong magic for anyone who has the gift of visions, as you have. Now I give it to you, little brother."

The tawny fur robe was soft and beautiful. When Touch the Sky tried to thank Arrow Keeper, the elder stopped him.

"We live on through the tribe. Boiled sassafras no longer comforts my old bones. Soon I must join Chief Yellow Bear in the Land of Ghosts. But the spirit of Arrow Keeper will live in Touch the Sky. Give this robe to your son, little brother, when your hair has turned to white frost like mine."

Upon mentioning Yellow Bear, Arrow Keeper had automatically made the cut-off sign as one did when speaking of the dead. Now, exhausted by the long days of celebration, the old shaman stepped back into his tipi to rest and prepare for the Sun Dance.

His mind full of many tangled thoughts, Touch the Sky headed toward his own tipi to put away his new gift. He was skirting the huge buffalo-rope pony corral when suddenly he drew up short. A trio of Cheyenne bucks had crossed his path. He recognized them as Black Elk, Swift Canoe, and Wolf Who Hunts Smiling.

"Our new 'shaman' has acquired some finery," said Black Elk, the oldest of the three.

He was a fierce young warrior with 22 winters behind him. One ear had been severed by a Bluecoat saber, then later sewn back on with buffalo sinew. This lent him an especially fierce aspect.

"Perhaps," added Black Elk, "he may use this skin as the bride-price for his own squaw instead of attempting to steal a bride from his betters."

Despite his impassive face, these mocking words were bitter. Black Elk had recently performed the squaw-taking ceremony with Honey Eater, daughter of the great peace chief Yellow Bear. Touch the Sky knew that the jealous Black Elk suspected him of holding Honey Eater in his blanket—making love talk to her despite her marriage.

Touch the Sky waited a few heartbeats until the first flush of anger had passed. He had recently made a sojourn to sacred Medicine Lake in the Black Hills. There, a powerful medicine vision had convinced him that his place was with the Cheyenne. Now he was determined to do everything he possibly could to convince his enemies he was a loyal Cheyenne, not a double-tongued spy for the hairy faces.

"Black Elk is my war leader and the brave who taught me the arts of combat," said Touch the Sky. "Thus, I freely admit he is my better. But never have I attempted to steal any brave's squaw."

These conciliatory words had little impact on Black Elk's scowl. But Touch the Sky was gratified to note that Black Elk's younger cousin, Wolf Who Hunts Smiling, seemed more subdued around him, less hateful and insulting than formerly.

They were still far from friends. But at least Wolf Who Hunts Smiling had revoked his long-standing threat to kill Touch the Sky. This was because Touch the Sky had bravely interceded during a Pawnee attack, saving the lives of Wolf Who Hunts Smiling and Swift Canoe. Now Wolf Who Hunts Smiling maintained a stone-eyed silence around him. But Touch the Sky knew the young warrior was intensely ambitious and he feared they must someday clash.

Swift Canoe, however, had not witnessed Touch

the Sky's bravery because he had lain in a creek bed wounded. And he still blamed Touch the Sky, wrongly, for causing the death of his twin brother, True Son. Unfortunately, Gray Thunder, the new peace chief, was a member of Swift Canoe's Wolverine Clan. Like Swift Canoe, Gray Thunder was suspicious of Touch the Sky.

Now Swift Canoe spoke up. "Arrow Keeper would teach this spy all the sacred secrets of our tribe. He will let him handle the sacred Medicine Arrows—yet he has contaminated himself forever by shedding tribe blood!"

"The only blood I have ever shed," said Touch the Sky, holding his face expressionless in the Indian way, "was spilled defending my life or protecting my tribe. I had nothing to do with the death of your brother."

"You speak in a wolf bark, white man's dog!"

Touch the Sky felt warm blood creeping into his face. Before he could reply, a familiar figure glided up close beside him.

"If it is three against one, brother," said his friend Little Horse, "I am here to help even the fight."

Little Horse was small, but quick and sure in his movements and built sturdy like a war pony. His steadfast loyalty to Touch the Sky had cost him friends in the tribe. But no one doubted his courage or ability in battle.

Copying the elders, Touch the Sky stepped back and folded his arms to show he was at peace. "There will be no fight, brother. This is a time of rejoicing. Come! Let us prepare for the Sun Dance."

Several naked Cheyenne children were playing near the river bend when the *Sioux Princess*, its sail as flat as a collapsed tipi cover, inched its way into the turn.

Some of the children dropped their toy bows and willow-branch shields, fleeing back toward the huge makeshift camp. Others just stood staring, their mouths dropping open in surprise as the huge keelboat loomed closer.

The *Sioux Princess* flew a white truce flag. She was 55 feet long, with shallow sides that sloped inward. These formed a pen for the horses and mules grouped tightly behind a plank cabin amidships. The boat was propelled upstream, depending on conditions, by its 22 oars, by poles thrust against the bottom, by two long ropes called cordelles—or, when fate chose to smile on the overworked crew, by a square sail filled with favoring wind.

But today there was no favoring wind. The river was too narrow at this point for proper use of the oars, the bottom too uneven for easy poling. So the mostly Creole French crew, hired on in New Orleans, manned the cordelles from either bank. Laboriously, muscles straining, they tugged the heavily laden boat against the current.

Wes Munro, a thin, hard-knit, rawboned man with the butts of two British dueling pistols protruding from his sash, stood in the prow. His face was clean-shaven, his collar-length salt-and-pepper hair clean and evenly trimmed, his linsey clothing immaculate. But his eyes—as flat and hard as two chips of obsidian—belied his genteel appearance.

His hands were folded atop a one-pounder cannon. Spaced at regular intervals around the rest of the heavily armed boat were swivel-mounted flintlocks that fired eight-ounce balls.

"Heave into it, you frog bastards!" shouted a

man behind Munro, calling out across the river to the crew on the banks straining over the cordelles. "You pack of spineless city squaws, *heave!*"

Hays Jackson lowered his voice and said to Munro, "Must be a big powwow. Christ, look how many red devils! This ain't no reg'lar summer camp marked out on the map."

Jackson was thickset, short, but built like a nail keg. His small eyes were set too close together. A nervous tic kept his left eye perpetually winking at whomever he spoke to.

Munro nodded as he waved to the children who still remained, curiously staring.

"Whatever's going on, it's no war council. We need replacements for those three men we lost in the Mandan raid. Time to announce our arrival."

The one-pounder was always kept loaded with black powder. Munro removed a flint and steel from the possibles bag on his sash and sparked the touch hole. A moment later the cannon exploded, belching black smoke and smoldering wadding. Its cracking boom echoed out over the calm river.

With terrified screams, the remaining children dropped their toy weapons and raced up the bank toward the safety of their people.

Hays Jackson threw back his head and laughed. His few remaining teeth were stained brown from tobacco. "Lookit them little red niggers scatter!"

Then he shouted out to the crew, "Snub the ropes to them cottonwoods, you raggedy-assed Pope worshippers!"

"Good thing they don't palaver much English," said Munro, "or they'd have opened your throat by now."

"Them lubbers?" Jackson hawked up a wad of phlegm and spat it overboard. "They wouldn't say boo to a goose, the white-livered cowards. You seen what a pack of wimmen they was when the Mandan hit us. Why, even that old codger we hired on at Bighorn Falls has got better oysters on him!"

At the booming roar of the cannon, the riotous camp had fallen silent. The Indians were more curious than afraid. Since the Fort Laramie accord seven winters ago, in the year the whites called 1851, keelboats had become a common sight in the Wyoming Territory. That crucial 1851 council had guaranteed the Cheyenne and Arapaho a broad tract of land that stretched from western Kansas to the toes of the Colorado Rockies. But it had also granted to the palefaces unrestricted transit rights across the territory.

Touch the Sky was among the first braves to reach the water. He noticed the two white men on deck, the drunken Creoles scattered along the banks, the horses and mules clustered in their shallow pen.

Then his eyes met those of a bearded old man standing amongst the animals. He was dressed in buckskin shirt and trousers with a slouch beaver hat.

A shock of recognition made Touch the Sky smile wide: It was his friend Old Knobby, the hostler from Bighorn Falls! Touch the Sky had been his friend back in the days when the Cheyenne youth was called Matthew Hanchon and lived among the whites.

"Knobby!" he called out, racing closer to the river.

Then he drew up short, confused and troubled.

Old Knobby had clearly recognized him. But now he made a quick, desperate gesture toward the other two white men, warning the youth with his eyes to stay quiet and pretend they were strangers to each other.

Then Old Knobby deliberately turned his back on his former friend, and Touch the Sky realized that trouble was in the wind.

Chapter 2

Old Knobby watched, hidden amongst the horses in his charge, as Hays Jackson barked out orders to the crew, mixing English with bad French. Crates were ripped open and merchandise heaped on the deck: gaudy military-surplus medals, bright beads, blankets, mirrors, sugar, coffee, tobacco, powder and ball and gun patches.

Knobby had been as surprised as the Cheyenne youth when he recognized his young friend Matthew Hanchon—Touch the Sky, the former mountain man remembered now. For Matthew's friend Corey Robinson had told him the youth's new Cheyenne name. But Knobby had seen enough, since beginning this ill-fated journey, to realize that Wes Munro and Hays Jackson spelled serious trouble to the red nations—and to anyone else who tried to block their trail.

After what Knobby had already seen, he sensed

it was a dangerous business to let these ruthless hardcases know that Touch the Sky knew him—or that the youth understood English. The best way to survive around men like this was by not calling attention to yourself.

Knobby had recently closed down his feed stable in Bighorn Falls and hired on as hostler at the mustang spread of John and Sarah Hanchon, Touch the Sky's adoptive white parents. The Hanchon spread was thriving now that their Cheyenne boy had whipped the gunmen Hiram Steele had hired to drive them out.

When Munro and Jackson had sailed into the Wyoming Territory, offering top dollar for good horseflesh for their journey, all had seemed well. Munro had presented credentials identifying him as an official with the United States Indian Department. This was a "goodwill" voyage, Munro had explained, to pour oil on the troubled waters of white man-red man relations.

Munro had offered Knobby a handsome salary to accompany them temporarily as hostler, and John Hanchon had readily agreed—Munro seemed friendly enough, and Hanchon welcomed any attempt to improve life for the Indians, especially now that his adopted son lived among them. Despite the fact that he had been forced to kill several of them in his younger days, Knobby too respected much about the red man and had learned many of their ways.

But then the *Sioux Princess* had anchored at the friendly Arapaho village of Chief Smoke Rising. And Knobby had soon learned that he was working for ruthless murderers who had a secret agenda of their own.

Munro had welcomed Smoke Rising aboard the

keelboat and showered him with gifts. But Knobby, ignored and unobserved, had also seen Munro trying to convince the old chief to sign some kind of document. Smoke Rising, who spoke some English, had remained friendly enough. But he'd stubbornly refused to sign the "talking paper."

Munro had not pressured the chief. But at a high sign from his boss, Hays Jackson had accompanied Smoke Rising ashore. Knobby had followed them and watched, in the moonlit darkness, as Jackson easily overpowered the ailing chief and smothered him to death with his own blanket. Munro had later concluded his mysterious deal with a rebellious subchief named Red Robe, who affixed his mark to the document.

Now, as old Knobby watched the braves crowd together along the shoreline, he realized the Cheyenne tribe was in trouble too. *All* the Plains Indians were. Somehow, despite the risk, he had to meet with Touch the Sky and warn him.

"I bring friendly greetings from the Great White Council in Washington," said Wes Munro. "These gifts are to show that the red man is brother to the white."

Munro spoke in the informal mixture of Cheyenne and Sioux tongues which was understood by most Plains Indians tribes. He and Chief Gray Thunder, surrounded by Arrow Keeper and the clan headmen, stood before the same hide-covered lodge where the chief-renewal had recently taken place. Gray Thunder had folded his arms over his bone breastplate to show the white man he was received in peace.

Touch the Sky, still deeply troubled by Old Knobby's strange behavior, watched from a distance. He had expected to be called forward to translate. Then he realized this neatly dressed white man spoke the Indian tongue with passable skill.

"Your gifts I welcome on behalf of my tribe. But these are indeed strange words," responded Gray Thunder. "The white man brother to the red? Then is it the white man's way to kill his brothers? To slaughter unarmed women and children in their sleep? To place a bounty on his brothers' scalps? And when the paleface hiders destroy our buffalo herds—is this too brotherly love? I would need to live another lifetime to understand such a cruel and murderous love."

The headmen murmured their approval of these words. Gray Thunder was still a powerful, vigorous warrior, though well past his fortieth winter. Even now, when the clan fires were lit and the clay pipes filled, the young warriors spoke with awe of his exploits against the Crow and Pawnee and Ute.

Nor could Touch the Sky in fairness resent Gray Thunder's coldness toward him. A good chief represented the collective will of his tribe, not his own feelings. Many in the tribe simply did not accept Touch the Sky, though few denied his skill and courage in battle.

"These sad things you speak of," said Munro, "are true enough. But they are the work of only a few whites. Do you stop eating all berries on the bush because a few are rotten? Are there not evil Indians who kill their own and steal from their people? The Great White Council wants peace throughout the land."

"Peace?" said Gray Thunder. "To the hair-faces this is only a word, a thing of smoke! The red nation was once at peace with the white. But peace was not good enough. Those Indians who choose the path of peace are told to stop hunting, to grow gardens like women. They are herded away to barren lands no white man wants. They are forced to dress like whites and pray to the white man's God. Peace is not worth such a price!"

Again the headmen murmured their approval.

"Seven winters ago, in 1851," said Munro, "your great Chief Yellow Bear"—here Munro made the cut-off sign for speaking of the dead, which impressed all the Cheyenne observers—"and many other chiefs signed the talking paper with the Bluecoats at the soldier house called Fort Laramie. That paper promised a vast and permanent territory for your people, a rich and beautiful land. Has the Great White Council east of the river called Great Waters ever tried to steal that land back?"

"No," said Gray Thunder, "certainly not all of it at one blow. But we are like birds who are told, 'You may have this limb, and this limb, for your nest. Only, we will cut down limbs and strip bark all around you.' The paleface hiders destroy our herds, and the Bluecoat pony soldiers build their soldiertowns in the midst of our best hunting grounds."

Munro had already decided this was a bad time to carry out the main part of his scheme. Clearly some huge ceremony was taking place, judging from the finery of the braves and the vast numbers of Indians congregated. Many chiefs could be bribed, but not when they were surrounded by their headmen. He would have to try again later—one way or the other, he would succeed.

Munro was a former "long hunter" from the Cumberland Gap. He could speak smatterings of many Indian tongues, and was familiar with Indian customs. Thus he had proved instrumental in the tricky negotiations which eventually had wrested a veritable nation from the Southeastern tribes.

After helping to swindle the Cherokee, Chickasaw, Choctaw, and Creeks out of their homelands, he had proved his worth to friends in high political places—including Missouri Senator Leigh Hammond, a stump-screamer whose considerable capital was behind this illegal expedition. Now, as Gray Thunder said, the once-proud tribes back East were farming and wearing shoes and answering roll calls like prisoners. And white land speculators had grown wealthy.

So now Munro was following the advice of a popular sentiment of the day: *The sun travels west, and so does opportunity.*

"I have listened carefully to your words," he told Gray Thunder. "I will speak the things you say before the Great White Council in Washington. I respect the red man. And I respect you, Chief Gray Thunder. I have counted the eagle tail feathers in your bonnet."

Gray Thunder's war bonnet trailed nearly to the ground, one feather for each time he had counted coup or slain an enemy.

"Perhaps you do truly respect the red man," Gray Thunder said. "You have troubled yourself to learn our tongue. Few whites do this. Though I fear it can do no good, I am grateful that you will speak for us at the white council. I do not deny that there are some good men among the palefaces. But there are never enough good men to stop the bad.

"Again, on behalf of my people, I thank you for these fine gifts."

Munro had given much away on this trip. But he knew the Indians had given much more. It had been the same almost everywhere he sailed. On the Missouri, the Platte, the North Platte, the Sweetwater, the Yellowstone, the Powder, the chiefs, or sometimes any brave calling himself a war leader, had affixed their marks to contracts which gave up the Indian homelands, millions of acres, for an annual payment amounting to a few wagonloads of trinkets.

Munro had felt it coming back in the 1840s. That was when the expansionists began to argue that it was absurd for the geographical unity of the U.S. to be broken up by groups of wild Indians. At the very least, they argued, the transportation routes must be cleared—an argument that especially pleased the railroad promoters.

And an argument, Munro knew, which was indeed true. Travel in the West was hard and dangerous. Places were god-awful far apart, with water often scarce. Sand wore out wooden axles, and green lumber shrank in the dry air. The sympathetic public back East was in an uproar over the terrible sufferings of the "handcart Mormons" and the immigrants who'd died by the hundreds in the massacre at the grassy swale called Mountain Meadows.

Now public sentiment called for a transcontinental wagon road first, to be followed by a railroad if the wagon road proved itself. And Senator Hammond already knew the proposed route, thanks to insiders on the key Congressional committee. It would follow the Platte Valley-South Pass-Humboldt River route, right through the heart of Plains Indian homelands.

And even if the railway plan failed, Senator Hammond was behind the not-yet-passed Homestead Act. This would grant 160 acres of Western land to settlers at $1.25 per acre—and Munro planned to own many of the best land parcels, Indians be damned.

"Gray Thunder," he said, "I have one request. Several sleeps ago, while my crew was freeing our boat from a sandbar on the Platte, we were raided by Mandan renegades. Three of my men were killed. I need replacements to man the poles and oars, the towing ropes.

"If you will loan me three of your strong young bucks to complete our journey, I will pay your tribe handsomely in new guns and ammunition. They will be gone perhaps for the duration of two or three moons. Then they will return to your tribe when my boat sails back to the St. Louis settlements."

Gray Thunder listened in silence, his face impassive. "I have no authority to grant or deny your request until I have spoken of this matter at council. I will speak with my headmen at the Council of Forty. However, I do not think they will approve such a plan. It is not the Shaiyena way to leave one's tribe. Still, I will give voice to your request. I will also tell the headmen you appear to speak one way to the red man, not with a double tongue."

Munro nodded. "*Ha-ho, ha-ho,*" he said in Cheyenne. "I thank you. I will wait aboard my boat for your decision. And I leave an offering to this place."

Munro opened his possibles bag and scattered rich brown tobacco on the ground. These Cheyenne words and gestures further impressed Touch the Sky and the other observers.

But even as Touch the Sky watched Munro return toward the river, a pebble bounced off the Cheyenne's back. Startled, he glanced toward his left.

Old Knobby peered out from behind a gnarled cottonwood, his grizzle-bearded face troubled. He gestured toward Munro, then bent his hand in Indian sign talk for the crooked arrow: the symbol of the liar.

Then Knobby cocked his head back toward a cedar copse behind him. Touch the Sky nodded once, slipping away to meet his old friend.

Chapter 3

"Well, cuss my coup if it ain't young Matthew!" exclaimed the old mountain man when the youth joined him. "Only, I best call you by your Cheyenne moniker now, Touch the Sky. I reckon *this* child never figgered on seein' you agin. You got some growth on you, tadpole, since I last seed you. Collected some battle scars too, by beaver!"

This was a reference to the gnarled mass of burn scar covering Touch the Sky's stomach—a legacy of his long night of torture in the camp of the whiskey trader Henri Lagace. There was also a jagged knife scar high on his chest. This had been inflicted by a white sentry after Wolf Who Hunts Smiling had deliberately alerted him in hopes of seeing Touch the Sky killed.

"I heerd Munro spilling all that chin music jist now about respect for the red man," said Knobby. "Respect. Pah! This hoss'll be ear-marked and hogtied iffen that murdering devil and his partner Hay Jackson ain't lower than snakeshit!"

Quickly, Old Knobby explained everything: that he now worked for John Hanchon and had hired on temporarily to accompany the keelboat crew on their "goodwill" voyage.

"Right from the get-go," said Knobby, "it made this hoss plain oneasy to see them two palaverin' in secret with subchiefs and givin' weapons to raggedy-assed renegade braves. I wanted to pack my possibles and git the hell out. But I figgered they might track me down and do for me. Then I seed with my own eyes when Jackson kilt Chief Smoke Rising pure as gumption. I doan know 'zacly what them two got on the spit. But it means bad cess for the red man."

Touch the Sky had listened with eager joy to the news that his adoptive parents' mustang ranch was now thriving. But the rest of Knobby's report left him full of cold apprehension.

Touch the Sky spoke in English. The words felt odd and stiff on his tongue after all this time without practicing them.

"My only friend among the elders," he said, "is Arrow Keeper, the tribe shaman who protects the Medicine Arrows. I'm his helper now, and we have to be present soon at the Sun Dance ceremony. But I'll go to him now and tell him what you've told me."

Knobby approved this with a nod, removing his slouched beaver hat for a moment to mop the sweat from his forehead. A patch of hideless bone at the top of his skull marked the spot where a Cheyenne warrior had almost raised the mountain man's scalp.

"You do that, sprout. This child best git back

afore he's missed. But jist you mind. That-air Munro and his queer-blinkin' pard Jackson will kill a man as casual as you or me'll let daylight into a prairie chicken. Doan go lookin' for your own grave!"

Touch the Sky nodded. While Knobby threaded his way through the trees toward the river, the youth sought out old Arrow Keeper at his tipi. The shaman was painting and dressing for the upcoming ceremony. He had donned his crow-feather war bonnet and his magic panther skin that was said to make Bluecoat bullets go wide. It was decorated with porcupine quills, feathers, leather fringes, and hair from enemy scalps.

The shaman frowned when he saw that Touch the Sky was not yet painted or dressed.

"Little brother, have you eaten strong mushrooms? The Sun Dance begins soon and you still wear your clout and leggings. You are one of the Dance Priests."

"I know, Father. But I would speak with you first before I dress."

"I have ears for your words. Speak them."

Touch the Sky repeated everything Old Knobby had told him. While he spoke, the cracked-leather seams in Arrow Keeper's face deepened.

"A word-bringer recently arrived from Smoke Rising's camp with word of his death," said Arrow Keeper. "There was no sign of violence, and his tribe assumed the old man had simply tired of life and given up his spirit to Maiyun. If, as your pale-face friend claims, he was smothered, this could have been done without marks. Now their acting chief is Red Robe."

Arrow Keeper was deeply troubled by Touch the Sky's report. There would be no reason for the white who spoke these things to be lying, and Red Robe was a notorious hothead who ruled by intimidation more than respect. It all made sense.

For a moment his eyes cut to the coyote-fur pouch resting atop his buffalo robes, as if drawing strength from it. Touch the Sky followed his glance. He knew that pouch held the four sacred Medicine Arrows. For these was Arrow Keeper named, in honor of his important mission to protect the four arrows with his very life, to keep them forever sweet and clean. The fate of the Medicine Arrows was the fate of the entire tribe. If the Arrows were sullied, the tribe was sullied; if they were lost, the tribe was lost.

And Touch the Sky knew that some day, when Arrow Keeper crossed over to the Land of Ghosts, the task of protecting the sacred arrows would pass on to him.

"Little brother, this man Munro seemed straight-arrow. He seemed to speak one way to Gray Thunder. Do you trust this white man named Knobby?"

Without hesitating, Touch the Sky nodded. "With my life. He has many winters behind him, Father, but his brain is strong and clear like yours. He is brave and true. Though he has fought and killed red men in his youth, he respects them. And he once saved my life when a Bluecoat officer meant to draw his weapon and shoot me."

Arrow Keeper nodded, his red-rimmed eyes pouchy with weariness. "Go now and prepare for the Sun Dance. Quickly. I will speak with Gray Thunder. But I fear the tribe is in grave danger. Last night, in a medicine dream, I saw blood on the Sacred Arrows!"

* * *

This season, as it was every ten years, the annual Sun Dance was combined with the chief-renewal dance, making it an especially important and grand occasion.

Arrow Keeper had carefully explained to Touch the Sky that the Sun Dance was not only to welcome the coming of the warm moons—it was also the Cheyenne tribute to their ponies, the most important element of their survival as Plains warriors. Today a newborn pony, the "gift horse," would be dedicated to Maiyun, the Good Supernatural.

Touch the Sky had been with the tribe long enough to attend two Sun Dances. But now Arrow Keeper was training him in the shaman arts, and this was his first occasion as a Sun Dance Priest. His nervousness was so great that, for the time being, the new danger Knobby spoke of was pushed to the back of his thoughts.

The drummers had begun late that morning, beating out a steady rhythm on hollow logs with their stone war clubs. Touch the Sky had donned his war bonnet, his new mountain-lion skin, and his best quilled and beaded moccasins. He had painted his face as if for battle: his forehead yellow, his nose red, his chin black. He had tied bright pieces of red cloth into his long, loose black locks.

Touch the Sky had carefully rehearsed his part with Arrow Keeper. Nonetheless, beads of nervous sweat felt like lice crawling through his scalp as all eyes turned upon him and old Arrow Keeper when they marched into the center of the camp clearing.

"Bring out the gift horse!" Arrow Keeper shouted in his gravelly but powerful voice, officially opening the ceremony.

This honor fell to Honey Eater as the daughter of their departed chief, Yellow Bear. Dressed in her finest doeskin dress, one adorned with shells and stones and gold coins for buttons, she led the bandy-legged roan colt into the center of the clearing by its buffalo-hair bridle.

Despite his nervousness, Touch the Sky was struck by Honey Eater's frail beauty—her magnificent black hair was braided in fresh white columbine. The high, prominent cheekbones were so perfect they might have been sculpted by the finest artist on the Plains. The long, thick eyelashes curved sweetly against them when she closed her eyes.

Arrow Keeper staked the gift horse in the exact center of the camp circle. Then Touch the Sky measured off ten paces from the pony—one pace for each of the ten main Cheyenne bands. Then he knelt and made a fire. When the flames leaped high like dancing spear tips, he lay four pieces of calico radiating out from the fire in the four cardinal directions of the wind.

At a word from Arrow Keeper, Honey Eater began the actual dance by singing a holy song. Her sweet, clear voice rang out with the purity of fine crystal. By the time she finished, a captivated hush had fallen over the entire camp. The air seemed to fairly spark with expectation.

Now, by custom, it was Arrow Keeper's task to call forth a lone brave to dance first by himself—one who had proven his bravery many times.

"Black Elk!" he shouted. "Begin the dance!"

The young war chief, fiercely magnificent in his full battle rig, stepped forth. First he and Arrow Keeper smoked the holy medicine pipe, lit only for this occasion. The drummers picked up their tempo and chanted *"Hi-ya hi-ya!"*—the Cheyenne war cry—over and over in a sing-song cadence. Black Elk danced in an ever-tightening circle around the gift horse, kicking his feet high and chanting with the drummers.

Black Elk finished his solo dance. Then, as the Dance Law required, he made a public recitation of all his coups in battle. When the war leader had finished describing his heroism, he turned toward their new peace chief and solemnly proclaimed the ritual words:

"Gray Thunder! As I have done it, so must you protect the people!"

Now, for the first time, the entire tribe raised a shrill cry of praise and began to dance together as one.

Touch the Sky heaved a great sigh of relief. His official duties as a Dance Priest were over. Now he was free to dance and rejoice with the others. The powerful and solemn ceremony had filled him with awe and drawn him close to the rest. He experienced a rare feeling of harmony, of oneness with the tribe. And when he smiled and nodded to his fellow Cheyenne, they smiled and nodded back.

Today, at least, he belonged!

But his new sensation of joy was fleeting.

During the course of the dance, purely by chance, he and Honey Eater were jostled close together by other dancers. This was the first time in a long while that they had found themselves so physically close to one another.

He stopped dancing, staring into the bottomless dark purity of her huge, wing-shaped eyes.

She too stopped dancing, matching his rapt gaze.

For a moment there was nothing else: no rhythmic drumming, no sing-song cadence of the dancers, only the two of them, locked in their forbidden love. Inside Touch the Sky, it was as if a dam had burst, and all the old feelings of love and desire burst forth, overwhelming him.

An iron grip like eagle talons fell on his shoulder, jolting him back to harsh reality.

He turned his head to confront the enraged, glowering face of Black Elk, who had witnessed their intimate moment of communion.

Quickly, Honey Eater spun away, resuming her high-kicking dance steps. But it was too late to palliate her husband's jealous rage.

"I have words for you, buck—now! Meet your war chief down by the river!"

Chapter 4

The dancers paid scant attention when the two young Cheyenne braves made their way through the crowded clearing. Black Elk remained several paces ahead of Touch the Sky as they reached the line of cottonwoods separating the clearing from the placid river.

Black Elk took care to avoid the anchored keelboat, aiming toward a thicket just beyond a sharp dogleg bend in the river. Only when the two Cheyenne were alone, safe from all prying eyes and ears, did the war leader face his subordinate and speak.

"Would you steal my ponies?" he demanded.

Confusion clouded Touch the Sky's dark eyes. "What does Black Elk mean by this odd question?"

"He means to be answered, Cheyenne! Would you steal my ponies?"

"You know I would not."

"Good. And would you steal my blankets, my buffalo robes?"

"Better to ask if a wolf would sleep with a rabbit! I cannot place these words in my sash."

Black Elk's eyes snapped sparks. His leathery hunk of sewn-on ear made him seem especially fierce. "Soon enough I will speak words you may carry off with you. But now, answer me. Would you steal my blankets and robes?"

"Not even if I were freezing!"

"And my meat racks, would you steal from them if you were starving?"

"I would not."

Black Elk nodded. "I believe you speak the straight word. I believe you would never steal these things. Yet you would steal my squaw from me, and do it in front of my face!"

"This is strong-mushroom talk. I would steal *nothing* that belongs to you—or any other member of my tribe."

"You lie like a hairy-faced Bluecoat, Touch the Sky! Just now, I saw how your eyes coveted Honey Eater. Why, the Bowstring Soldiers who enforce the Dance Law might have punished you had they seen you stop dancing without leaving the clearing first. You know this is not permitted, yet you were so full of thoughts for Honey Eater, your brain became tangled!"

"*She* stopped dancing too!"

As soon as he spoke the defiant words, Touch the Sky regretted them. Hot blood flowed into Black Elk's face, flushing his clay-colored skin even darker.

"Yes, she stopped too. Arrow Keeper is right to see the shaman's power in you. Long have you held her in your spell and charmed her as a snake might charm a bird."

"No! I—"

"Your war chief is still speaking, be silent! I do not completely blame Honey Eater. She is a woman, and women are weak in matters of the heart. This is why our unmarried maidens wear knotted ropes below their waist to protect them from the rut. It is the man's job to be strong, to do the right and honorable thing according to our Cheyenne way.

"*You* are the culprit, Touch the Sky! It is you who plays the fox, you who beguiles her. The cow only receives—it is the bull who mounts and penetrates."

Now anger began to kindle in Touch the Sky's keen eyes. "This talk of rutting and bulls mounting dishonors both myself *and* your good, chaste wife. Neither I nor Honey Eater have given you cause to speak so recklessly."

"Would you swear this thing?"

"Gladly, if only for Honey Eater's sake."

"Wait here," said Black Elk.

In a moment he was gone, disappearing rapidly beyond the thicket. Before long he returned. Now he carried a smoothly finished flap of doeskin. Four arrows had been drawn on it with claybank paint, two rising vertically and two more crossing them horizontally.

"You know what these represent?" said Black Elk.

Touch the Sky nodded.

"These are the Sacred Arrows. Swearing on this painting is no different than swearing on the Arrows themselves. I will say this much for you, tall warrior. On matters not concerning Honey Eater, you have always spoken one way, the straight way. I do not believe you would speak in a wolf bark while your hand is on these."

"You are right, I would not."

"Then touch them now and swear this, that you have *never* held Honey Eater in your blanket for love talk since she became my bride."

Without hesitating even the space of an eyeblink, Touch the Sky did so.

For a moment, some of the clouds seemed to clear from Black Elk's brow. But when Touch the Sky started to remove his hand, Black Elk grabbed it and held it in place.

"We have not had done yet. Swear *this* thing too, that you will *never* hold her in your blanket so long as you live."

These words caught Touch the Sky by surprise. Black Elk's strong grip trapped his hand in place. The two warriors faced off for the space of several heartbeats, their eyes locked in mutual challenge.

How, Touch the Sky agonized, could he ever swear such a thing? Had he not placed a rock in front of his tipi, swearing to Honey Eater that his love would melt only when that rock too melted? More important—did she not steal away alone each day to check that rock, to make sure it had not melted? Though Cheyenne law and the weight of tribal opinion opposed their love, it was a true and eternal love. And true love kept itself alive by feeding on one thing only—hope. Hope that somehow, some way, against all odds, the lovers would someday be together.

Chief Yellow Bear's prophetic words, spoken from the Land of Ghosts during Touch the Sky's powerful vision at Medicine Lake, echoed again in his mind: *I have seen you bounce your son on your knee, and I have seen you shed blood defending that son and his mother.*

His mother . . . he had no proof she would be Honey Eater. But neither did he have proof she would not be.

With a sudden surge of strength that surprised Black Elk, Touch the Sky tore his hand away. Now the blood of anger filmed the younger warrior's cycs. His mouth was a determined slit.

"Never! Black Elk asks too much. I have sworn that his bride has been faithful, that I have respected his marriage vows. I will swear to nothing else."

Black Elk's rage was instant. A huge vein in the side of his neck swelled with angry blood. In a moment his bone-handle knife was in his hand.

"You squaw-stealing dog! Now swear with your blade!"

Touch the Sky leaped back, at the same time drawing his lethally honed obsidian knife from its sheath.

"I would never stain the Sacred Arrows by being the first to draw Cheyenne blood," he told Black Elk. "But I have seen how sick jealousy has ruined Black Elk's manly goodness. There was a time when, though covered with hard bark, you were always fair and just.

"Then, when I journeyed to Medicine Lake, you gave in to your jealous, diseased fancies. You sent your cousin and Swift Canoe to murder me in cold blood! This was the act of a coward, not a warrior. Now I will defend myself as any warrior must. Come at me, then, I am for you! This day one of us goes under!"

With a snarl like an infuriated wildcat, Black Elk leaped at him. Touch the Sky used his war chief's own momentum against him, dropping quickly onto his back and lifting his feet to catch Black Elk's stomach. He continued rolling back as he heaved mightily, sending the older brave crashing into the brush behind them.

In an instant Touch the Sky was back on his feet. He had time, before Black Elk recovered, to plunge his knife home. But the taboo against drawing Cheyenne blood was powerful. The putrid stink of the murderer would cling to him for life. Even if the Headmen ruled his action self-defense, never could his lips again touch the common pipe, his hands hold a utensil used by others. And never could he be a shaman—anyone killing a fellow Cheyenne, even by accident, was forbidden from taking part in the Renewal of the Medicine Arrows or any of the other ceremonies.

All of this whirled through his mind in a heartbeat. Again he moved back instead of closing for the kill. And now Black Elk was on his feet again, his face still distorted with murderous hate.

"Look at you!" said Touch the Sky. "When I joined the tribe, how often was I mocked for letting my feelings show in my face? How many times was I called Woman Face? And now it is my war chief who lets his feelings distort his countenance! Do I follow a double-tongued war leader?"

Touch the Sky did not speak in a taunt, but in a plea to Black Elk's better self—the better self who had recently recounted his coups before the tribe. And his words were not without effect. Though he still clutched his weapon, chest heaving like an enraged bull's, Black Elk pulled up short in his next lunge.

"We have enemies enough outside our tribe for a lifetime," said Touch the Sky. "Do not sully the Arrows!"

Before either buck could speak another word, the unseen camp crier's voice rang out above the rhythmic hubbub of the dancing.

"Black Elk! Touch the Sky! Report at once to the lodge of your chief!"

Chapter 5

For a moment Touch the Sky wondered if he and Black Elk had been reported by the Bowstring Soldiers who enforced the Dance Law. Then he realized the crier had no idea where they were.

His sudden curiosity was mirrored in Black Elk's eyes.

"Our chief would not summon us during the dance," said Black Elk sullenly, "unless it is an important matter touching on the tribe." He sheathed his knife. "Our personal battle will be settled later."

Neither brave, however, wished to be in the company of the other any more than necessary. Touch the Sky let Black Elk leave first. Then, when his war leader had been swallowed up in the knot of whirling dancers, he followed.

His curiosity only deepened when, upon arriving at Gray Thunder's hide-covered lodge, he discovered Arrow Keeper waiting with the new chief.

"I looked for the two of you myself," said the old shaman, dividing his piercing gaze between the two new arrivals. "But I could not find you among the dancers."

His pointed tone held sharp reproof for both of them. Neither Cheyenne answered, their eyes flying from the elder's.

Gray Thunder, only vaguely aware of the personal conflict between the two bucks, was clearly bothered by some more weighty matter.

"Black Elk," he said, "we have new trouble. You are our battle chief and must be informed. However, after listening to Arrow Keeper's report and advice, I have decided to keep this matter out of Council. I trust the Headmen. But nothing which passes at Council remains secret for long. And this matter must be tucked under your sash."

Quickly, he summed up what Old Knobby had reported about Wes Munro and his partner Hays Jackson. When he described the murder of Chief Smoke Rising, Black Elk went livid with anger—the old Arapaho was a longtime ally of the Shaiyena. Alongside their Cheyenne and Sioux brothers, the Arapaho had courageously driven the murdering Kiowas and Comanche well south of their present homeland.

When Gray Thunder finally looked at Touch the Sky, a certain distance entered the chief's eyes. His tone too was more remote.

"This white beard who told you about these things he saw, does he speak one way?"

"Always, Father. And he has respect for the red man."

"Respect. This is what the other paleface said

too. Now I am told he is a murdering liar."

Gray Thunder fell silent, musing. He was young for a chief, his thick dark hair only now showing the first frosted streaks of age.

"I suspected him from his very first words," said Black Elk hotly. "Words coated with honey! Let me take a few good warriors down to their boat now, and we will dangle their scalps from our lodge poles!"

"I was once like you," said Gray Thunder. "Quicker to sharpen my battle-ax than to parley. But now I would rather look before I wade into deep waters."

"Everyone knows that Gray Thunder has the courage of a silvertip bear fighting for its cubs," said Black Elk. "But only think on what happened to the red man east of the Great Waters. They too were slow to paint their faces against the Long Knives. Indeed, they greeted them with smiles and helped them survive the short white days of the cold moons.

"And now, only look! The Iowas, the Sacs, the Foxes, the once-proud Shawnees on the Meremec—now they crowd into the white man's stinking cities to trade their best furs for strong water. Now they are so unmanned by drink they no longer remember the Warrior Way or the old cure songs."

Gray Thunder nodded. Black Elk was quick to rise on his hind legs, but this was well spoken.

"All this is true enough, fiery buck. But nothing draws more hairy faces than the murder of their own. This paleface claims enough power to address the Great White Council. I have the welfare of my tribe to consider. If we kill these dogs, a pack far larger may descend on us in wrath.

Should the women and children suffer because I choose the warpath?"

Arrow Keeper approved these words with a silent nod. Gray Thunder, Touch the Sky realized, had a more realistic grasp of the sheer numbers of the whites. Black Elk still thought of them as merely one more tribe, capable of extermination.

Gray Thunder addressed Touch the Sky again.

"We must listen and watch, learn what their plan is. You understand their tongue. I have decided to grant the white man's request. He did not lie about the Mandan raid. Word-bringers from the south have confirmed it. We will loan him three capable bucks to help with their journey.

"It will surely be dangerous. If they have killed Smoke Rising, a great chief, they will not hesitate to slaughter three young Cheyenne bucks. Therefore, I will send only strong warriors. You will go with Wolf Who Hunts Smiling and Little Horse. Do you understand the importance of this mission to the red nation and to your tribe?"

Touch the Sky nodded. "Yes, Father."

"Good. And do you understand that there is no room for personal battles within the tribe?"

Touch the Sky understood. All in the tribe knew that he and Wolf Who Hunts Smiling were enemies. But they were also the best of the younger warriors.

Again Touch the Sky nodded. "I have ears for your warning, Father. My tribe comes first."

Gray Thunder looked at Black Elk.

"Send your cousin and Little Horse to me. I will speak the same warning to Wolf Who Hunts Smiling. And, without telling them what is in the wind, have your warriors make ready their battle rigs and keep them ready. This double-tongued white man is clever like a fox, and I fear our wise Arrow Keeper is right. The tribe faces great danger!"

Camped just to the west of the Cheyenne's permanent summer camp on the Powder River were their close allies, the Arapaho. Descended from the same ancestors as the Cheyenne, ancestors who had once roamed the wooded lake country of Minnesota until forced west, the Arapaho too were divided into Northern and Southern branches.

The Cheyenne and Arapaho had experienced minor clashes on occasion. But these amounted to family squabbles. They were close enough that the Arapaho, like the friendly Dakota, would receive Cheyenne exiles into their camps with no questions asked—and even let them take Arapaho wives.

The two tribes also looked remarkably similar in face and body type. Which was why the white militiaman named Fargo Danford was not sure, at first, whether the riders approaching his position overlooking a bluff near Roaring Horse Creek were Arapaho or Cheyenne.

Danford adjusted his Army-issue field glasses, squinting for a closer look.

"Durned if them ain't Arapaho," he finally announced to his men. These riders all wore their hair braided, which most Northern Cheyenne braves did only for ceremonies or in old age.

Danford sat astride a big claybank. He wore a flat leather shako hat, his trophy after murdering a Mexican *vaquero* in California. His Colt Navy pistol was tucked into his holster butt forward to accommodate his left-handed cross-draw.

"If them's 'Rapahos," said Heck Nash, the big, balding man on the roan stallion beside him, "that means they're from Smoke Rising's band."

"That it do," said Danford, "that it do. And it also means these red A-rabs has seen their last sunrise. They're breaking white man's law now. This is wagon road right of way. According to that treaty they signed, they're spoze to steer clear of this land."

Nash held a sawed-off scattergun loaded with a double load of buckshot carefully balanced across his saddletree. The riders clustered behind them were also heavily armed.

These "militiamen," and others like them, had been employed by Wes Munro. They were scattered all along the river routes where Munro had entered into private treaties with the various tribes. Technically illegal, these bands were mostly out-of-work miners who had gone bust in California. Many had been riding the outlaw trail for years, on the dodge from the law. But the only law this far out on the frontier was the U.S. Army. And generous payments to the right commanders ensured that the ragtag militia remained mostly unchallenged.

Their job was to enforce the illegal private treaties—treaties most of the Indians understood little, if at all.

One of the militiamen carried a wooden guidon with a white truce flag flying from it. At a nod from Danford, he rode out in front of the group. The others fell in behind him, spurring their mounts to a long trot.

The white truce flag snapped in the breeze. They descended the long bluff in a loose wedge formation. They bore down on the small party of Indians, who had led their ponies to the creek to drink.

"C'mon, boys, let's put paid to it. It's like shootin' at a bird's nest on the ground," said one of them.

"Damn good thing, Tom," another joshed him. "You couldn't hit a bull in the butt with a banjo."

"Real slow and careful-like now, boys," said Danford. "Don't draw any steel until I give the signal. We don't want to spook 'em. Don't give 'em any time to get out of the weather when it comes!"

The small party of five Arapaho braves was hunting fresh game for its tribe. They were led by a brave named Smiles Plenty.

Smiles Plenty, one of the friendliest braves in the tribe, was in an especially joyous mood today. This despite the recent death of Chief Smoke Rising, whom the tribe was still mourning.

On the day before, his son Fleet Deer, who had only 11 winters behind him, had killed his first eagle with his bow and arrow. Proudly, Smiles Plenty had stood in the door of his clan's dance lodge until late that evening, announcing this feat to all who came. Would such a son not be a great warrior?

Smiles Plenty had spotted the paleface riders even before they rode forward to meet the Indians as if to parley. Despite their truce flag, he was wary. He remembered ten winters ago when the hairy-faced fools tore across the country toward the far-off land of the Modoc tribe, the land beyond the sun which the Long Knives called California. In their mad dash for the yellow rocks, they had broken every promise in their talking papers.

Now Smiles Plenty was worried. But it was no use trying to outrun them. Fleeing from whites was an invitation to be shot. Besides, these whites did not seem intent on any serious mischief. They had slowed from a trot to a walk. Now their horses came forward with their heads down, setting their own pace. Nor had any of the whites drawn his weapon.

His braves were armed only with their bows, their lances, and one old muzzle-loader. So fighting was out of the question. Best to parlay and count on his good disposition, his skill as a diplomat, to get them through. He was the tribe's best negotiator, and had kept them off the warpath more than once with no loss of honor.

"Just let your ponies drink," he instructed the rest. "This thing will pass."

When the whites were close enough that he could make out their faces, Smiles Plenty stepped out to meet them.

Smiling the broad, ear-to-ear, toothy smile that had earned him his name, he lifted one hand. He turned it in a slow circle from the back of the hand to the palm, a universal Plains Indian greeting of friendship. Then he folded his arms to show his band was at peace.

The paleface in the silly leather hat seemed to be their chief. He said something in the white tongue. Smiles Plenty stepped closer, shaking his head to let them know he did not understand.

"Game's over, pards," Fargo Danford had said quietly to his companions. "Time to call in the cards."

A heartbeat later the smile was literally blown off of Smiles Plenty's face when Heck Nash emptied the double load of buckshot almost point-blank.

Suddenly, more rifles and short arms spat fire. Before Smiles Plenty's heels had quit scratching the dirt, the other four braves lay dead or dying.

"Lift their scalps, boys," said Danford as he holstered his Navy Colt butt forward. "I'll need somethin' to prove to Munro that we're doing our job."

Chapter 6

Despite the fact that the Cheyenne seldom ate the plentiful trout which the blue-bloused soldiers loved, rivers were essential to their existence. Every major camp, summer or winter, was erected near a river. Yet, not until he became a member of the crew of the *Sioux Princess* did Touch the Sky begin to truly understand the constant dangers and grueling hardships of river life.

Wes Munro had expected disappointing news when Chief Gray Thunder sent a delegation of headmen to his boat. Instead, to his considerable surprise, the new Cheyenne leader agreed to lend him three strong young bucks for the journey.

As a good-faith gesture (and a practical move through such dangerous territory) the Cheyennes were allowed to bring their weapons. Besides their knives in their beaded sheaths and well-honed throwing axes, all three owned good long guns. John Hanchon had given his adopted son and Little Horse their choice of weapons when they rode to Bighorn Falls to help him defeat Hiram Steele's gun-throwers. Touch the Sky had selected a percussion-action Sharps, Little Horse a four-barrel flintlock shotgun with barrels that were rotated by hand.

Wolf Who Hunts Smiling owned a Colt Model 1855 percussion rifle. It had once been Touch the Sky's. But when Wolf Who Hunts Smiling had made the gesture of returning it, after Touch the Sky saved him from Pawnees, the tall Cheyenne had told him to keep it.

Despite this offering, however, the two young Cheyennes were far from friends. Instead, a grudging, temporary peace of sorts had developed between them. Between them was the mutual respect one brave warrior always feels for another, even an enemy.

But both were of opposite temperaments. And Wolf Who Hunts Smiling, who had watched his father cut down by Bluecoat canister shot, would never accept a Cheyenne raised in the white man's world. Especially one who was so clearly his rival in the warrior arts. His ambition to be powerful within the tribe was great, and they both sensed that someday they must clash.

For the moment, however, all three Cheyenne bucks were united against new enemies. First of all was the mysterious Wes Munro, who talked like a red man but lied like a white. There were also the hostile Hays Jackson, the hostile crew of voyageurs or boatmen, and not least formidable of all, the hostile river itself.

Old Knobby carefully avoided any contact with Touch the Sky. He also clearly preferred the company of his horses and mules over the company of Hays Jackson or Wes Munro.

They departed almost immediately after the three youths had reported aboard and stowed their gear. For the first few hours a strong favoring wind from the southeast had filled the canvas sail. Only occasionally were a few of the crew required to assist the boat through an embarrass, a spot where floating debris had formed chokepoint, with long wooden poles.

Then the breeze suddenly died, the square sail went limp, and the *Sioux Princess* halted all forward progress.

"Man the cordelles, you raggedy-assed lubbers!" bellowed Hays Jackson, his left eye winking open and shut from his nervous tic.

The Creoles groaned. The river was too narrow at this point to fix the long oars into their locks along the gunnels.

Men scrambled over the gunnels and splashed ashore on either side. They trailed long, thick ropes connected to metal rings on both sides of the prow.

"The hell you blanket asses waitin' for? An invitation from the Queen of England?" demanded Jackson, glowering at the Cheyennes. They stood together amidships, curiously watching.

Little Horse did not understand one word, though the powerfully built paleface's hateful tone was clear enough. Wolf Who Hunt Smiling spoke slow English and understood some of this. Touch the Sky, however, understood every word. He was grateful that the Cheyenne way had taught him to hold his face expressionless and not let his feelings show.

Jackson gestured impatiently. The three bucks

slipped into the river and up onto one of the banks. They took their place on the cordelles and strained with the rest of the crew.

It was slow, agonizing work. Despite their strength and youth, their hands were not thickly callused for such work. By the middle of the first afternoon, Touch the Sky's hands were raw and blistered. Nor were their thin elkskin moccasins designed to dig into the rocky, uneven ground of the banks. Soon their feet were bloody and lacerated from sharp pieces of flint.

The Creoles despised them and the whites, sticking to themselves. Their informal leader was a small but wiry and tough man of about 30 named Etienne. His skin was even darker than the Cheyennes'. He led his fellows in singing strange songs in French, an odd language which, to the Cheyennes, seemed to be thrust forth out of the nose, not the mouth. It was Little Horse who dubbed them the Nose Talkers.

Clearly, one condition of the voyageurs' service was an unlimited supply of alcohol. They began drinking early in the day and remained drunk. They were constantly broaching another keg of rum or whiskey.

Each night the boat anchored and two camps were made, the three Cheyennes on one bank, the Creoles on the other. Wes Munro and Hays Jackson slept in the plank cabin. Knobby slept on deck under the stars, erecting a small canvas awning when it rained.

The boat's lazaret, the storage area under the deck, was well stocked with provisions: dried fruit, jerked beef and venison and buffalo meat, slab bacon, hardtack, coffee. The Nose Talkers caught trout and cooked them in their camp at night, the smell causing the three Cheyennes to wrinkle their faces in disgust. Old Knobby made biscuits each morning. It was the Cheyennes' responsibility to occasionally supplement the fare with fresh game. Rabbits and pheasants were plentiful near the river. Sometimes they even shot them from the boat.

Three sleeps after their departure, Touch the Sky's aching muscles began to condition themselves to the cordelles. But his feet, like those of Little Horse and Wolf Who Hunts Smiling, were still bloody and lacerated. Some of the deeper cuts had even begun to ulcerate.

They tried all the natural remedies which Black Elk and Arrow Keeper had taught them, but none was powerful enough to help much. Old Knobby took pity on the trio of badly limping bucks. One evening when Munro and Jackson were conferring inside the plank cabin, he quickly showed them how to mix river mud with crushed marigold and myrtle leaves, forming a soothing poultice. Slowly their feet began to mend and toughen.

But there was no end of new troubles and hardships.

On the fifth day of their journey, they passed the fork where the headwaters of the Shoshone River joined the Tongue. The current abruptly picked up strength, slowing the *Sioux Princess* almost to a standstill. Suddenly the boat hit a spot where the opaque river water was boiling furiously.

"Sawyer!" shouted Jackson. "Tack around 'er!"

A sawyer was a submerged tree or huge clump of tree limbs. Trapped in the water unseen, they "sawed" back and forth snagging anything that passed over.

The banks on either side were too steep to man

the cordelles, and too many gravel bars made rowing impractical. So the entire crew lined both sides of the keelboat, thrusting their long poles into the river bottom.

"I said tack around!" Jackson raged. "*Heave*, you pack of spineless maggots!"

He constantly carried a knotted-leather whip in his sash. Normally he used it to lash the deck and gunnels, goading the crew to greater effort. But now, as the keelboat balanced on the feather edge of becoming entangled in the sawyer, Jackson brought the whip across the shoulders of one of the Creoles.

Etienne saw this. Touch the Sky, his shoulder and back muscles straining as he manned his pole, watched the crew leader's eyes narrow with hatred when he stared at the white tyrant.

Wolf Who Hunts Smiling too saw this.

"Hear my words," he said in a low tone to his two companions. "We are on a mission for our tribe, and I have orders directly from my chief. But I am no cowering dog like these Nose Talkers. I swear this thing, if that stinking white pig's afterbirth touches me with his whip, I will use his guts for a new bowstring!"

Such talk troubled the other two. The hotheaded Wolf Who Hunts Smiling had been making more and more threats of this nature lately.

"As you say," said Touch the Sky, "we are on a mission for our tribe. Our task is to discover what these whites are really doing on this journey. I hate the filthy dog too. But our personal feelings do not matter. Perhaps later our chance will come. But for now we must remember that we are warriors and will endure anything rather than place our tribe in danger merely to taste revenge."

"Merely?" said Wolf Who Hunts Smiling. "Revenge can be a sweet dish, and I am ready for it *now.*"

"You blanket-asses shut your damn gobs and *heave!*" shouted Jackson, his face bloating with rage. "This ain't no time to palaver!"

The Cheyennes fell silent and threw their all behind the poles. Etienne shouted something in French, rallying the voyageurs. Slowly, inch by inch and just in the nick of time, the keelboat slipped sideways and edged around the furiously boiling water.

Wes Munro, who spent much of his time in the cabin poring over papers and charts, tried to be more diplomatic than his abrasive lackey. He never struck members of the crew and seldom even raised his voice. This was not the result of compassion. To him, men were like dogs—sometimes a pat on the head got better results than a kick on the rump.

That night, to reward them for their hard work earlier in avoiding the sawyer, he broke out rations of expensive Scotch whiskey. The Cheyennes refused their share, opting for rich white man's coffee heavily sweetened with raw sugar.

There had not yet been contact with another Indian tribe. Slowly, as the summer days lengthened and the Wyoming sun's heat grew warmer, they made their way north toward hostile Crow Indian country.

The Crow Nation was currently at war with all whites, the result of a cavalry massacre of one of their villages. Munro had no intention of trying to deal with them. Instead, his plan was to acquire land rights all around them, hemming them in. Then he would convince the Army to drive them south to Kiowa and Comanche country as they had once before.

Soon, as the *Sioux Princess* drew closer to the Yellowstone River, it reached a nearly impassable stretch of water.

At times the Tongue was so clogged with hidden boulders that several oars and poles were snapped. Gravel bars suddenly scraped against the hull with a grinding shriek, forcing the boat to a complete stop. One gravel bar was so long and wide that it took the crew hours to drag the boat free with the cordelles. Other times, thick and well-constructed beaver dams stretched across the entire width of the river, and had to be laboriously torn down after blowing them apart with the cannon.

Once, even Old Knobby was impressed into hard labor, tugging on the cordelles with the others until he coughed up phlegm. Then, ten sleeps after the Cheyennes had departed from their camp, the dreaded confrontation between Hays Jackson and Wolf Who Hunts Smiling took place.

The *Sioux Princess* had cleared a sharp dogleg bend only to encounter the white-churning waters of dangerous, rocky rapids. A narrow and relatively small channel of water skirted the rapids on one side. Only one bank was passable, and half the crew was tugging one cordelle, with the other half poling from the opposite side of the keelboat.

"Tack to starboard!" screamed Jackson. "Tack hard to starboard! Hurry, goddamnit! *Heave* into it!"

In his agitation he made the mistake of singling out Wolf Who Hunts Smiling, who had paused for a moment to get a better grip on his pole.

"Maybe you mistood me, whelp! I said *heave*!"

And then he brought his whip singing smartly across Wolf Who Hunts Smiling's bare back.

The young Cheyenne brave held his face impassive. But his swift-as-minnow eyes blazed with murderous hatred. Quick as a wink, the hot-tempered Cheyenne threw down his pole, whirled around, and seized the knotted whip. One sharp tug, and Jackson was sprawled on the deck.

"You heathen sonofabitch!"

Jackson moved with surprising quickness for such a stout man. In a heartbeat his .36-caliber Paterson Colt pistol was in his hand. But just as quickly, Wolf Who Hunts Smiling's bone-handle knife was raised overhead, ready to be thrown.

Munro happened to be on deck, worried by the rapids. They had not been marked on his navigation charts. As Touch the Sky and Little Horse leaped on their companion, Munro simultaneously caught Jackson's arm.

"Let it alone," he said sharply. "We don't clear that rapids and quick, we'll all be doing the hurt dance!"

Jackson glowered at Wolf Who Hunts Smiling. "Don't miscalculate yourself, Innun. I've scalped better bucks 'n you!"

But Munro had already ordered the Cheyennes back to work. The horses and mules, upset by the turbulent pitching of the keelboat, had quickly become agitated. Old Knobby worked hard to calm and control them.

Again Etienne rallied the Creoles in rapid French. The boiling, churning waters tossed the boat around like a helpless cork in a child's bath. Several crates lashed to the deck broke loose and tumbled into the river, and a buckskin pony leaped over the gunnel in panic.

With a sharp snap, Touch the Sky's pole became wedged between two boulders and broke. At the same moment, one of the Creoles manning the cordelles slipped on the sharp bank and tumbled down into the water, injuring his left leg.

Seeing that the Nose Talker was in no immediate danger of drowning, Touch the Sky leaped into the river, fought his way up the bank, and gripped the thick cordelle in the voyageur's place.

"Heave!" Jackson shouted, fear replacing the surliness in his tone. "Jesus God almighty, *heave*!"

For a moment the *Sioux Princess* balanced between sure destruction and uncertain salvation. Then, like a skittish pony making a sideways little skip, it literally bounced into the narrow, calmer channel.

The heavy boat missed crushing Touch the Sky to death only by inches. But the hapless crew member trapped in the river was not so lucky. His face draining white, he tried to scramble up out of harm's way.

But he was too late. As Touch the Sky watched horrified, the injured Creole was instantly crushed to a human paste against the rocks.

Chapter 7

The *Sioux Princess* survived the rapids with only a few rough gouges to her keel and the loss of some expendable trade goods. But Touch the Sky noticed a change occurring among many of the Creole voyageurs.

The loss of a fourth man on this godforsaken journey was bad enough. But the attitude of their white employers left them noticeably sullen. There was no attempt to recover and bury the remains, no pause for even the simplest of ceremonies. Their comrade's death meant no more to Munro and Jackson than the slaughter of a rabbit.

The Cheyennes were sympathetic. Their tribe placed great importance on recovering the bodies of their dead and preparing them for the final journey. Although the Nose Talkers were an odd lot, and hostile toward the Indians, the three bucks couldn't help feeling a certain brotherhood—were these dark-skinned men, who might have been mistaken for red men if they wore leggings and clouts, not despised by the whites?

On the day after the incident at the rapids, the *Sioux Princess* anchored early so Old Knobby could exercise the horses and graze them in the lush bunchgrass bordering the river.

As a gesture of sympathy toward the voyageurs, Touch the Sky shot a fat mule deer and dressed it out. Assisted by Little Horse, he carried it to the boatmen's night camp and presented it to Etienne. They were limited to sign talk, but the Creole leader understood their purpose. He was not exactly friendly, and did not invite them to visit. But at least he was polite as he thanked them.

Wolf Who Hunts Smiling, however, scorned this gesture.

"These men live in cities and dress as whites," he said when Touch the Sky and Little Horse returned to their camp. "A true Cheyenne does not hunt for lazy, fish-eating drunkards."

The keelboat was visible in the grainy twilight behind them. Fires blazed from the voyageurs' camp on the opposite bank of the river.

"When our chief crossed over," countered Little Horse, automatically making the cut-off sign, "the Lakota Sioux presented our tribe with much antelope meat. It is the red man's way to be generous in a time of sadness."

"Perhaps," said Wolf Who Hunts Smiling. "But the Lakota are our cousins. They raise their battle lances beside ours. Their enemies are our enemies."

"I have ears for this," said Touch the Sky. "But only think, the enemies of the Nose Talkers are also our enemies. Have you not seen how they are treated by the palefaces?"

"So you say, buck. But you too have accepted devil water from the hair-mouth whites, just as these nose-talking fish eaters do. *I* drink nothing of my enemy's except their blood!"

Touch the Sky fell silent, an angry pulse throbbing in his temples. Wolf Who Hunts Smiling had scored a good hit. Once, at the trading post at Red Shale, Touch the Sky *had* drunk strong water with whites who worked for the whiskey trader Henri Lagace. But he had only been tricked into doing so in a desperate attempt to get them to listen to his pleas.

Little Horse could bear no more of this.

"Your tongue is bent double from foolish hatred and jealousy," he said to Wolf Who Hunts Smiling. "You saw how Touch the Sky behaved when those same white dogs held him prisoner in their camp. Did he drink with them then? No! He was prepared to ram an arrow down his own throat rather than cooperate with them."

Wolf Who Hunts Smiling was silent at this. Perhaps he was also recalling the time when Touch the Sky, returning from his vision at Medicine Lake, had bravely saved him from Pawnee marauders—this in spite of the fact that Wolf Who Hunts Smiling had been sent by Black Elk to kill him.

"He was brave," he finally conceded begrudgingly. "He is no coward, certainly. But he also disobeyed his war leader and caused the death of High Forehead by doing so."

Little Horse was about to respond. But Touch the Sky laid a hand on his arm, quieting him. It was no use to argue further with Wolf Who

Hunts Smiling. His mind was stubbornly set, and it was pointless to antagonize him further. Their survival on this dangerous journey would depend on cooperation.

The next day brought a brief respite for the crew. The river widened and deepened as it passed through a verdant valley of hip-deep buffalo grass. A gentle favoring breeze puffed out the square sail.

This gave Touch the Sky an opportunity to do what, so far, he had been too busy to accomplish very often—eavesdrop on the whites as they met in their cabin.

He sat on the plank deck, close enough to the cabin to hear the voices within. He was using a bone awl and buffalo-sinew thread to repair his badly torn moccasins. The cabin had only an open archway for an entrance. But the whites, unaware he knew even one word of English, ignored him as they would a camp dog.

Wes Munro was consulting a U.S. Army map.

"Dakota land," he said to Hays Jackson, "doesn't officially begin until we reach the Whistling Rock fork. So this is still open land. Better put a shack out just in case the Territorial Commission sends out an inspector."

Jackson nodded and whistled to a few of the idling crew. The order was given, and the *Sioux Princess* was moored close to shore.

What followed next was something Touch the Sky had witnessed several times since the voyage began.

With Jackson bellowing out orders, a small wooden shack mounted on wheeled axles was lifted off the keelboat and set ashore. Old Knobby hitched up a team of horses to traces, and the shack was positioned well back from the water. Then the wheels were removed. Fresh white letters on the side of the new pine boards proclaimed THE OVERLAND COMPANY.

Other shacks like it were being knocked together daily by the crew. There was no attention to workmanship. Huge gaps were left between the boards, and they did not even include doors and windows. In addition to setting out the shacks, Jackson used a tomahawk to blaze traces in the area around them.

Touch the Sky had been burning with curiosity about these shacks. Now, as Knobby led his team back up the boarding ramp, the old hostler saw the question in the Cheyenne's eyes.

Knobby glanced carefully around. Then, as he came abreast of the spot where Touch the Sky sat, he squatted as if to examine one of the horse's fetlocks.

"This child has finally got it figgered," he whispered quickly to his friend. "Them piss-ant shacks and the tomahawk claims is mainly to bolster the Overland Company's claim that they're 'proving up' gum'ment land betwixt the reservation lands. Gives 'em a legal claim to it later."

Knobby rose, stiff kneecaps popping, and led the horses back to the shallow pen at the rear of the *Sioux Princess*. Now Touch the Sky listened intently as Jackson's bullhorn voice spoke up.

"You know this Dakota chief?" he asked, his left eye twitching open and closed. "This here Chief Bull Hump?"

"I never palavered with him," said Munro. "But I've heard talk of him."

"Will he make medicine with us?"

Munro was silent for several heartbeats, carefully considering that question.

"From what I've heard, it's not likely. He'll hobnob with whites, but he won't make medicine," Munro finally replied. "But one way or another, there's a wagon road going up. I've made plans. Old Bull Hump is going to join Smoke Rising in the Happy Hunting Ground."

Jackson grinned. "That shines fine by me. Injuns are nits—and nits make lice."

Now Touch the Sky felt his face drain cold as he finally grasped the gist of Munro's scheme. The heart of the red nations was being stolen out from under the Indians to build a road for the whites!

Absorbed in what he had heard, eager to hear more, he was staring intently through the open doorway when Hays Jackson suddenly met his eye.

Hastily, the Cheyenne looked down and pretended to concentrate on repairing his elkskin moccasins.

But a little nubbin of doubt festered at the back of Jackson's mind. This was several times now that he had caught the tall Cheyenne buck apparently listening.

It could just be curiosity, he told himself. The savage had probably never been around whites before.

Still . . . he sure's hell *acted* guilty.

"Hey, you on the deck," Jackson said to him quietly in English. "Look at me."

But Touch the Sky, nervous sweat making the bone-sliver awl difficult to hold, refused to look up.

Old Knobby was worried.

He hadn't heard the eerie sound in a long time—not since his fur-trapping days in the great mountains he still called the Stonies, though most now called them the Rockies. But he thought he had heard the sound again this morning, when he rolled out of his blankets just as dawn rimmed the eastern horizon in pink light.

The light, fluttering tweet of a bone whistle: the favorite signaling device of the dreaded Crow Crazy Dogs.

Knobby had known the Crow tribe as the Absaroka in the days when they still hunted in the Yellowstone Valley. But as they moved west, encountering more enemies, they became known simply as the Stub-hands. This was a reference to their custom of cutting off their fingers to mourn their dead. Knobby had seen Crow warriors with nothing left but a thumb and a trigger finger.

The Crows were the great thieves of the plains, roaming everywhere in search of booty. And Knobby knew that the Crow Crazy Dogs were the most feared Indian soldier society in the West because they were suicide warriors. Once they entered combat, they were bound by sacred oath—violation of which brought certain shame—to either win or die in the attempt. Joining the Crazy Dogs gave a Crow warrior a special, almost supernatural status—in the eyes of his tribe he was already dead.

Again Old Knobby heard the sound, even closer now: a low, hollow, fluting whistle almost like a whippoorwill. It came from a thicket about 70 yards back from the fog-shrouded river.

Knobby felt his bowels go loose and heavy as his nagging worry turned to sudden fear.

He looked at the one-pounder cannon mounted in the prow, debating. Normally it was fired only in farewells and salutes, though it could also be loaded with up to 16 one-ounce musket balls. It made a hell of a roar, he knew, and would wake everyone instantly.

He was still debating when his favorite horse, a chestnut mare with a white sock on both forelegs, pricked her ears forward toward the thicket. Then Knobby knew for sure.

They were out there.

All hell's soon gonna be a-poppin', he told himself.

As usual, the cannon was loaded with powder, but no musket balls. The old-timer limped forward quickly, tugging at the rawhide drawstring of his possibles bag. He produced a sulphur match and lit it with his fingernail. He held it over the touch hole, and a booming report split the calm silence of dawn.

"What in tarnal *hell*?" Hays Jackson stumbled out of the cabin with his shirt-tails flapping. He clutched a cavalry carbine against his hairy belly. Munro emerged behind him, one of his dueling pistols in each hand.

The three Cheyennes were already racing toward the *Sioux Princess*, their loose black locks flying. The voyageurs, hung over as usual from a late night of revelry, were rising more slowly from their camp.

"You goddamn soft-brained old coot!" said Jackson to Knobby. "The hell are you doing?"

"Stow the chin music," said Knobby grimly as the three Cheyenne bucks raced up the boarding plank. "Best tell your crew to hump it. And break out the spare rifles for 'em. We got Innuns on the warpath."

"Where, you stinking old goat?"

"Over yonder," said Knobby, nodding toward the thicket.

The Crows, the element of surprise already ruined, had decided to attack immediately before the bulk of the crew could form up against them. As if timed for dramatic effect, they charged even as Knobby finished speaking.

With harsh, guttural barks, they streamed out of the thicket on the backs of painted ponies. There were at least two dozen of them. And Knobby knew for a fact now that they were indeed the feared suicide warriors: They wore horse tails gummed into their already long hair, making it trail down below their buttocks. This was the fashion preferred by the Crazy Dogs.

Little Horse too recognized the feared suicide warriors.

"Crazy Dogs!" he shouted to his companions as he raised his scattergun. "*Now* we are in for a battle, brothers!"

The attackers carried no rifles. But their fox-skin quivers were packed tight with new, fire-hardened arrows. They were also armed with their deadly skull-crackers, stone war clubs that could split an enemy's head like a soft melon.

With the suddenness of a prairie storm, arrows began raining into the wooden keelboat all around them. Touch the Sky felt a harsh, fiercely hot stinging in the meat of his right thigh as a flint-tipped arrow found him. He could feel that it had not sunk deep. He ignored it, firing the Sharps and knocking a Crazy Dog off of his horse.

Another arrow found Hays Jackson's right shoulder, and one pierced Old Knobby's slouch beaver hat. But more Crazy Dogs in the first wave went down as they, or their horses, were dropped by the first volley of fire from the *Sioux Princess*.

However, there was no time to reload or insert fresh primer caps. The attackers were too close and advancing too swiftly. Already one warrior was charging up the boarding ramp. Touch the Sky drew his knife from its beaded sheath. In the same smooth movement that drew it, he brought his arm back and threw the knife hard into the warrior's chest.

Several fire arrows thwacked into the keelboat, one dangerously close to the powder cache. Old Knobby hustled to put them out.

Munro had emptied both pistols. Now he leaped toward one of the swivel-mounted blunderbusses. The 22-inch barrel had a two-inch flared muzzle which accepted eight-ounce balls. Unlike the prow cannon, these were kept constantly loaded. He fired it, missing his target. But the smoky explosion spooked several of the Crazy Dogs' horses.

One of the Crows had leaped into the river and jumped over the gunnel unnoticed. Now, as he raised his stone skull-cracker to bash Touch the Sky's head in, Old Knobby screamed in English:

"Look to your right flank, tadpole!"

Touch the Sky spun, glimpsed a movement in the corner of his eye, ducked. The club passed so close he felt the wind from it. His battle-ax was already in his hand. Before the Crazy Dog could recover his balance, Touch the Sky shattered his breastbone.

"Hi-ya!" screamed Wolf Who Hunts Smiling, rallying his comrades. *"Hi-ya hi-i-i-ya!"*

Now all three Cheyenne braves stood shoulder to shoulder, repelling boarders with their knives, lances, and axes. Old Knobby fired a blunderbuss, and a charging Crow warrior literally lost his head.

The body, carried forward by nerve momentum, took three or four more steps while blood spumed from the severed neck.

The first wave had been broken, but the second was now rushing the boat. Munro was desperately loading the one-pounder with musket balls.

"Where the hell's them white-livered frogs?" bellowed Jackson.

Touch the Sky glanced back at the opposite bank. The Creoles had all gathered behind Etienne, watching the battle in wide-eyed astonishment. They were not afraid, Touch the Sky realized. They simply felt it wasn't their fight.

Etienne's eyes met Touch the Sky's. The Creole leader saw the arrow protruding from his thigh, the streaming blood where a spear had torn a ragged gash in Little Horse's side.

Munro fired the one-pounder, and two Crazy Dogs were turned into stewmeat. This slowed the assault and bought precious time.

The leader of the Nose Talkers abruptly shouted something in French, leaping into the river. With a chorus of answering shouts, his men leaped in behind him. In moments they were scrambling aboard the keelboat and accepting the carbines which Jackson hastily threw out from the cabin.

Chapter 8

Once the voyageurs joined the battle, it was quickly over.

The Crow Crazy Dogs, true to their fanatical oath, died to the last man. Touch the Sky and Hays Jackson had taken arrows, neither serious wounds, and Little Horse would be laid up for a day or two until the wound in his side started to mend. Two of the Creole crew received minor wounds, and one had been seriously hurt. A stray bullet had killed one of the mules.

But despite the sudden ferocity of the attack, no one aboard the *Sioux Princess* had been killed. For two more days the keelboat limped along, again short of crew members while the wounded recovered. The seriously injured boatman, laid out by a Crow war club, would survive but would be useless for any hard labor. These losses, plus the death of the voyageur crushed at the rapids, held the boat to as few as 15 miles a day.

Then favoring winds again sprang up, and the daily distance was more than doubled for a few days.

Munro's mood noticeably improved, and he was generous with rations of good whiskey and coffee. Even Jackson, to whose surly face smiles were total strangers, cursed less at the crew. Under strict orders from Munro, he avoided any further confrontation with Wolf Who Hunts Smiling.

But Jackson and Munro now had reason to keep a close eye on Touch the Sky.

On the night after the attack by the Crazy Dogs, the two men had met in secret inside the plank cabin.

"That tall red nigger palavers English," said Hays Jackson with conviction. "During the fight, did you hear the old codger warn him to look to his right flank? And by God, he looked."

Wes Munro nodded. As usual he was neatly dressed in a clean linsey-cloth shirt and trousers, his face smoothly shaven. His eyes seemed like hard, flat chips of obsidian in the light of the coal-oil lamp. The two men sat at a crude deal table which had been spiked to the deck. A bottle of good liquor gleamed like topaz among the charts spread out between them.

"That would explain," said Munro slowly, thinking out loud, "why Gray Thunder changed his mind. They wanted to send a spy along. But why? Is it just natural suspicion of the white man, or did the chief receive some kind of warning?"

"Well, I kilt Smoke Rising clean," insisted Jackson. "Just like you told me. No marks on him. The old pus-bag was close to death anyhow.

Even if the Cheyenne got wind of him goin' under, why should it make them uneasy about us?"

Munro glanced away, irritated as usual by Jackson's twitching left eye. Munro always tried to stay downwind of the man too. Munro had grown more fastidious since his days as a long hunter, and Jackson always smelled like a whorehouse at low tide.

"It could just be natural suspicion of the white man," Munro suggested again. But then something else occurred to him. "How does the old man know he spoke English?"

Jackson pondered that, his small, close-set eyes staring into the lamplight. "Might be he don't. Might be it was just natch'ral to yell out in the heat of the fight. It don't strike me as too likely that old sot could know him."

Jackson was no great intellect, but Munro nodded agreement.

"It's also possible," said Munro, "that we're wrong about the buck knowing English. The old man yelled loud, and the warning was clear in his tone. The buck might've understood the warning without understanding the exact words."

"That could be," conceded Jackson. "The crew're dumb as dead stumps, but even they'll sometimes hop when I say 'jump' in English."

Both men wanted to believe that possibility because it was comforting.

"At any rate," said Munro, "we'll keep a close eye on him. We need bodies, and he's a strong worker. But at the first sign he's bamboozling us, kill him."

The three Cheyenne braves had covered most of this Tongue River territory during their warrior training with Black Elk. So when the *Sioux Princess* sailed into view of the Eagle-tail Mountains, their snow-capped tips probing into the blue dome of the sky, they knew they were approaching the Dakota village of Chief Bull Hump.

The Dakota were not such close allies as the Arapaho. But they were on a friendly footing with the Shaiyena nation and had sent generous gifts to the chief-renewal. Once each year a Dakota subchief sat in as an honorary member of the Cheyenne Council of Forty.

So the three Cheyenne braves worried when, once again, the crew began to break open crates of trade goods and heap them on the deck. By now, of course, thanks to what Touch the Sky had overheard, they knew the gist of Munro's plan to steal Indian homelands for the paleface wagon road. Now their attention was concentrated on some plan to interfere with Munro, to disrupt the well-oiled machinery of this engine of destruction.

When and if the opportunity came, they had to get word back to their camp. But now they had a more immediate concern. Chief Bull Hump had been a good friend to their tribe. They wanted desperately to protect him from the fate which had befallen Chief Smoke Rising.

But the keelboat did not stop close to the village of Bull Hump. Munro gave the order to anchor about an hour's hard horseback ride to the south. And the lone brave who was waiting for them there, hiding from his own tribe's scouts and lookouts, was not Chief Bull Hump. It was a rebellious young subchief of 25 winters named Cries Yia Eya.

Cries Yia Eya waited on a buckskin pony. The Dakota tribe did not like riding bareback, but preferred their flat, stuffed buffalo-hide saddles. The powerful young warrior wore a leather shirt adorned with intricate beadwork.

For a moment he glanced with curiosity at the three young Cheyennes. But though they knew him, from brief councils he had held with Black Elk during their warrior training, he did not remember them. He dismissed them with one haughty glance and turned his attention to Munro, greeting him in English.

Touch the Sky had noticed that, since the battle with the Crow Crazy Dogs, Munro and Jackson would not speak around him as openly as before. He was not aware they had heard Old Knobby's shouted warning to him. But a worm of suspicion gnawed at him—the fear that they somehow knew he spoke English.

Munro and Cries Yia Eya disappeared inside the plank cabin. Much later the brave emerged and departed, taking none of the goods heaped on deck.

Munro did not give the order to weigh anchor. Touch the Sky guessed that, whatever was afoot, they were waiting for the cover of darkness—Dakota lookouts must surely surround the area, as all tribes maintained constant security from surprise attack.

Whatever was in the wind, Touch the Sky thought grimly, it could not bode well for Bull Hump. Most of the trade goods on deck consisted of new scatterguns, Hawken rifles, and percussion-cap pistols.

Little Horse too had made a somber inventory of the munitions. He and Touch the Sky were employed in repairing frays in the cordelles while the boat lay idle. Wolf Who Hunts Smiling had been sent ashore by Munro to hunt fresh meat.

"Brother," said Little Horse, "soon comes a storm of trouble. What can we do?"

Frustrated and miserable, Touch the Sky shook his head.

"I wish my medicine were as strong as Arrow Keeper's. Then I might quickly summon magic to help us. Already our shadows grow long behind us. Whatever these dogs have planned, it will happen when our sister the sun has gone to her resting place. Somehow, some way, we must follow them under cover of darkness."

When the Sun Dance ceremony had ended, Gray Thunder's Cheyennes made ready to return north to their permanent summer camp at the fork where the Little Powder joined the Powder.

This operation was impressive in its efficiency. While Black Elk sent scouts out to make sure the route was secure, the women and children broke down the camp. The tipis, which would take much longer to erect than dismantle, came down in minutes. Everything they owned was lashed to travois, along with the very old and the very young incapable of walking or riding ponies.

The warriors formed a double column, the rest of the people traveling between them. Black Elk sent out flankers and point riders. The ponies, well rested and grazed, made good time. In only a few sleeps the summer camp was reestablished along the Powder.

By tradition, each clan pitched its tipis and lodges in the exact spot where they had stood previously. These spots had been carefully marked by buffalo ribs stuck into the earth. A place developed strong medicine that was special to that clan.

The tipis of Little Horse and Wolf Who Hunts Smiling were erected, in their absence, by their clans. However, Touch the Sky had no known blood clan among the Cheyenne. But old Arrow Keeper made sure that two young boys erected the tipi for him on the lone hummock where it had always stood near the shaman's.

Few in camp knew of this new trouble with Wes Munro. They were told only that the three missing braves had been sent to assist the journey. The recent hunts had been good, filling the meat racks with jerked buffalo and ensuring plenty of pemmican for the cold moons. This and the elation following a good Sun Dance left the tribe in unusually high spirits.

However, word of new trouble soon arrived.

On the third sleep after the return to the Powder River camp, River of Winds showed up outside Black Elk's tipi. He was one of the scouts Black Elk had sent out and one of the most trusted warriors in the tribe.

"Black Elk!" he called from outside the elkskin entrance flap. "I would speak with you. It is an urgent matter."

Black Elk lifted the flap and bade him enter. A small cooking fire blazed in a circle of rocks, the smoke curling through the hole at the top of the tipi. Honey Eater sat amidst a pile of buffalo robes at the back of the tipi, finishing a hide on pumice stone.

Despite the obvious importance of River of Winds' message, Cheyenne custom was strong and a visitor always an important thing. Honey Eater prepared hot yarrow tea and bowls of spiced meat for the two men. After they had eaten, Black Elk packed his long clay pipe and both men smoked, speaking of inconsequential matters. Finally Black Elk lay his pipe carefully between them. This was the signal for the serious discussion to begin.

"Brother," said River of Winds, "I did as you told me. I scouted for several sleeps along the Tongue, following the route of the white men's boat.

"Strange little lodges without entrance holes have been erected at places near the river. I cannot read the symbols painted on them in white. Around these lodges, the trees have been blazed with tomahawks.

"More than once I was forced to find cover. Large groups of heavily armed white men are patrolling the area. They are not Bluecoats. I watched one of these groups approach a band of Arapaho hunters near Roaring Horse Creek. Brother, I saw . . ."

Here River of Winds was forced to stop, sudden emotion choking his words off. Honey Eater knew it was important to stay out of the affairs of men. Nonetheless, she stared openly now at their visitor. The hide lay ignored in her lap.

Black Elk noticed this. A fierce frown wrinkled his brow. He knew full well why his bride was so concerned.

"I have ears for your words," he said with impatience to River of Winds. "But I have no medicine to understand them unless you finish speaking them."

"Brother, I saw these hair-faces ride down under a truce flag, as if to parlay with the hunters. Then, with no warning, they slaughtered the Arapahos! They scalped them and mutilated the bodies. They sent them under to an unclean death with no chance to sing their death song—and the leader of the hunters was Smiles Plenty!"

A choked sob escaped from Honey Eater. Even Black Elk, who despised public displays of emotion by men, was stunned into a long silence. Like River of Winds, he too automatically made the cut-off sign. Smiles Plenty was popular among the entire Cheyenne village. Worse, they both knew that by strict Arapaho custom, the names of those who died unclean could never be mentioned again. Their tribal history had ended with their deaths.

Keeping her face averted, Honey Eater suddenly rose and hurried outside. Black Elk watched her, his eyes smoldering with furious jealousy. He realized it wasn't just Smiles Plenty's death that had upset her—clearly, she was fearful for her tall young buck, the squaw-stealing Touch the Sky.

"You have reported this thing to Gray Thunder?"

River of Winds nodded. "He ordered me to report it to you immediately. It will be discussed tomorrow in council."

"These murdering white dogs," said Black Elk, "do they know the palefaces on the boat?"

"I do not know this thing, Black Elk. But they always ride close to the river, and they are thickest everywhere where the boat has been."

After River of Winds had left, Black Elk rose in agitation and paced around the dying fire. This was indeed grim news for the tribe. But something else bothered him, something much more personal—something that pierced him hard in a place where his warrior's armor was useless.

He knew where Honey Eater was right now.

Not wanting to confirm his suspicion, yet driven by some morbid need to know for sure, he slipped out of the tipi. Night had gathered her black cloak over the camp. Fires blazed everywhere, casting eerie shadows. In the clearing at the center of camp, the younger braves were congregating to bet on the nightly pony races.

Keeping to the shadows beyond the fires, Black Elk made his way toward the lone hummock where Touch the Sky's dark, empty tipi stood.

A scud of clouds blew away from the moon, bathing the camp in soft, silver-white light. And there, on her knees before Touch the Sky's tipi, was Honey Eater.

She clutched a smooth, round stone to her breast. In the moonlight limning her pretty face, he could see the glistening tears streaming down.

Bitter bile rose in Black Elk's throat as the words drifted back from the hinterland of memory. Words he had heard Touch the Sky shout to Honey Eater when she and the tall youth were both held prisoner in the camp of Henri Lagace's whiskey sellers:

Honey Eater! Do you know that I love you? Do you know that I have placed a stone in front of my tipi? When that stone melts, so too will my love for you! These white dogs can kill me now, but they will never kill my love for you!

Black Elk's rage was instant.

He rushed forward and seized his wife hard, lifting her from the ground and shaking her.

"What? Are you in rut for your randy buck? For *him* you would gladly get a child in your belly, yet where is *my* son? I will cut off your braids, you unfaithful she-bitch! Then the entire camp will know you are in heat for him!"

Honey Eater was frightened by his terrible wrath. But she was the daughter of a great chief, and her pride was also great. Her own indignant rage was immediate and deep.

"Then cut them off! I am weary of your childish accusations! Do women in rut shed tears? I am worried for him! While you sully the Arrows with this unmanly strong-mushroom talk, *he* faces great danger for his tribe.

"Here! Take this! Cut my braids off now and be done with your threats!"

All Cheyenne women fiercely valued chastity. Thus they carried a "suicide knife" on a thong under their dresscs. These were used to kill themselves rather than face rape from captors. Honey Eater pulled it out now.

But already Black Elk regretted his rash outburst. In his overweening pride he would never publicly mark his wife for shame—this would be an admission of his own weakness, a public acknowledgment of his inability to control his squaw.

Roughly, he threw her back down to the ground.

"Then cry for him! Make rivers with your tears, flood the plains. You are wise to do so, for if the whites do not kill him, *I* surely will!"

Chapter 9

Once again unexpected help came to the three Cheyennes in the form of Old Knobby.

Night had descended over the river and, as usual, the braves had pitched their camp on shore. They had been anxiously watching the anchored keelboat since the earlier meeting between Munro and Cries Yia Eya. But they were still without any plans as they waited for the next sign of trouble for Chief Bull Hump's Dakota village. So far all had remained ominously quiet except for the rowdy, drunken singing from across the river at the camp of the Nose Talkers.

"Listen," said Little Horse quietly, "someone approaches our camp!"

A heartbeat later all three youths had slipped back out of the circle of firelight, weapons at the ready. A figure glided closer from the surrounding shadows. Moments later, Old Knobby stood in the eerie orange glow of the fire.

"I swan, you boys faded quicker'n scat!" he said with a chuckle. "This hoss figgered to catch you with your clouts down. C'mon out now 'n' let's parley. There's bad fixin's on the spit."

Touch the Sky spoke briefly to Little Horse, translating this, and they all joined Knobby around the fire.

"I tolt Munro and that pig-eyed Jackson I got the droppin's bad when I et green chokecherries fir breakfast," he explained. "They think that's how's come I'm beddin' down ashore tonight. I doan 'spect it matters much nohow. Them two is too busy layin' big schemes to worry 'bout a toothless old fartsack like Knobby."

Wolf Who Hunts Smiling understood only some of Knobby's talk. Quickly, while Touch the Sky translated for the other two, Knobby explained that he had managed to overhear some of their plans.

In a little over an hour, Munro and Jackson planned to leave the boat with several packhorses loaded with weapons and ammunition. They were meeting Cries Yia Eya at a secret place well back from the river and the rest of the tribe. Several key night sentries for the tribe were in on the plan and would not sound the alarm, though others were loyal to the tribe and would be avoided.

"The pint is," said Knobby, "this Cries Yia Eya is a consequential brave, a real nabob 'mongst the hothead younger warriors. Any way you lay your sights, it's gunna spell trouble for Bull Hump and the rest of the tribe. *This* child doan know the when and the where of it."

Touch the Sky came to the same conclusion Old Knobby had already reached: Munro and Jackson would have to be followed tonight. But they were in unfamiliar terrain and the night was moonless. And both Munro and Jackson were experienced in the wilderness—they would carefully cover their back-trail and could not be too closely followed.

To make matters worse, Knobby now informed them that some of Munro's militiamen were in the area.

"Sure as hell's afire," added the old mountain man, "if they sniff us out, our scalps'll be danglin' off their coup sticks. We best do some fancy night scoutin', nazpaw? Doggone my buckskins for ever signin' on this trip. *This* hoss'll be glad when he's quits with the whole shitaree."

Touch the Sky was grateful to hear Old Knobby speak of "we." Because of the taboo against fighting and traveling at night, Cheyenne warriors did not, unlike the Pawnee, become very proficient at nighttime scouting and tracking. He and Little Horse had managed well enough in Bighorn Falls, when they fought Hiram Steele's thugs. But that had been on mostly open terrain long familiar to Touch the Sky. The country surrounding them now was rife with thick forests, steep cutbanks, rocky bluffs, and blind cliffs.

Old Knobby wasted no time in giving them their first lesson.

Near-total darkness like tonight, he explained, drastically changed appearances and apparent sizes of objects because details were obliterated. Rapid, safe movement was impossible unless the night scout learned to fill the details back in.

He pointed to a nearby tree that rose high into the sky. It looked much smaller than it would during daylight, he explained, because the new twigs at the tips of the branches couldn't be seen. Such size and distance miscalculations could be fatal.

Don't look at any one object too long, Knobby cautioned them, and remember that sounds are transmitted a much greater distance at night or in damp air. He also repeated the advice of Arrow Keeper and Black Elk: Smells could be a valuable warning, especially horse smells and the distinctive damp-earth odor from bodies of water.

He instructed them to get their weapons and equipment ready now. He also reminded them to make sure everything was ready and to hand while they were on the move—on a night this black they would have to rely on sense of touch instead of their eyes to find and adjust equipment.

When everything was ready, Knobby called them back to the fire one last time.

"If we get caught out by Munro or his raggedy-assed militia and hafta bust caps," he said, "stay frosty 'n' shoot plumb. Now, this child figgers we got mebbe a hour afore they leave the boat."

They had to prepare, he said, by wrapping their heads in blankets or robes and remaining in total darkness until the whites left. Their pupils would become as big as watermelon seeds and thus gather from the night any stray bit of light.

They did as instructed. As he lay in pitch-black darkness waiting, Touch the Sky listened to the rapid, hollow thump of his heart. His isolated mind naturally turned to thoughts of Honey Eater.

She and the rest of the tribe should have returned to the Powder River camp by now. Some instinct deeper than language told him that right now, at this very moment, she was also thinking of him.

That thought consoled him somewhat whenever he thought about the danger they were about to face. But why did that nagging sixth sense, which Arrow Keeper insisted he must develop as a shaman, also keep painting another picture on his mind's eye: the picture of an angry, jealous, murderously raging Black Elk?

As Knobby had predicted, about an hour later Munro and Jackson led their packhorses away from the *Sioux Princess*.

Knobby made his companions wait another quarter of an hour. Then he and the Cheyennes emerged from their self-imposed total darkness.

"It's only embers now, but doan look at the fire," Knobby cautioned them. "It'll shrink your eyeballs back up."

Touch the Sky was amazed. The clouded sky was completely empty of moon or stars. Yet he could clearly distinguish objects close at hand. Ever farther off, where before he had seen only the black shroud of night, he could distinguish the shapes of trees and hills.

"Write this on your pillow case," Knobby instructed Touch the Sky as they set out. "When you're scouting near enemies at night, never move until you've picked a landmark to aim for first. I know what direction they struck off in. So I'm a-drawin' a bead on that-air stand of pines yonder, see it?"

Touch the Sky nodded and they set out. When they reached the pines, on a bluff beyond the river, Knobby halted them.

"First off, we need to know their gait. Iffen we move too fast, we'll end up on their hinders. Move too slow, they'll meet us on their way home fir breakfast. And this is the safest time to light a match, now that we know they be well ahead of us."

Knobby struck a sulphur match and soon located their tracks.

"Lookit here," he said, grunting as he knelt. "These hoofprints is nigh to overlappin'. That shows them movin' at a walk or a trot. Now a trot's deeper, like these. So we best hump it some."

They made good time at first, Old Knobby always moving them by predetermined bounds between landmarks. The heavily laden packhorses were tearing up divots of earth with their shod hooves. So now and then Knobby simply felt about in the darkness with his hands to make sure they were still on the trail.

After they had been on the move for nearly half an hour, he knelt again to listen to the ground.

"Doan put your ear right on the ground," Old Knobby whispered to him when Touch the Sky too knelt down. "Else you'll hear your own heart a-pumpin', not the horses. Put it *close* to the ground."

Faintly, like a weak, slow drumbeat, Touch the Sky picked up the sound of iron-clad hooves.

"We're nigh onto 'em," cautioned Knobby. "Slow down. Wait till there's natural sounds like the wind to cover our movement."

Soon the sound of nickering horses ahead was carried to them on the wind. The four of them were moving up out of a long draw. Touch the Sky felt his pulse thudding in his palms as they grew nearer and nearer to some unknown danger.

With Knobby leading, the three youths crawled up a long, rocky slope above the draw. Now they could clearly hear the sound of voices, of impatient horses stamping the ground. They were downwind, so they didn't need to worry about their smell spooking the horses.

Touch the Sky reached the edge of the bluff, and peered over. The sight below made ice run in his veins.

A fire had been built in the lee of a ridge, protected from the wind. Wes Munro and Cries Yia Eya stood beside a huge, flat boulder shaped remarkably like a table. The Cheyennes recognized this spot from their days in warrior training. It was called Council Rock, a place where Dakota headmen often met in outdoor council.

Jackson stood between his boss and Cries Yia Eya, both hands holding a piece of paper flat against the rock. The packhorses were picketed just behind them. Their panniers were still unloaded.

In a ring about the three men, still mounted, was a circle of at least 30 young braves—and the flickering tongues of firelight showed that their faces were painted for battle!

"You understand your end of the deal?" said Munro. Cries Yia Eya had learned some English during the year he'd spent as a guide for the Northwest Fur Trading Company. "In exchange for these weapons, and another generous payment every year, the Dakota tribe agrees to surrender rights to a tract of land that stretches from here . . ."

Munro pulled a second sheet of paper out from under the first and pointed. "From here, at the juncture of the Tongue and Medicine Creek, to here at the foothills of the Red Shale Mountains. You agree that your tribe will not hunt nor roam over this territory so long as this treaty is in effect."

Urgently, Wolf Who Hunts Smiling nudged Touch the Sky. According to the Fort Laramie accord of 1851, the tract which Munro had just described ran through the heart of a great buffalo range owned jointly by the Sioux, the Arapaho, the Dakota, and the Cheyenne.

Below, Cries Yia Eya nodded impatiently.

"You also understand," said Munro, "that you are acting as the legal agent for your tribe? Meaning, of course, that Bull Hump will either have to be in agreement with you or somehow removed from leadership?"

"Cries Yia Eya knows full well what the talking paper means," said the bold warrior, his beadwork shirt glittering in the firelight. "He does not mince around the truth like a pony avoiding a snake. This paper is nothing. Give me and my braves our guns *now* and Bull Hump crosses over this very night!"

Munro nodded and Jackson grinned. Cries Yia Eya affixed his mark to the private treaty.

"My militiamen are waiting back near the river," said Munro. "It's best if you take care of this yourself. But if the fight goes bad for you, send a word-bringer back to my boat. I'll signal with the cannon, and my boys will give you a hand."

"The fight will not go bad," Cries Yia Eya assured him. "Even now you are looking at the best warriors in the tribe. The rest are loyal to Bull Hump. They would rather dig turnips with the squaws than tread the warpath with men. Tonight Cries Yia Eya takes over his people!"

"All right, *Chief*," said Munro, nodding with satisfaction. "First let's break out the weapons and make sure your braves know how they operate. Then the next move is yours."

Chapter 10

Knobby and the three Cheyennes had seen and heard enough. At a high sign from the old man, they quickly retreated down the bluff. They hid inside a jagged erosion gully to counsel.

Wolf Who Hunts Smiling's grim face showed clearly that he had understood the slow, clearly spoken English. Touch the Sky quickly filled Little Horse in on the treachery afoot, though the sturdy little brave had guessed enough without words.

"What do we do?" Touch the Sky asked Knobby, despair clear in his tone. "Bull Hump's village is still well downriver from here. We'll never get there on foot in time to warn them."

"Simmer down, sprout," said Knobby. "If we hump it, there's more time than you kallate. This hoss helped load them weapons. The pistols is all brand-spankin' new Remingtons that was broke down for shipping. They got to be put together agin. Them Innuns ain't never seed that model 'n' won't know sic 'em about the mechanism. Munro'll hafta learn 'em how they work.

"Plus, the whole shitaree—the rifles too—is packed thick in oil to protect the workin's from rust on the river. All that gun oil will hafta be cleaned off the firing pins 'n' loading gates afore them irons will crack caps."

Knobby's calm voice had its effect on Touch the Sky. He too calmed down and began to think more clearly. He continued speaking in English to Knobby.

"We won't have to worry about noise, so we can make good time back to the boat. You've got the horses grazing near the river. We can cut out three fast ponies and ride hard to the camp and warn Bull Hump. We *might* be able to beat the others."

"That's the gait!" said Knobby approvingly. "Now you're roarin' like a he-bear Cheyenne. This hoss by God wishes he could ride with you. But there'll be trouble a-plenty as it is, comin' up on a red village at night. Ye doan need no hair-face to draw down fire from the sentries.

" 'Sides, the rheumatic has already got this old bag o' bones stiff 'n' tied up. A hard ride'll crack his tailbone. C'mon, pards—time to make tracks back to the river!"

The three Cheyennes read it as a good omen—at least for now—when a full ivory moon suddenly emerged from the boiling mass of dark clouds. With the silver-white moonlight aiding them, they made the trip back to the river in good time.

Knobby cut a sorrel, a paint, and his favorite, the chestnut mare, from the ponies grazing the bunchgrass in a temporary rope corral. There were leather saddles aboard the *Sioux Princess*. But the three Cheyennes settled for bridles and reins.

Wolf Who Hunts Smiling and Little Horse had used only buffalo-hair hackamores. Old Knobby had to show them how to slip the iron bits into the horses' mouths. Though they said nothing, Touch the Sky could tell they were thinking the same thing—this was yet one more proof of the white man's barbarous treatment of horses.

As they were about to set out, Touch the Sky ready to mount the chestnut, Old Knobby caught hold of his arm.

"Might be that your trail will cross with the others afore you git to Bull Hump's camp. Or mebbe you'll be caught in the lead when the renegades show up. So poke this last bit o' advice into your sash.

"Like I said, that-air Cries Yia Eya is a mighty consequential brave. You knock the wind out o' *his* sail, the whole fleet is dead in the water—you catch my drift?"

The younger braves following the rebellious subchief drew their reckless courage from his example. If Cries Yia Eya were taken out of the picture, the others would have no leader in their traitorous uprising. Touch the Sky considered this a fatal weakness of the red man's warrior code. He secretly believed that red men needed to be more like the Bluecoats on this point—white soldiers rigorously maintained a strict chain of command to ensure a leader in battle at all times, even if the original commander was killed or wounded. But when Indians lost a battle chief, too often they were quickly thereafter defeated.

Touch the Sky nodded. "I catch your drift. Thanks, Knobby."

The hostler slapped him on the back. "Doan forget Munro's gun-throwing militia is in this neck o' the woods. Keep your powder dry, buck, and give 'em a war face! Good huntin' to all three o' ye!"

Touch the Sky grabbed a handful of shaggy mane and swung up onto the pony, laying his rifle across its withers. Moments later the three braves, assisted by generous moonwash, were racing up the sloping bank of the river toward the open flats.

After so many long days cramped up on the boat, it made their blood sing to be on horseback again. The cool wind lifted their long, loose locks like black streamers, flying as one with the manes of the ponies. Touch the Sky drew strength from the feel of the chestnut's powerful, tightly bunched muscles moving with fluid grace beneath him.

The mare too seemed glad for the hard run after so much inactivity. She responded only reluctantly when Touch the Sky drew in her reins as they neared the final rise overlooking the Dakota camp.

The brief exhilaration of the ride was behind him. Now there was only the worry cankering at him: Would they be in time to do anything useful? Or would Bull Hump be dead, and the camp under command of Cries Yia Eya?

They had already discussed their plan on the return trip to the *Sioux Princess*. Sentries would be ringing the camp, stationed in the encircling belt of cottonwood and pine trees which surrounded the village. Those loyal to Cries Yia Eya would be grouped at the north approach to camp—the route from Council Rock that his band would almost surely be taking. So the three Cheyennes approached now from the south.

It was not a night sentry's main responsibility to fire on intruders, but rather to immediately rouse the tribe to possible danger. Nor, with full moonlight showing the Cheyennes' identity, would Dakota sentries be likely to fire on their allies. Though of course, armed Cheyennes approaching at night were clearly violating normal customs and might well be up to no good. Some rebellious Dog Soldiers of the Southern Cheyennes had been known to sneak this far north on raiding missions. Even tribes normally friendly to each other had learned to be suspicious.

Still, they agreed the best plan was simply to ride boldly up and let the sentries rouse the village—this was exactly what they wanted to do anyway. The next step was to confer, as quickly as possible, with Chief Bull Hump.

Touch the Sky was grateful for the calm silence as they approached. At least the still night air was not yet disturbed by the sounds of attack.

As soon as they topped the last rise, clearly skylined now against the full moon, a sentry sounded the Dakota's shrill, yipping alarm.

By the time they were halfway down the rise, iron-shod hooves drum-beating, they heard riders galloping out to intercept them. A party of about a dozen warriors, several still naked but armed, formed a skirmish line to stop them. They had no rifles. But all had already strung an arrow into their green-oak bows.

"Halt there or blood must flow!" commanded one of the warriors. "Why do you approach our camp at night, armed like this for battle? We know you as our friends."

Little Horse, who when he was younger had played with a Dakota child taken in by the tribe, spoke for them. He mixed their words with Cheyenne and Sioux words, knowing most Dakota also understood those two tongues a little.

"Because blood *will* flow, and soon, brothers! We must speak with Bull Hump. Even now the hotheaded Cries Yia Eya bears down on your village, backed by rebellious warriors with blood in their eyes. They met this night with paleface dogs at Council Rock. They have new guns and plan to kill your chief. Some of your sentries are playing the dog for Cries Yia Eya and will not sound the alarm."

His words momentarily stunned the others into silence. Then they conferred rapidly in Dakota. One of them leaped to the ground on all fours and bent his head low, listening.

"The tall stranger speaks straight-arrow," he confirmed. "Riders approach! Many, and rapidly!"

"I will alert Bull Hump and check the tipis," said another, "and see who is missing." He rode quickly back down toward camp.

Still, the remaining sentries were cautious.

"Sadly, we do not find your words about Cries Yia Eya difficult to believe. But you must surrender your weapons before we take you to Bull Hump," said the first brave. "You may speak from two sides of your mouth."

The Cheyennes did not object, knowing this was only a proper precaution. The Dakota braves quickly led them into camp. Dogs, upset by these unfamiliar actions, barked and yowled. Already the women and children and elders were gathering near the river. They were desperately searching out places where they had cached buffalo-hide rafts. At the first signal, they would ferry across the river and take to the secret escape routes.

Chief Bull Hump met the new arrivals in front of his tipi. He was an old man of perhaps 70 winters, and clearly in ill health. His skin sagged off his bones like the loose coat of an old hound. He wore his long white hair parted in the middle and brushed back behind his ears. But in a defiant gesture, he had donned his bone breastplate over his blanket.

Bull Hump spoke the Cheyenne language. Quickly Little Horse explained the desperate situation facing his village. Bull Hump's leather-cracked face showed nothing. But it was clear from the deep furrow between his eyes that all of this seemed highly suspicious to him.

"You say you are from Gray Thunder's band? Then do you know Arrow Keeper?"

It was Touch the Sky who spoke up. "I am his assistant in the shaman arts, Father. He is training me to be a medicine man."

Bull Hump leaned close to Touch the Sky, squinting. Arrow Keeper was the most respected Cheyenne on all the Plains. If Arrow Keeper had truly chosen this tall young buck to be his assistant, his honesty would be beyond challenging.

"If you know Arrow Keeper well," said Bull Hump, "tell me this. What does he always carry in his medicine bag, besides the totem of his Owl Clan?"

This question stumped Little Horse and Wolf Who Hunts Smiling. But Touch the Sky spoke up without hesitating.

"He always carries his magic bloodstone, Father, which makes his tracks difficult for his enemies to find."

Bull Hump nodded once, his face still an impassive mask of cracked leather. But he turned to the sentries, and his next words showed that he was now convinced.

"These brave Cheyenne youths speak with one tongue. Every warrior must make ready his rig for battle, now!"

But more bad news arrived. The sentry who had checked the tipis now rode up.

"Bull Hump, our best fighters are missing! Your cousin Red-tailed Hawk and his party are not due back from the trading post in Red Shale for two more sleeps. The others must be following Cries Yia Eya. We have only a handful of blooded warriors, none with fire sticks."

Now Bull Hump was desperate as he remembered—Red-tailed Hawk and his band of 15 seasoned fighters, all loyal to Bull Hump, had taken travois loaded with beaver pelts to trade for rifles and bullets.

And even now, from the north approach to camp, came the sound of many riders drawing closer.

"Dakota Father," said Touch the Sky, "I ask your pardon for speaking up so boldly. But we are the fighting Cheyenne, and we are keen for this battle! Cries Yia Eya plays the dog for whites who are stealing our homeland along with yours. We have discussed a plan to remove the tip from the lance. Give us ropes, Father. Then form up your warriors around your tipi and wait. If we fail, soon enough the bloody battle will come to you."

Bull Hump had no choice but to place his fate in the hands of these three brave Cheyennes. Perhaps, after all, they had been sent by the Great Spirit for just this purpose. He nodded, ordering one of the sentries to give the young warriors buffalo-hair ropes.

The three braves had followed Knobby's advice in forming their plan. They would use the strategy of the buffalo hunt. Hunters never attacked an entire herd—they isolated part of it from the rest, then closed for the kill.

Now the attackers had nearly gained the final tree-pocked slope which descended into camp from the north end of the village. The Cheyennes raced forward, knowing that every moment counted now. Touch the Sky and Little Horse had successfully used ropes to disrupt an attack on the Hanchon spread at Bighorn Falls. They had decided to try their rope trick once again. They knew that the fiery Cries Yia Eya would be riding in front of his warriors.

They reached a spot where a cottonwood and a scrub pine grew across from each other on opposite sides of the sloping approach. Quickly, Wolf Who Hunts Smiling rode out ahead and took up a position behind another tree with his Colt.

Touch the Sky and Little Horse dismounted and slapped their horses hard on the flanks, scattering them. Then, moving rapidly, they stretched the rope out between them and then each hid behind one of the trees.

They were not a moment too soon. Throwing all caution to the wind, Cries Yia Eya raised a hideous war cry as his powerful buckskin leaped over the top of the rise and plunged down toward the quiet village. The ground thundered and vibrated as the main body poured over the rise behind him.

Cries Yia Eya held his new Hawken under one arm. Touch the Sky and Little Horse waited until the last possible moment. Then Touch the Sky shouted, "*Now,* brother!"

Rapidly, deftly, they snubbed each end of the rope several turns around the trees. This left it almost three feet off the ground. The sure-footed pony saw it and leaped at the last moment. For a heartbeat Touch the Sky's hopes sank—now the village was doomed!

Then one rear hoof snagged hard on the rope, it held, and with incredible speed and force the buckskin crashed muzzle first into the ground.

Cries Yia Eya lost his rifle as he tumbled forward in a fast somersault. He slammed into the ground, stunned. Before he could recover and rise, Touch the Sky had raced out from the right flank. Now he rammed the muzzle of his Sharps into the rebellious subchief's neck. He spoke in Cheyenne, but his meaning was deadly clear.

"One twitch, and you cross over tonight!"

The surprised warriors, following hard upon Cries Yia Eya's heels, reined their ponies hard to avoid trampling him. They flowed past their downed leader like a raging river parting around a huge boulder in midstream. As a brave lifted his rifle to fire at the lone, brazen Cheyenne, a shot rang out from Wolf Who Hunts Smiling's position.

The brave's shield flew from his hand as Wolf Who Hunts Smiling's bullet struck it. The Cheyennes had already agreed to avoid shedding blood after dark—a serious taboo to their tribe—except as a last resort. A second Dakota brave raised his pistol to fire at Touch the Sky.

Now Little Horse fired his scattergun into the trees, the buckshot raising a loud clatter. He quickly rotated all four barrels and fired them in succession. The roar of the shotgun was deafening and spooked several of the Dakota ponies. Deflected buckshot rained down on the warriors and many of them flinched.

By now Wolf Who Hunts Smiling had loaded another primer cap and blown a brave's war bonnet off his head. This unexpected armed resistance, and the capture of their leader, confused the others. Where had the tribe gotten guns, and how many? Rumors suddenly flew through their midst that Red-tailed Hawk and the rest must have returned early with new munitions. Many now believed they were under heavy defensive attack and retreated back over the rise.

"Your war leader is only a bullet away from death!" shouted Little Horse in his odd blend of Dakota and Cheyenne. "Look near the river! Your wives and children and old grandmothers huddle in fear—those whom you are sworn to protect! Even now your old chief stands bravely in front of his tipi, prepared to die like a man. Who among you will shamelessly shed Bull Hump's blood?"

Cries Yia Eya tried to shout out something. But Touch the Sky growled like an angry beast and threw his weight into the rifle. The notched sight pressed into Cries Yia Eya's throat hard enough to choke his words off.

About half the warriors remained, uncertain what to do, wondering if they were surrounded by Cheyennes—certainly no warriors to be trifled with. Then one of them shouted something and pointed down toward camp. The others looked where he pointed and fell silent.

Chief Bull Hump, alone, walked slowly up the slope toward them. Eerie silver moonlight gleamed off his bone breastplate. In the ghostly light the pale, gaunt figure looked almost like a spirit wraith from a medicine vision. Ten paces out from Touch the Sky and the prisoner, he stopped.

"Dakota warriors!" he shouted. "Here stands your chief unarmed, with the yellow leaves of age clinging to the brow where once a dark mane flew as he raced into battle! Kill him, then, and follow Cries Yia Eya! Follow the red traitor who has sold your buffalo ranges for brutal power!

"Kill your chief now, as the women and children watch from the river. *Kill* him! And let he who sends this old warrior under also boast how, like Cries Yia Eya, he played the white man's dog, while young cheyenne strangers fought for the Dakota people!"

These words had a profound effect on the remaining warriors. Their shame now was almost palpable. One after another they lowered their weapons, some dropping them to the ground.

Then, to the last man, they folded their arms in the universal Indian sign for peace, and Touch the Sky knew the immediate crisis was over.

Chapter 11

Fargo Danford sat astride his big claybank on a long ridge overlooking Bull Hump's Dakota village from the south.

In the generous light of the full moon, he had watched the drama unfold below as if he were a spectator in a huge outdoor theater. The action had been exciting enough, he conceded. Damned entertaining, actually. Those three bucks were young, but clearly not the type to rabbit at the first sound of a war whoop.

But Wes Munro was definitely going to be unhappy.

To one side of Danford, Heck Nash sat his saddle on the big roan stallion. The sawed-off scattergun which had destroyed Smiles Plenty's face was balanced across his saddletree.

"Where in blazes did them three come from?" said Nash, watching three Indians ride away in single file from Bull Hump's village. "From Smoke Rising's camp?"

Danford shook his head. The brim of his flat leather shako hat left most of his face in shadow. "Them ain't 'Rapaho. Them's Cheyennes."

"In a pig's ass! There's no Cheyenne camp hereabouts."

"Well, then, could be they just dropped down from the moon. But them's Cheyennes."

"Might be Cheyennes," said a third man in the group, which remained slightly down ridge from the other two. "But I scouted for the 2nd Cavalry, and I by God know shod horses when I hear them. Those red varmints're ridin' shod horses."

Danford nodded. "That they be, that they be. Makes a man a mite curious, don't it?"

Wes Munro had ordered Danford and his men to stand by during the assault by Cries Yia Eya and his renegades. Their orders were to sit tight unless the fight went badly for the rebels.

But *what* fight? Danford thought now. Those three upstart braves had quickly unstrung the attackers' nerves, and not one drop of Indian blood had stained the earth.

Danford realized it was pointless to attack the village now. His militia group was some two dozen strong, a formidable, well-armed force. But he knew the point was not simply to kill redskins—it was to make sure that the big chiefs were all drinking out of Munro's trough.

And those three Cheyennes, wherever the hell they'd come from, were obviously dead set against letting that happen. But how did they know about the plan for tonight? Munro had sworn it was secret.

He watched the three Cheyennes crest a long bluff, riding due east. The fat, butter-colored moon sat suspended on a low line of hills beyond them. For a moment the three figures slid across the lunar face, darkly silhouetted. It almost seemed as if they *had* fallen down out of the moon just in the nick of time, and were now returning inside.

White man's shod horses. They stole them then, thought Danford. That made them hostiles. But then, he agreed with the philosophy of some of the army commanders: *All* Indians were hostiles.

Wherever they came from, it was time to settle their hash. Danford had a job to do if he wanted to collect his wages. He told himself he damn straight wasn't about to let a trio of flea-bitten blanket asses come between *this* dog and his meat.

"Gee-up, you ornery, ugly, hard-cussin' bachelors of the saddle!" Danford called out to the rest. "Let's take some of the starch outta them red A-rabs!"

He put hard spur to his mount, and the big claybank leaped off down the side of the ridge. With a whoop, his men followed him.

As they returned to the river, the Cheyennes boasted as all Indian braves do after a victory.

"Brothers," said Little Horse, "did you see Cries Yia Eya's face as he flew over his pony's ears? I did not—all I could see was his rump!"

"And did you see the others flinch and duck when Little Horse rained buckshot down on them?" said Touch the Sky. "From their frightened faces, I thought we had perhaps woken the children!"

"Their bull was down," said Wolf Who Hunts Smiling, "so the herd ran over a cliff!"

All three Cheyennes laughed at that. For this moment, at least, the enmity between Wolf Who Hunts Smiling and the other two seemed forgotten.

But much had been left in doubt, and the three young bucks did not celebrate long as reality again set in. Cries Yia Eya had been taken prisoner even as they left, true. But how strong was his influence among the younger braves?

Exile from the tribe might not remove the threat. Unlike the Cheyenne, the Arapaho did practice capital punishment. But would Bull Hump, an old and ailing chief, be strong enough to enforce such a punishment?

Even worse, what lay ahead as the Tongue River wound its way into the country of the Shoshone, the Gros Ventres?

"Brothers," said Little Horse suddenly, "*why* ride back to the keelboat at all? True, we might be able to help as we did this night. But we already know the plans of the white dogs. Why not hurry back to our people, report this at council, and join the war party which will surely return?"

The other two reflected on this. It was Wolf Who Hunts Smiling who spoke.

"Because," he replied slowly, "it is better to stay and do the thing ourselves. The old hair-face spoke right. Kill the queen and the hive is lost. It will take many sleeps to return to camp, then ride out again painted for battle. *We* can kill these two whites and help our tribe avoid a terrible battle."

"But this decision would be without benefit of council. Chief Gray Thunder spoke wisely," objected Little Horse, "when he said no people are more terrible than the whites in their thirst for revenge when Indians kill their own."

"So? The war party you speak of would attract even more notice from the whites," said Wolf Who Hunts Smiling.

"True," agreed Touch the Sky. "But what if the two paleface dogs met a terrible accident? A death that could not be blamed on the red man? This is not unlikely on so hard and dangerous a journey."

Now the other two braves watched him closely, hungry for more.

"This time I think the hot-tempered Wolf Who Hunts Smiling is right," said Touch the Sky. "True, we have no permission from the Councillors to act on our own. But are we not warriors? Is our tribe, and many others, not in grave danger? These white devils have killed Smoke Rising. How many others would have gone under this very night? I say, we return to the boat and watch for our chance. These paleface swindlers drew first blood!"

Wolf Who Hunts Smiling stopped riding and thrust out his lance.

"I have ears for these words! This is not drawing first blood, so we are not sullying the Sacred Arrows. Let us swear on it, bucks! If we fall, it will be on our enemy's bones!"

All three warriors crossed lances and pledged themselves to the victory.

Yet despite this warrior's oath the three swore as one, Touch the Sky was worried. There was a strong, ambitious gleam in Wolf Who Hunts Smiling's eye—the same urgent glint he had seen on the night when, disobeying orders, Wolf Who Hunts Smiling had tried to raise a sleeping Pawnee's scalp. He had thus roused the enemy camp and caused the death of Swift Canoe's twin brother, True Son. To this day Swift Canoe blamed Touch the Sky for that.

Wolf Who Hunts Smiling was young, with only 17 winters behind him. But his ears were full of tales of Indians with only 20 winters who had nonetheless led great tribes into battle. And Touch the Sky now suspected that the good of the tribe had little to do with Wolf Who Hunts Smiling's intentions—it was personal glory he wanted to wrap himself in. No doubt he was determined to have Munro's scalp dangling off his clout.

"Brothers!" said Little Horse, abruptly scattering Touch the Sky's thoughts. "Listen!"

They sat their ponies without moving, all three falling silent. Little Horse's keen ears were already legendary among the tribe. The trio was downwind in a gentle breeze fragrant with the smell of prairie flowers and sweet grass. The fat moon shone big and yellow almost straight overhead.

Now Touch the Sky heard it—the stiff, low creaking of saddle leather, the jangle of cinches and latigos and rowel-tipped spurs.

Caught up in their discussion, and still heady with thoughts of the tense encounter at Bull Hump's camp, none of the braves had paid attention to the long ridge on their right. Now, even as they stared in that direction, dozens of well-armed riders charged over the ridge straight at them, gun muzzles spitting fire.

Touch the Sky realized immediately, as he dug his knees hard into the chestnut mare's flanks, that this must be Munro's militiamen.

"Ride like the wind itself, brothers!" shouted Little Horse. "Be one with your pony or sing the death song!"

Now lead whizzed past their ears with the sound of angry hornets. All three braves automatically dropped low and forward, into the defensive riding position for which their tribe was famous when bullets whined too close—hugging the pony's neck close, presenting a minimal target away from the direction of attack. All the whites might glimpse was a leg hooked over the pony's back, a face momentarily peering from under its neck.

"*Hiya*!" they urged their horses and rallied each other. "*Hiya hi-i-i-ya*!"

The attackers whooped and shouted curses behind them, their blood up for the kill. The ground thundered, horses nickered, more guns spoke their piece. Flying lead nipped at the braves' heels and tore up clumps of sod all around them.

Touch the Sky knew their only hope now was the strength and speed of their horses. These were all broncos, selected by Knobby as the best in the herd. Broncos could make fine and gentle horses. But Touch the Sky also knew that, despite the water-starving, beatings, blindfolds, and other tricks used by white men to break their spirit, now and then their former wildness came out. When that happened, broncos galloped with a reckless abandon that was dangerous for horse and rider.

Fortunately for the Cheyennes, the broncos' former wildness came out with a vengeance this night.

To the pursuing whites, the Cheyennes seemed to be simply an extension of the swift-as-lightning horses they rode with such astonishing skill. Steadily, one by one, the tamer mounts of the militiamen began to falter; the trio of wild Indians gradually opened the distance. Finally, when the

Cheyennes were swallowed up by a dense pine forest bordering the Tongue, Danford gave the command to cease the chase.

"Leave it alone for now, boys," he called out to his men. He holstered his big Navy Colt, butt forward to accommodate his left-handed cross-draw. "The horses are played out. We'll ride closer to the river and make camp for the night. I got me a gut hunch we'll be seein' them bucks again real soon."

Chapter 12

But Fargo Danford didn't realize exactly *how* soon he'd be seeing the Cheyennes again.

As it turned out, he and his men made their camp less than a mile from the three braves' camp near the *Sioux Princess*. Danford picked this spot on purpose because he was due to report to his boss at the crack of dawn.

While his men snored in their bedrolls, Danford boiled himself a can of coffee. Then, with pockets of white mist still shrouding the river, he untethered the claybank and rode downstream to meet Wes Munro.

The three Cheyennes had already discussed this potential new danger of the militia reporting last night's chase to Munro. But they mistakenly believed the militia had crossed their trail by chance—they had no idea the hired outlaws had actually watched them ruin Cries Yia Eya's raid.

Very few whites, they all agreed, could distinguish tribes, especially in the dark. Chances were good the militia would have mistaken them for Dakota braves or neighboring Arapahos.

Thus lulling themselves with false security, exhausted, they slept soundly as Danford reported. He approached the boat quietly from upstream, and the Indian camp was well downstream from the keelboat. Thick mist separated their camp from the boat. The hissing chuckle of the current filtered out noises and made their sleep deeper. Danford had left his claybank in a spruce thicket before disappearing almost immediately inside the plank cabin.

"How'd things turn out last night?" Munro said in greeting. The keelboat skipper was still bare to the waist. A metal mirror was nailed to the wall. In the weak light of the coal-oil lamp, Munro was carefully shaving.

Hays Jackson sat at the deal table. His face was still sullen and lopsided with sleep, the left eye winking open and shut spasmodically. He poured whiskey into a metal cup of coffee and tossed it down in a few gulps.

"Jesus Christ in a buckboard!" said Danford, removing his shako hat and fanning it in front of his nose. He stared at Jackson. "Smells like something died and swole up bad in here."

"A bunch of goddamn wimmin worry about how they smell," said Jackson.

"Never mind that," said Munro impatiently. "Why do you two have to scrap like dogs?"

He concentrated closer in the mirror as he slid the straight razor over the bumps of his throat. "I asked you," he said to Danford, "how it turned out last night."

"It turned out flatter 'n a one-sided pancake," said Danford without further explanation.

Munro's hand stopped moving. His eyes shifted upward to find Danford's reflection in the mirror.

"Spell it out plain. I don't pay you top dollar to speak in riddles."

"Cries Yia Eya is trussed up tight in ropes, a prisoner of his tribe. And every damn one o' them weapons you give him is in the hands of braves loyal to Bull Hump. Is *that* plain enough?"

Red-mottled rage crept up from Munro's neck into his fresh-shaven face. He splashed water from the wash basin, rinsing off the remaining shaving soap. Only when the first, tight-templed throbs of anger passed did he speak again. His voice was dangerously low and calm.

"You mean to tell me you stood by and watched Bull Hump's braves whip Cries Yia Eya? And you and your men didn't pitch in?"

"Pitch in? Pitch in to *what*? Wes, I'm here to swear by the two balls of Christ there was no battle to pitch into! Thanks to three Cheyennes, it was all over faster than a starvin' man could swallow a chokecherry."

Danford was surprised. His remark about the Cheyennes nearly floored the other two men.

"Cheyennes?" repeated Munro in that same low, dangerously calm tone. "Three of them?"

Danford described the part the braves had played in defusing the raid.

"I tried to do for 'em," said Danford. "My word on it, we give 'em jip. But they had fresh, faster horses. White man's horses, though. They was all shod."

"Was one of the bucks," said Munro, "noticeably taller than the others? And the two smaller ones, was one stocky built, the other wiry and tough with slinking eyes that never stop moving?"

Danford's jaw went slack. "That they be, though I couldn't see no eyes. You know these Innuns?"

"Know them? Why, man, they've been drinking my coffee every day!"

Danford finally took his meaning. Understanding flashed in his eyes. "Say! You mean, them three jackleg boatmen you mentioned to me?"

His jaw clamped so hard the muscles were tightly bunched, Munro nodded. The same three boatmen who were coming between him and a wagon road that was only the beginning of huge profits and almost unlimited power.

Hays Jackson pushed away from the table, rising. He slid the Paterson Colt out of its holster. "The hell we waitin' on? Let's kill them slippery red niggers now."

"Put that iron away and sit down, you fool," said Munro. "You think you're just going to waltz up and kill *those* Indians? They might be young, but Gray Thunder knew what he was doing when he sent them. Don't sell a Cheyenne warrior short.

"Besides, I don't want them dead just yet. I need to know how much Gray Thunder knows. I need to know how he got wind of the scheme. And I damn sure need to know how much they've told to anyone else."

"See there? See there?" said Jackson. "I *told* you that red devil palavers English. Didn't I say he did?"

Munro ignored him, looking at Danford. "Did anybody see you come aboard?"

"Don't seem likely. I was quiet-like, and the mist is thick."

Munro glanced through the cabin doorway and

nodded with satisfaction. "It still is. Leave now. For all I know, they didn't even come back last night. But if they did they'll be coming aboard soon. I don't want them to see you."

"Should I have the boys resume the routine patrols?"

Munro shook his head. "No, not yet. Look here."

He stabbed an index finger into the navigation chart on the table. "There's a huge clbow bend in the river right before it reaches the fork with Frenchman's Creek. You know the spot?"

Danford nodded. "That I do. There's big salt licks there."

"That's the spot," said Munro. "Here's what I want you to do."

If Munro and Jackson harbored any new suspicions, Touch the Sky noticed no warning. Jackson was no more or less surly than usual when they reported on deck with the rest of the crew.

Munro, as always, spent most of his time over his charts and maps. Old Knobby greeted the trio with a stealthy wink and a reassuring nod. Then he turned quickly away again to tend to the horses and mules.

Nonetheless, as he glanced upriver through the clearing mist, Touch the Sky felt his still-developing shaman's sixth sense nettling him again.

Unfortunately, he had little time to ponder the feeling. He and Little Horse were both forced to keep a close watch on Wolf Who Hunts Smiling. Both braves had conferred in secret after yesterday's plan was formed. They agreed that the hot-headed, arrogantly proud youth would now seize the weakest excuse to kill Jackson and Munro.

They were determined not to let his blind quest for personal glory jeopardize the entire tribe.

If the *tribe* must be blamed, then *all* the Cheyenne warriors would tread the warpath first and earn the bloody punishment that would surely come. Otherwise, with luck and help from Maiyun, the Good Supernatural, the deaths of these two murdering land-grabbers would be "accidents" spawned by the dangerous river. The tribe had suffered enough from the white man's wrath.

All this tumbled like loose scree through Touch the Sky's head as he manned his pole to help shove the *Sioux Princess* away from the grassy bank. As usual the square sail lay flat and crumpled against the mast, as dead as a spent cartridge. When the boat reached midstream, the crew manned the oars. The river was wide hereabouts, fairly unencumbered for smooth rowing.

Something suddenly occurred to Touch the Sky: Despite Wolf Who Hunts Smiling's almost taunting stares and gestures, Jackson was just as deliberately ignoring him.

Why? He had never before shown such restraint. Why now? wondered Touch the Sky.

That feeling was back, a nagging little awareness like something half-remembered, half-forgotten. But once again he had no luxury to turn over and poke through his own thoughts. Now they were approaching a huge, sharp bend. The river suddenly constricted, boiling into white froth and making rowing impractical. Nor would poles ensure safe progress through all the boulders and other debris which naturally massed at river bends.

But smooth shelves of rock had been cut out by centuries of wind and current. They followed the bend around on both banks until the river widened again. The banks were easily wide enough to accommodate many men.

"Man the cordelles!" shouted Jackson.

This was followed by the usual chorus of groans from the Creole voyageurs. The two teams grabbed the thick towing ropes and clambered over the gunnels. Those waiting on deck fed the ropes overboard to their comrades as they swam ashore and climbed up onto the rock ledges.

As the three Cheyennes prepared to leap out, Touch the Sky again glanced upriver. Now the sharp bend cut off most of his view.

Still, a cool feather of apprehension tickled the bumps of his spine.

"Brothers!" he said suddenly to the other two. "We are in danger! An enemy is hard upon us!"

Little Horse looked at him sharply. The sturdy little brave was one of the few who had noticed the mulberry-colored birthmark, shaped like an arrowhead, buried past Touch the Sky's hairline. This tall youth was also marked as a receiver of visions. Arrow Keeper would never select any brave to learn the shaman arts unless that brave already possessed strong medicine.

"What do you mean?" demanded Little Horse. "Quickly, brother! Speak words that fit in our sashes!"

Touch the Sky shook his head, again staring toward the bend. "I cannot. Yet just now I felt it."

"You felt only your own fear," scoffed Wolf Who Hunts Smiling. "Like women will do, you have dwelled too long on the dangers we face. Now the bowstring of your courage has frayed. Be a man and do not fear any 'feeling.' That is a thing of smoke."

"You goddamn red devils quit stalling!" shouted Jackson. "I said man that damn cordelle!"

"You are a pig's afterbirth!" Wolf Who Hunts Smiling said to him aloud in Cheyenne. "It is common knowledge that white men rut on sheep and turn the offspring into soldiers!"

Though Jackson couldn't understand these taunts, the other two quickly shut their companion up.

"Hump it!" Jackson snapped his whip on the deck. "Move your flea-bit asses!"

They leaped into the cold river, swam a few strokes, then waded ashore and pulled themselves up onto the nearest rock ledge. They took their usual place at the end of the line of men tugging the cordelle. Each man gripped the thick rope and strained. Little Horse was in front, followed by Wolf Who Hunts Smiling. Touch the Sky brought up the rear of the line.

"*Heave*!" shouted Jackson from the deck, establishing the cadence. "*Heave . . . heave . . . heave!*"

Soon sweat beaded up in his scalp and rolled down into his eyes. Sometimes Touch the Sky was bent almost double as he heaved forward against the rope. He tossed his head once to throw the sweaty, long locks back out of his eyes.

For a heartbeat, in the corner of his right eye, he saw the butt of the huge Navy Colt descending fast toward his skull. A moment later a color wheel exploded inside his head. His bones seemed to become all soft marrow as he collapsed on the ledge.

Chapter 13

Pain throbbed over his right temple, one moment dull, the next sharp. His entire body felt hot, and rivulets of sweat flowed down out of his thick hair, making it hard to open his eyes.

He opened them anyway, to nothing but the salt sting of sweat and a harsh yellow orb of relentless sun. Quickly he closed his eyes again. He tried to move his arms, his legs, but they refused to respond. Every slight movement of his head sent a fresh jolt of pain hammering into his skull.

"Thisen's comin' around," said an unfamiliar voice.

Touch the Sky cocked his head out of the sun and opened one eye. From this angle he saw the white canvas flap of the square sail, now billowing as a favoring wind finally filled it.

A boat, he remembered the keelboat. These hard

boards must be the planks of the deck beneath him, then. He still wasn't quite sure yet how he got there. But it felt like the boat was gliding along at a good clip. Why couldn't *he* move?

The sweat cleared from one eye. Now he saw Little Horse stretched out spread-eagle beside him on the deck. His wrists and ankles were bound in lengths of green rawhide. The rawhide had then been staked into the deck. Congealed blood traced the edges of a fresh wound on Little Horse's forehead. Flies had begun to land in the tacky mess.

He glanced to the other side and saw Wolf Who Hunts Smiling in the same plight, his jaw bruised and swollen, perhaps broken.

"Welcome to the white man's West," said Jackson's voice. A moment later the toe of a leather boot smashed into his ribs. Touch the Sky flinched as fresh pain wracked his body.

Now two faces peered down at him, harshly back-lit by the sun. Jackson's close-set eyes he recognized immediately, even without the nervous wink. The other man was a stranger. But no, he remembered that odd, flat hat—the leader of the exterminators of red men, who called themselves militia!

From the angle and warmth of the sun, Touch the Sky guessed it was late morning. Now the gates of memory had been flung wide, and he recalled being knocked cold on shore.

Jackson kicked him again harder, in the same spot. The force of the pain lifted Touch the Sky's strong back up inches off the deck, straining the green rawhide. But the strong thongs held.

"Thought you was a pretty crafty Injun, dintcha?" said Jackson. "Thought you was slicker 'n snot on a saddlehorn, hah? I wager this, blanket ass. Before that green rawhide shrinks all the way, you'll not only palaver in English, we'll have you singin' 'Loo-loo Girl!' "

Jackson kicked him in the face this time. The hob-nailed sole of his boot raked over Touch the Sky's cheek and split it open. Warm blood trickled into one eye.

Now Touch the Sky remembered why green rawhide had been used. It would shrink tight and firm in the sun, cutting off the blood and causing excruciating pain.

"Here's a lick for you too," said Jackson, kicking Little Horse in the groin. "Don't want to make you jealous of your pard."

The sickening thud of the kick made Touch the Sky wince. Another white man, the big baldhead one he had seen riding beside the militia leader last night, stood over Wolf Who Hunts Smiling.

"Thisen ain't quite woke up yet," said Heck Nash. "I hit him a mite hard. Maybe a little tonic water'll do the trick."

Moments later something warm splashed off the deck near him, and Touch the Sky realized with a shudder of disgust and murderous rage—the pale-face devil was making water in Wolf Who Hunts Smiling's face!

"H'ar now!" Touch the Sky recognized Old Knobby's angry voice. "Them's Injuns, mebbe, but a Christian man doan even treat a *dog* that low."

"You put a cork in it, you old pus-gut," said Jackson, "or we'll stretch your worthless, Injun-lovin' hide out beside 'em."

"Doan step in nothin' you can't wipe off," Knobby warned him defiantly. Now Touch the Sky could see him. The old man brandished his Kentucky over-and-under flintlock. "Ye'll speak direct to this gal afore ye hurt her sweetheart."

"You hear that old fart threaten me, Heck?" he said to the baldhead paleface. "I reckon old dogs growl even after they lose their teeth."

Wes Munro spoke quietly from the open doorway of the cabin, his words meant only for Jackson. "That old dog might yet kill both of us, you jackass. He had plenty of teeth when the Mandans and Crows hit us, didn't he? Don't force his hand. And you better chew on this too—the old man had to know the Indians have been riding the horses. Why do you suppose he's kept his mouth shut about it? Just whose colors do you think he's flying?"

"Sonofabitch," said Jackson. "Why, that old fart *has* got a set on him!"

Touch the Sky could hear only the sound of their voices, not the words. Munro added something else in his quiet voice. Then, mercifully, their tormentors left them alone for a while. But the sun and the shrinking rawhide quickly took over where the white devils had left off.

The pain in his wrists and ankles soon made his throbbing temple seem like a breeze caught in a tornado. He felt his hands and feet going numb as the thongs shrank in the hot sun. It felt like all four limbs were slowly being amputated.

Occasionally, Munro glanced out of the cabin at the three supine prisoners. He knew the Cheyenne tribe well enough to know that torturing a good brave for information was a tricky business, much like breaking green horses to leather. The spirit had to be broken first; the will to fight had to be destroyed.

That would be the job of those rawhide thongs,

plus a little extra hell thrown in for good measure now and then by Jackson and the militiamen. Hell, they had to have some fun. But Munro kept an eye on his men—he didn't want the Cheyennes beaten so senseless they couldn't answer his questions when the time came.

And they *would* answer his questions. All in good time. Plenty of investors back East had sunk capital into this venture. How could he return and report to them that savage, half-naked people who couldn't even record their own language had stumped him?

He had a plan. The threat of bodily harm to themselves might not be enough to break these stone-faced young warriors. But how would they respond if their refusal to cooperate hurt their companions instead?

Munro had studied the bucks closely during the voyage. The tall one who obviously knew English was tight as ticks with the powerfully built smaller brave. The other one, the sullen one with the furtive, swift-moving eyes, seemed aloof from both of them.

It was time to test his plan.

He went out on deck. The *Sioux Princess* still made good time, her square sail fat with favoring wind. A dozen men were rowing, assisting the wind against the current. Munro felt Etienne's gaze on him. But as usual when he glanced in the Creole leader's direction, the man was looking somewhere else.

That's another good reason, thought Munro, for cutting short the men's fun with the captives earlier. Though the voyageurs had remained aloof from the Cheyennes, a certain esprit bred from mutual suffering and hardship had sprung up. Etienne had watched Jackson with contemptuous hatred when he was kicking the braves, Munro recalled.

So it was best to keep it fast and quiet and effective.

Jackson and Heck Nash were sharing a bottle of whiskey at the stern of the boat. Munro waited impatiently until he had Jackson's attention. Then he nodded once. Jackson nodded back and handed the bottle back to Nash. On his way to join his boss, he paused to snatch a belaying pin out of its hole in the gunnel. It was a short but solid and heavy iron peg used for securing gear.

Touch the Sky was lost in a foggy delirium of pain. He was slow to register the image when Munro squatted down beside him and looked square into his face. His captor spoke in his halting but serviceable mixture of Cheyenne and Sioux.

"I know you speak English. For now, just tell me this. What orders did Gray Thunder give you?"

"Get downwind of me, you stinking mound of manure," said Wolf Who Hunts Smiling. He spoke with difficulty, the words slurred through his swollen jaw and lips. "Cheyenne braves will live to bull your mother and sisters while you watch!"

Munro ignored the snarling youth behind him. "I said, what orders did Gray Thunder give you?"

"He told me, as he told all of us, to work hard and not to shame our tribe."

"That's *all* he told you? You're sure?"

"He also said," Wolf Who Hunts Smiling interrupted, "that white men eat their newborns as will a cat! And that they smell worse than a camp dog's crotch! In these things he spoke straight."

"Cheyenne!" It was Little Horse who spoke, admonishing Wolf Who Hunts Smiling. "Are you a woman, to chatter so at our enemy? *Men* save their anger for deeds, not words."

"I'm saying it one last time: What else did your chief tell you?" repeated Munro.

"He reminded me to follow the Cheyenne way in all matters."

"Did he now? What else?"

"Nothing else. What have we done that is wrong?"

"What *you* just did wrong," said Munro, giving the signal to Jackson, "was that you refused to cooperate. And that refusal may have crippled your friend for life."

Pain jolted through Touch the Sky as Munro suddenly seized his head and turned it, forcing him to watch. Moving swiftly in spite of his bulk and drunkenness, Jackson pulled the belaying pin out from his sash. He bent low over Little Horse, took quick aim, then swung the pin with all his might, grunting loud at the effort. His blow smashed the tied-down warrior's right kneecap.

There was a fast, hard crack like green willow snapping. The surprised shriek this forced from Little Horse spooked the horses and made Nash drop his bottle overboard. Moaning, Little Horse went into shock and semiconsciousness.

Despite the terrible pain caused by the shrinking cords, Touch the Sky strained against them in rage. His murderous dark eyes shifted between Munro and Jackson. The latter chuckled as he rose again and slipped the iron peg back into his sash.

"Hell, it was like smashing a clamshell with a brick. *That* buck won't be doin' no war dances for a while."

Munro brought his smooth-shaven face within

inches of Touch the Sky's. "I'll be back later to ask you some more questions. Now you've seen what your refusal to help causes. Think about it. At least this time your friend is still alive."

Chapter 14

Touch the Sky did think about what Munro said. He thought long and deep, when the increasing pain from the shrinking rawhide would let him think.

He thought about it while Little Horse groaned at the double torture of shrinking cords and a shattered knee—this brave and true friend whose swift, sure movements had earned him his name. Never again would he glide with the lithe grace of a shadow.

Touch the Sky thought of this and much more. When Munro and Jackson returned, toward the end of the long afternoon, Touch the Sky had made up his mind. They were dead no matter what he said or didn't say. But saying one thing might get him untied. And that, at least, would be one last chance.

"How about it, friend?" Munro greeted him in

English. "You ready to talk terms?"

"I'm ready," he replied in the same language.

"Well, shit-oh-dear!" said Hays Jackson. "That belayin' pin must've inspired him."

"All right," said Munro. "Start by telling me what your chief knows."

"My chief," said Touch the Sky, "is Major Bruce Harding, Commanding Officer of the 7th Cavalry at Fort Bates."

Wolf Who Hunts Smiling had been about to hurl another insult in Cheyenne at the white dog. But he understood Touch the Sky's unexpected announcement. The words struck him with the force of fists. Now the rebellious Cheyenne buck fell silent, waiting for more.

Munro's face registered nothing at this. "What are you saying? Has your tribe signed a treaty with him? He's your treaty chief?"

"No. I'm saying he's my commanding officer. I was a forward observer with the Indian scouts assigned to his regiment. Now I'm on a longer mission to infiltrate the Cheyenne."

Jackson suddenly slapped his meaty thigh in amazement. "Hell 'n' furies! This is better 'n them shows where they got the two-headed cows! You believe the gall of this red nigger, sayin' he's a soldier?"

Munro was careful here. The claim did seem preposterous. On the other hand, this buck's English was spoken easily and with no accent. It was clearly the first language of his youth. And the War Department had indeed recently begun experimenting, infiltrating savage tribes with Indian spies loyal to the Stars and Stripes.

"If you're a spy," said Munro, "why did you speak up only after we hurt this brave?" He pointed at Little Horse.

"I'm not cooperating to protect the other two. I have nothing against them, they're good fighters and I share their blood. If I can help them, I will. I kept my mouth shut because that was my orders from Major Harding. But now I want to save my own bacon if I can. When you ordered that knee smashed, I knew then for sure you weren't just playing the larks."

Munro nodded. He was far from convinced, but it was a good, sensible answer.

He didn't know Major Harding personally, but he knew of him. Now Munro said, "What kind of man is your C.O.?"

Touch the Sky winced again at the tight-cutting pain of his rawhide bonds. He was aware that Wolf Who Hunts Smiling was listening to every word.

"A rulebook commander," said Touch the Sky, recalling what his friend Corey Robinson had told him. "A spit-and-polish man who can't tell a Sioux from a Cheyenne. He lets his junior officers make his decisions for him."

Munro said nothing. But this was exactly what he had heard about Harding.

"Who's your immediate superior?" said Munro. "The one you report to?"

"Lieutenant Seth Carlson."

In naming his enemy, Touch the Sky had taken a chance—Carlson had in fact been transferred far north of Ft. Bates as punishment for cooperating in Hiram Steele's attempt to run John Hanchon out of the mustang business. But if Munro knew this, he showed no sign of it.

"So what exactly *is* your mission for the Army?" said Munro.

This was the easiest part of his ruse. Touch the

Sky had grown up near a fort. Military formations, strategies, and thinking had been the stuff of everyday life.

"I communicate with forward observers by leaving messages in the forks of trees. I report anything that might be useful military intelligence. Exact numbers of braves, what kind of weapons and how many they're armed with, plans for major movements or raids. The Army already knows where most of the tribes pitch their summer camps. But by summer the horses are strong from the new grass, and the braves can fight on horseback naming their own terms. The Army wants to learn where the secret winter camps are located. Then they can attack when the snow and ice have the valleys locked. The ponies and the braves are weakest in winter."

"Hell, all that shines right to me," said Jackson. "I think this buck is tellin' the straight."

Wolf Who Hunts Smiling, ignored now, was ominously silent. He thought about everything he had just heard. What was Touch the Sky's motivation for saying these things? Everything he had just confessed to was an accusation hurled at him by members of the tribe. Had he cleverly made up a confession based on false accusations? Yet hearing him matter-of-factly state the words just now gave them a certain, bothersome ring of truth.

Could he be a spy after all? And even if he wasn't, could he not be claiming he was one to save himself from the fate awaiting the other two Cheyenne prisoners?

Munro too was wondering. This was a full-blooded Cheyenne. But if he was also an Army spy, he was a Cheyenne whose word would count for something with the military brass. True, he could prove true-blue soldier and ruin the wagon-road scheme—he certainly knew enough about it by now, if he chose to expose the plan.

But a man who had no qualms about selling out one race would just as quickly sell out another, if the price was right. And Munro could use such a man. His reports might be enough to bring in the soldiers against those tribes—like Bull Hump's—that refused to cooperate.

But Munro, unlike Jackson, was not yet convinced of the tall buck's story. Munro had survived on the frontier by taking nothing on faith and never trusting the next man. He left Touch the Sky and called Fargo Danford over.

"Where's your men?"

"Waitin' for me to meet 'em at Singing Woman Creek."

"We'll be there around nightfall," said Munro, gauging the remaining sun. "Listen, that new man you just put on the payroll . . ."

"Meeks? Sam Meeks?"

"That one. Didn't you say he was a snowbird? One who just deserted from the new regiment at Fort Bates?"

Danford nodded. "That new regiment formed special to hunt down Innuns. He slipped out after the first spring melt, said he was sick of eatin' beans and singin' 'Boots and Saddles.' "

Munro smiled at this news, adjusting one of his cuffs. He was the only man on board whose shirt was not fouled by dirt or sweat or blood. But a hard life spent following no law but his own had lent him a spur-trigger uncertainty it was not wise to challenge. Everyone who met him sensed it.

"Good. Tell him to come aboard when we reach the Singing Woman."

He returned to Touch the Sky's side and knelt down. "If you're telling the truth, we'll soon know," he told the Cheyenne prisoner. "And if you're telling the truth, I'll deal you in like a man and start by setting you free. The other two I can't do anything about, you have to understand—it's the same pressure a chief faces.

"Danford's men got their blood up chasing you three, but the kill never came. They want blood now. An Indian scout I can save. Not them. I'm not a strong enough chief. They've been drinking, and with women scarce, they're feeling mean and looking for a little fun. But you and I will talk some real terms, if your story proves out. You nail your colors to Wes Munro's mast, you'll come out of this a rich man."

Munro's eyes, two flat, hard chips of dark flint, held his.

"But if you're lying, buying time at my expense, all three of you die right there where you lay. Danford's men are upset. They've heard some story about Comanches dragging a white baby naked through cactus. Believe me, they plan on having some fun, and Cheyennes will do fine if Comanches aren't available."

Munro was watching him closely. Looking for the least sign, Touch the Sky knew, that all of this was a lie. That sign would also signal his death.

"That's fine by me," said Touch the Sky. "But these cords hurt like hell. You're all armed—can't you at least cut me loose while we're waiting?"

One chance, Touch the Sky thought. One wild chance was all he asked. One lunge for the knife in

Jackson's sheath. Knobby was no doubt watching everything. The old mountain man would get off at least two good shots, buying some time to cut the other two free. Wolf Who Hunts Smiling could fight, at least try to escape. But Little Horse could not even move.

Still, he could hold a weapon! What was the alternative to such wild schemes? Only slow, sure, agonizing, and humiliating death. Better to die like Cheyennes, uttering war cries with their last living breath. One chance was all he asked.

Munro considered the request for some time, watching the Cheyenne's face closely. Whatever he read there, his response showed that he did know Indians.

"No. We'll wait until Sam has a good look at you."

The green rawhide not only constricted around his limbs, it also drew tighter and tighter at the stakes until Touch the Sky was arched like a warrior's bow, forced to bend his back to relieve the pressure.

This same pressure bent the others too, causing incredible contortions of pain to Little Horse's ruined right knee. Now he had regained awareness and bore his pain in a numb silence.

Sunlight bled slowly from the sky, and the air took on the first evening chill. Touch the Sky knew, from the detail of voyageurs ordered to the poles, when they had reached the juncture with Singing Woman Creek. The sail had already been lowered. The first frogs of evening were beginning to sing when the *Sioux Princess* tacked close to shore and threw down her boarding plank.

Touch the Sky guessed, from the amount of whooping and cheering and shouting at the nearby camp, that the drinking had begun early. The planks trembled under him as more men in heavy boots boarded, clumping their way heavily toward the bound Cheyennes.

"That's what I'm sayin', Mr. Munro," said the voice he guessed was Sam Meeks. "Fort Bates ain't never used but Pawnees for scouts. And this Seth Carlson, he got orders out just after I joined up. He had a set-to with a big tall Cheyenne buck, and he lost."

Moments later the harsh smell of liquor assaulted his nose. Daylight was fading fast now, and several coal-oil lamps were already lit. Somebody thrust one close to his face.

"And right there's the buck who whipped him!" said Meeks triumphantly. "Spy? My sweet aunt! This here's the slippery hoss that sent Carlson somersaultin' 'cross the plains! Hell, half the 7th Regiment was poking steel after this one and his pard here with the swole-up knee. Can't say I've ever seen the other one, though, and I'm one tends to mark down an Indian's face for later."

For a moment Munro looked as if he'd just swallowed something that didn't agree with him. But it passed, and his face took on its usual calm wariness. He slipped one of the dueling pistols out of his sash and fired it into the air.

The flat report startled everyone into silence.

"You men on shore!" he called out. "Tonight it's good liquor and it's compliments of the Overland Company! Come aboard and broach a keg in friendship!"

A rousing cheer greeted this and men began hurrying onto the boarding ramp.

"There's also entertainment tonight!" shouted Munro. "We've captured three Cheyenne savages that tried to slit our throats while we slept!"

This brought another cheer and a few shouted oaths. The current Apache and Comanche uprisings to the south had paralyzed Texas and the Arizona Territory and spread fear far north. Now all was pandemonium as more of the hardcase militiamen joined the knot boarding.

It was one of Danford's men, having crossed to the pen to admire some of the horseflesh, who first saw it—the rapid sweep of flames just now engulfing the stern!

"Sweet Jesus Christ!" he said to himself. Then, almost as an afterthought, he yelled as loud as he could, "Fire!"

Chapter 15

Lying trapped on the deck, Touch the Sky felt the mood change from hostility to panic.

"Fire!" someone shouted again. The deck shook and vibrated under him as the men rushed toward the stern. The same stiff breeze that had filled the square sail all afternoon now wafted the first billowing clouds of harsh smoke to Touch the Sky's nostrils.

The boat pitched wildly at anchor as the horses panicked, rearing up, leaping up out of the shallow pen and forcing men to jump overboard to get out of their way.

"What's on the spit, tadpole?" a familiar voice suddenly said in his ear.

"Knobby!"

"Boy, you better hump it like a hound with his ass afire," said the old-timer grimly as he sliced his Bowie through the rawhide thongs binding Touch the Sky. "That-air blaze I set ain't gonna burn forever."

Knobby leaped across to free Wolf Who Hunts Smiling as Touch the Sky, body protesting in pain, sat up and quickly rubbed some life back into his dead, swollen limbs. Knobby must have ducked into the cabin first: Their weapons lay piled on the deck nearby.

"Shove that cut rawhide in your legging sash," said Knobby. "No need the others findin' it quick and knowin' how you was sprung."

"What about Little Horse?"

"Doan be a bigger fool 'n God made you, sprout! Lookit! Twixt that-air smashed knee and that bash he took on the brain-pan, he ain't goin' nowheres. You two jist rabbit for help or all three of ye're as good as planted!"

Old Knobby was right and Touch the Sky knew it. The old man had just risked his life for them, and he still had a lot to explain to Munro. Either they insisted on taking Little Horse, and died now trying to get him ashore, or they ran hard and lived to fight another day, perhaps saving Little Horse. It wasn't much of a choice, nor was there time to debate—already the flames were under control. Any second now someone would glance forward and see them.

Wolf Who Hunts Smiling too stumbled a few times trying to take a first step on his numb limbs.

"This hoss is dust," said Knobby, heading back toward the hubbub at the rear. "Keep your powder dry, lads!"

In a moment he had disappeared in the confusion. Touch the Sky was casting a last, regretful glance at Little Horse when Wolf Who Hunts Smiling urged in his ear, "Into the river, buck, and cry for your friend later!"

They leaped off the prow, stiff muscles screaming in pain, and sliced into the cool river water. Behind them, horses still nickered in fright and greasy black smoke clouds still darkened the twilight sky. No one had seen them leap. They decided to strike for the opposite, more heavily wooded bank.

They had not quite reached the middle of the river when Hays Jackson's voice roared, "What in tarnal hell? The Innuns're loose!"

"There!" someone else shouted. "There, in the river, see 'em?"

"Put at 'em, boys!" yelled Fargo Danford. "It's like shootin' fish in a barrel!"

The sun was down, but there was still plenty of light for aiming. A terrific volley of rifle and pistol fire churned the water into foam all around the two fleeing Cheyennes. Touch the Sky took a quick breath and swam deep, his chest scraping river bottom. The deadly hail of lead followed him down, making hollow pinging noises underwater.

He lost track of Wolf Who Hunts Smiling. His lungs were soon bursting for air, but Touch the Sky refused to surface again until he struck the opposite bank. His head emerged at the same moment as his comrade's. They scuttled up out of the water like wading birds fleeing from a snake, bullets still humming past their ears and zwipping through the tall bunchgrass.

There was a savage explosion from the starboard gunnel as someone fired a blunderbuss. The eight-ounce ball whistled between Touch the Sky's legs and ploughed into the bank, kicking up a geyser of dirt and grass. Another blunderbuss fired, and a sapling just beside Wolf Who Hunts Smiling snapped in two.

Bullets nipping at their heels, they finally reached the protection of the trees. But now they could hear the sounds of pursuit as their white enemies, mounted on horseback, began fording the Tongue.

Anyone watching the two youths move would have thought they were old men tied up with stiff joints. Feeling had still not returned to Touch the Sky's swollen feet, and Hays Jackson's brutal kicks had left his rib cage a mass of tender bruises. Each deep breath felt like a spike being stomped into him.

But the sounds of deadly pursuit, not far behind them, turned those clumsy feet into wings. Unencumbered by horses, they were able to penetrate the thickets and brambles that riders would have to bypass. By the time darkness had finally settled in, the sounds of the chase had given way to the usual nocturnal chorus of the forest.

"I am for traveling through the night," said Touch the Sky. "It is all downriver to our camp. We follow the Tongue to Bear Creek, then to the Powder."

"I have ears for this," said Wolf Who Hunts Smiling. "We can hollow out a canoe from one of these soft logs. We must return to camp, alert the council, then join the war party which must intercept the keelboat and destroy those white devils."

"And save Little Horse and Knobby," added Touch the Sky.

"Little Horse will be dead," said Wolf Who Hunts Smiling flatly. "Nor do I think the old hair-face will still be above the ground. The whites will soon guess that he helped us."

"This one has helped you more than once," said

Touch the Sky, "yet you say you hate all whites."

"He is a warrior to be respected. He knows even more than my cousin Black Elk about the warrior arts. But never forget that for all we have seen the hair-face do, there is even more we did not see. He has scalped red men in his youth—I have seen the scar on his head, his cold eye and steady hand when the battle is on! *You* have seen trouble, but never have you been forced as I have to watch while Bluecoats cut your father down like cattle, laughing and congratulating themselves and paying off bets on the kill!"

For once Wolf Who Hunts Smiling had not spoken merely to taunt him. But almost as if sensing he had shown too much feeling, the younger brave now spoke in his usual, arrogant tone. It was another reminder of the battle looming between them, a reminder that their two ambitions took vastly different forms.

"Put your friends out of your mind. This leaves more room to nurture vengeance after we return. Those stinking dogs lifted their legs and made water on me! I will lead the young warriors in their first combat. We shall kill so many that Arrow Keeper will have to declare a Scalp Dance to give thanks! Little Horse and the brave old hairy-faced one shall be avenged many times over."

Still, as the two Cheyennes began desperately whittling the center out of a cottonwood log to make a hasty dugout, Touch the Sky clung to hope for his two friends.

"Alert the bands all up and down the river," said Wes Munro. "Watch the land routes and post sentries along the water. And make the order clear: Shoot to kill. These are dangerous braves."

Fargo Danford merely nodded, too disgusted to muster the usual false congeniality toward his employer. He had promised his boys a big shebang tonight, and now Munro was closing down the show.

"I'll put the word out," he said. "But say, who can blame 'em if they ain't too keen for it? They was promised top-shelf liquor. Now they're sent off without any."

Munro was quiet after this, staring out across the dark silence of the river. He, Hays Jackson, and Fargo Danford stood just outside the cabin of the *Sioux Princess*. Most of the men had gone ashore to their old camp, sent by Munro in his rage after the escape.

Now he had cooled off enough to know it was dangerous to push it with these men.

"You're right," he told Danford. "They can take the liquor with them. Just leave me in peace on the boat."

"Say! That's mighty white of you, Wes. I'll see to it personal that them two Cheyenne whelps get kilt. What about the one that's left?"

"Leave him. He's unconscious now anyway. He might draw the other ones back. Just make sure you alert the rest of the bands. I want that Powder River camp watched. The first sign of a war party forming, all the militia will rendezvous at the boat."

"Got 'er," said Danford.

Danford's boot heels were still drumming on the boarding ramp when Munro turned to Jackson.

"How do you figure that fire got set?"

Jackson's face was a blur in the darkness, but Munro could smell him plain enough. He stepped carefully upwind of his lackey.

"One of the horses kicked over a coal-oil lamp, mebbe?"

"Maybe. But where was the old man when the fire broke out?" said Munro. "I saw him later, returning from this direction."

"I catch your drift," said Jackson. "The old fart lit it hisself, then cut the bucks loose."

"That's what I'd wager," said Munro.

"Pus-gut old sonofabitch."

Both men stood in the slanted shadow cast by the cabin, watching Knobby measure out grain for tomorrow's feed.

"He's been in this right from the jump," said Munro with sudden conviction. "He knew the tall buck from before. He must have sneaked ashore during that ceremony, met with him. It's been that old codger all along."

"Like he told us, he's got his rifle to hand. He's expectin' us."

Munro nodded. "But he'll drink himself to sleep like he always does. Just be patient."

Old Knobby did get drunk, as usual. But he also took extra precautions when he fell asleep.

Instead of his usual bedroll on deck, he made a crude shakedown bed right in the middle of the pen amongst the horses. He knew from long years of experience that horses would avoid stepping on humans. Curled up around his Kentucky over-and-under, he drifted off to sleep hidden behind a score of milling horses.

Sometime late in the night, one of the horses nickered. The old mountain man sat up, instantly wide awake.

There was a loud, menacing click as he cocked the hammers. The river was silent except for the low hum of insects, the gentle lapping of the water against the hull. A clear night sky had been dotted wide with blazing stars.

"Come on, then," he said softly into the horse-fragrant darkness around him. "Ol' Patsy Plumb here has got a kiss fir ye."

Another horse nickered, several moved nervously. Knobby kept his head down below their bellies, watching for legs wearing pants.

Suddenly he heard a soft plop as something was thrown in among the animals. There was a slither of movement in the corner of his eye, an abrupt stirring among the horses. Then Knobby saw, in a stray patch of moonlight on the deck, that it was a fat brown river snake that had been tossed into the pen.

The snake panicked at all the dangerous hooves. The horses were equally panicked by the sudden presence of a reptile. They reared back all around it, leaving Knobby exposed in his crude pallet.

A light suddenly flared inside the cabin, and Knobby swung his rifle in that direction, distracted.

That was when Jackson stepped up behind him and slugged him hard on the side of the head with the belaying pin.

The flintlock clattered to the deck. Knobby gave one surprised grunt before he sprawled over on top of it.

Jackson kicked him several times for good measure.

"Drag him up here," said Wes Munro quietly from the cabin. "Stake him out next to the Indian. A man likes to be surrounded by his friends when he's dying."

Chapter 16

Touch the Sky and Wolf Who Hunts Smiling quickly discovered that death now lurked at every turn in the river, behind every deadfall.

They finished hollowing out their dugout while the Grandmother Star still blazed brightly in the north. They lugged the canoe down to the river and slipped into the quick-moving current. For the rest of that night they made good time. Only an occasional embarrass or beaver dam slowed them down.

By sunrise they were exhausted and hungry. They stashed the dugout in a thicket and killed a pair of rabbits. Spitting them on the same arrows that killed them, they risked a small fire and roasted them. After feasting on tender rabbit meat and cold river water, they forced themselves to move well downriver from that spot in case their smoke had been spotted. Then they crawled into a cedar copse and slept until the sun's warmth signaled mid-morning.

Almost immediately after they took to the river again, they encountered danger.

The Tongue had narrowed as it passed through a rock canyon. The banks rose steep and craggy on both sides, slippery, deep-seamed rock carved out through countless eons. They steered the canoe with crude paddles they had fashioned out of squares of bark lashed tight to willow branches. Several boulders, made dangerous by the speed of the current, lay just beneath the frothing surface of the river. These hidden dangers required all their concentration.

Neither of them saw the telltale glint high overhead as sunlight caught the brass butt plate of a Sharps percussion carbine. Word of their escape was rapidly being relayed downriver. Marksmen were being positioned at key points.

The churning of the river was deafening in this constricted, rock-lined gorge. The two Cheyennes never heard the report of the carbine.

A narrow water spout shot up just in front of Touch the Sky's paddle. Another. His curiosity was deepening into a sense of danger when a bullet thwacked into the front of their dugout, chipping bark into his eyes.

"Jump!" shouted Touch the Sky.

He flew out one side of the dugout, Wolf Who Hunts Smiling the other, just as the next shot embedded itself where Touch the Sky had been sitting.

They were forced to trust their weapons to the dugout. Once again the two Cheyennes swam deep, surfacing only when their lungs ached hard for air. They continued swimming deep until they reached a flat, peaceful stretch of forest well past the small canyon.

"Look!" Touch the Sky pointed.

The dugout had become wedged between two boulders. Several bullets were embedded in it. But none had penetrated under the waterline. Their rifles would have to be dried off some, but were still safely stowed along with their bows and fox-skin quivers filled with arrows.

"Buck," said Wolf Who Hunts Smiling, "we are alive only because Maiyun chose to smile on us. We must be more vigilant. Word of our escape precedes us by land."

Touch the Sky nodded. Again the rigorous warrior training first taught to them by Black Elk came into crucial play. By day and by night the two Cheyennes moved swiftly, silently, stopping only during the day to snatch a few hours' rest. Often they took turns fitfully napping in the dugout

They looked like the walking wounded after a terrible and long battle campaign. Deep pouches of exhaustion formed under their eyes. Wolf Who Hunts Smiling's jaw was still bruised and swollen, as were Touch the Sky's ribs. Raw scars circled their wrists and ankles like bloody bracelets, the legacy of the rawhide thongs.

Despite their exhaustion, they remained ever alert for the warnings of frightened shore birds and the angry scolding which jays reserved for intruders. Their new vigilance was rewarded: Twice they were able to spot hidden marksmen before they themselves were sighted.

They eluded the first one, hidden in a deadfall where Bear Creek joined the Tongue, by lugging their dugout ashore and laboriously carrying it around his position. But this was time-consuming, exhausting work, especially in their present condition.

"The next one we see," vowed Wolf Who Hunts Smiling, "will taste the edge of my knife! At this pace we will be in the cold moons before we reach our village."

"We cannot kill all of them," said Touch the Sky. "Nor outwit so many. Travel on the river is too dangerous and slow. We need horses."

"As long as you are wishing," said Wolf Who Hunts Smiling, mocking him, "why not wish for wings so we might simply *fly* back? Just how do you plan to get these horses? With shamanism?"

"There are ways without magic," said Touch the Sky. His constant worries about Little Horse and Knobby made him desperate to cover more ground more quickly. "You are too quick to rush in fighting, when using your brain would be better."

"And you," said Wolf Who Hunts Smiling, "are too quick to make clever plans like a woman when a warrior's rash courage is the best plan."

"When it is time to close for the kill," said Touch the Sky, "I think of nothing but finding my enemy's warm vitals. But until that time forces itself, I put the welfare of my tribe before personal glory."

"So you say now. This is not what you told the white pig Munro when you begged him to loosen your bonds. *Then* you were ready to play the turncoat Ute for him!"

Anger sent hot blood into Touch the Sky's face. He had been lying to buy time, and Wolf Who Hunts Smiling had to know that. But now their dugout was nearing a wide bend and Touch the Sky bit back his retort. The militiamen liked to wait at such places. It was time to leave words behind and rely on his senses.

They had just entered the bend when a flock of startled sandpipers rose from the shore ahead of them, from a point out of sight just past the bend.

Both Cheyennes saw the birds at the same moment. Tired muscles screaming at the strain, they quickly back-paddled against the current and angled toward the bank. They hid their dugout behind some hawthorn bushes. Then, sticking to the thickets and willow rushes, they crept forward with their rifles held close to their chests.

When they were almost through the bend, they spotted them.

About a half-dozen well-armed whites sat their horses, sharing a smoke break with another man on the ground.

"The hair-face militiamen," whispered Wolf Who Hunts Smiling, "checking with one of their sentries."

Touch the Sky nodded. "Your knife will not silence all these."

"No," Wolf Who Hunts Smiling said grimly. "Now we lose more precious time carrying the dugout."

"Not this time," said Touch the Sky, thinking again of Little Horse and Knobby. Both men had saved his life, had fought beside him in pitched battles and proven themselves brave warriors. If there was a chance that either of them was still alive, that chance got slimmer with every hour wasted.

"On horseback," said Touch the Sky, "we can reach our tribe in one sleep. This is where we trade our dugout for horses. Hear my words."

His plan was simple and reckless, and thus it appealed to Wolf Who Hunts Smiling. They worked quickly, before the riders could leave. First the younger brave returned to the dugout for the rest of their weapons. Then, leaving his rifle with Wolf Who Hunts Smiling so he could move unencumbered, Touch the Sky worked his way into the thick brambles and bushes beside the river.

He waited until Wolf Who Hunts Smiling had sneaked into position behind a huge elm tree near the white men.

Then, quite boldly, he stepped into the open as if unaware the others were present.

"Look yonder!" shouted one of the militiamen.

The growth hereabouts was too dense to chase a man on horseback. As Touch the Sky leaped back behind cover, his heart thumping hard against his ribs, the first bullets sliced through the brush all around him. He made plenty of noise as he ran, hoping the whites would give chase on foot.

They did, though he couldn't be sure how many. Their clumsy, heavy boots made it ridiculously easy to track their progress as he led them on a wild run away from the river. Occasionally, when they seemed to be slowing, he showed just enough of himself just long enough, teasing them into another shot and more clumsy pursuit. But now and then a bullet whanged past his ears, dangerously close, and reminded Touch the Sky this was no child's game.

Then a single rifle report back near the river made Touch the Sky's blood surge with hope—and sent the whites back to the bend in a near panic.

Touch the Sky made his way quickly downriver to the copse where he had arranged to meet Wolf Who Hunts Smiling. The younger brave waited impatiently for him. His face was triumphant and arrogant as he handed the reins of a powerfully built bay to Touch the Sky. He also led a spotted gray mare whose chest was thickly ridged with muscles. Both animals had clearly been selected for endurance.

"As you said, they left only the one paleface to watch their mounts," he said. "And though I had no time to raise his hair, another white enemy has crossed over!"

The horses were saddled, which caused Wolf Who Hunts Smiling considerable trouble and scowling at first. But soon they were making good time as they crossed the open tableland between the Tongue and the Powder, every heartbeat bringing them deeper into Cheyenne country and closer to their people.

"Wolf Who Hunts Smiling and Touch the Sky approach camp!" shouted the crier, racing his pony up and down the clan circles. "They ride in on white man's horses!"

It was early morning, the mist still floating like pale smoke over the Powder River. Curious Cheyennes spilled forth from their tipis, congregating in the central clearing before the council lodge. Honey Eater was among them, her lower lip caught between her strong white teeth in her nervousness. She felt Black Elk's angry, jealous eyes watching her every moment. She tried to keep the deep concern and relief from showing in her face.

But when she finally spotted Touch the Sky, her breath snagged in her throat.

The blood-encrusted gash over his temple, bloody and raw bracelets around ankle and wrist, the huge, grape-colored bruises on his ribs, the arrow wound in his thigh—these spoke eloquently of such suffering that tears of pity formed on her eyelids.

Then, as the two warriors rode up, Touch the Sky's eyes found hers.

The hunted-animal hardness left his troubled gaze. The suggestion of a smile replaced the grim, determined slit formed by his lips. Her fragile beauty again took his breath away and made the blood throb in his temples. And he told himself again, *this is why I fight*.

But Black Elk was watching both of them, and the light smoldering in his eyes was clearly not a welcoming fire as was hers.

"Father!" said Wolf Who Hunts Smiling, spotting Chief Gray Thunder as he swung clumsily down from the saddle. "Have ears for my plea and call the Councillors together *now*!"

Gray Thunder silently studied his two bruised and bloodied young warriors.

"You left on the white man's boat," he said at last, "and now you return on stolen ponies, bearing the marks of much suffering and pain. This is how the white men used you, Cheyennes, in spite of their word that you would be respected. Yes, the Councillors will meet as is the way. I would hear your tales. But the greater part of them is told in these scars and hurts you bear. Soon the Arrows will be renewed for battle!"

Now Gray Thunder nodded at the camp crier, who was soon covering the well-packed paths of camp as he summoned the Council of Forty to the meeting lodge. The sense of urgency was strong, and the usual ceremonies of prayer and smoking to the directions were suspended.

Gray Thunder called on both braves to speak. Touch the Sky reported in detail everything he had overheard about the scheme to build a wagon road through the heart of Plains Indian homelands. Wolf Who Hunts Smiling admitted he understood less of the English, but verified these things.

Gray Thunder showed little emotion, though he nodded with approval at Wolf Who Hunts Smiling's description of the aborted coup by Cries Yia Eya, and his subsequent capture by the Dakota people.

"There is nothing else for it now but a battle!" said Touch the Sky when his companion had finished. "Chief Smoke Rising has been murdered. More villages will be divided, more of the 'private treaties' signed. If Munro is allowed to complete this journey, his talking papers will speak against us, and they will speak a death sentence! Soon all red men will lose the lush grass and the buffalo. They will be confined to the arid, empty lands where the Apaches hide."

These words stirred several headmen to voice agreement. Touch the Sky had only spoken from his heart. But when he finished, he saw Arrow Keeper eyeing his apprentice with pride and admiration. A red man who could speak well at council would go far indeed!

"The stones will speak," said Gray Thunder. "These whites have killed not only Smoke Rising, but Smiles Plenty and his fellow hunters. For these crimes and others, I too counsel for war against these whites. Our fight is not with the hired boatmen. Those who do not fire at us will not be fired upon. But the dogs named Munro and Jackson must die with their murdering 'militia.' "

"My warriors are ready," said Black Elk. "I was for greasing their bones with war paint from the first moment I heard his honeyed tongue spreading its lies!"

Black Elk and Touch the Sky had carefully avoided meeting each other's eye. Both were well aware there was an unsettled score between them. And Black Elk had noticed the approval Touch the Sky's words inspired from some elders. But rumors about Black Elk's jealousy had spread through camp, and he knew it would not be wise to speak against his enemy. So now he passed a quick signal to Swift Canoe, who was eager to snipe at his enemy at every opportunity.

Swift Canoe spoke: "Fathers and brothers! It has not been so long since River of Winds, one of our most trusted warriors and hunters, reported that Touch the Sky is a spy for the Long Knives! I saw with my own eyes when he met with a Bluecoat chief, when he left messages for this chief in the forks of trees! Is it wise to rush into battle against whites now at *his* bidding?"

"Wolf Who Hunts Smiling is your friend," said Touch the Sky. "He has been with me for this entire voyage, and he too counsels for war."

A long silence followed this comment. All of the Councillors looked at Wolf Who Hunts Smiling, waiting.

"Yes, I counsel for war," he said. "But as for Touch the Sky's loyalties, I say Swift Canoe is wise to advise caution."

Now Wolf Who Hunts Smiling looked only at Gray Thunder. "Touch the Sky begged that white jackal Munro to loosen his bonds. He boasted how he was a spy for the hair-faced soldiers. He boasted how cleverly and easily he spoke out of both sides of his mouth. He compared himself to those Indians who raise one hand in greeting while with the other they kill you!"

Wolf Who Hunts Smiling had not missed the increased tension between Black Elk and Touch the Sky. Now Wolf Who Hunts Smiling met his older cousin's eye and held it as he added, "He also boasted openly of the joys of tasting the fruits of both race's women, without owing responsibility to either."

The furrow between Gray Thunder's eyes grew ominously deeper as he stared at Touch the Sky. "Are these charges true?"

The youth felt his face flush. These last words were an outright lie, but the first part had been true enough. "I spoke some words like these, Father. But they were bent words. I wanted the white dog to untie me."

"I was in pain too," said Wolf Who Hunts Smiling. "So was Little Horse. *We* did not forsake our tribe just to be untied and made more comfortable."

Touch the Sky rose in anger from his spot beside the center lodge pole. "You know full well that I did not seek 'comfort.' I only wanted the chance to free you and Little Horse and go for my enemy."

Though he held his face impassive, inwardly Wolf Who Hunts Smiling was gloating. Here stood his worst enemy in the tribe, showing his embarrassed anger in his face like a white man! Of course the wily Cheyenne buck knew Touch the Sky hadn't intended to cooperate with the whites. But it was dangerous to let this tall newcomer win too much influence among the elders. Again Wolf Who Hunts Smiling had managed to sew seeds of doubt amongst Gray Thunder and the Council of Forty.

"This incessant bickering only turns over old dirt," said Gray Thunder, "without bearing fruit. Our purpose now is to vote with our stones. Do the Cheyenne people ride the warpath against this land-stealing murderer?"

Half of the Council of Forty were voting Headmen. A pouch containing 40 stones—20 white moonstones and 20 black agates—was passed among them. Each voting Councillor removed a stone of his choice and kept it hidden in his palm. When the pouch returned to Gray Thunder, he shook it out on the robes in front of him: 20 white moonstones formed a pile.

Gray Thunder stared at the unanimous yes vote. Then he gazed around at the Headmen and addressed them as one:

"The red man did not send out the first soldier, we only sent out the second. Now the tribe has spoken with one voice. The Shaiyena people are at war!"

Chapter 17

No time was wasted after Gray Thunder's announcement.

Cheyenne warriors seldom mounted an offensive battle without painting and dressing and making their offerings to the sacred Medicine Arrows. Warriors often chose to run away, with no loss of honor, rather than fight before they had thus acquired strong medicine. So it was announced that the Renewal of the Arrows would take place that same day. The war party would then ride out well before the sun went to her resting place.

Cheyenne and Sioux scouts had already reported on the militiamen, and the warriors knew these well-armed hair-faces would likely join the battle as mercenaries for Munro. However, no one knew their actual numbers. But between the militia and the big-thundering guns of the *Sioux Princess*, a hard, bloody fight was expected.

In the past Touch the Sky had made offerings to the Medicine Arrows before riding into battle. But today, for the first time, he would assist Arrow Keeper in conducting the ceremony.

Always at the back of his mind was his concern for Little Horse and Old Knobby. Though he knew that escaping had been the only chance for *all* of them, he still felt gnawing doubts—despite Little Horse's crushed knee and the lack of time, could he have freed him? But how? And Knobby—Munro and Jackson would not be slow to guess who must have cut the Cheyennes loose. The old man had known that when he did it, sacrificing his life to give them a slim hope of escape.

This constant worrying about his friends alternated with rage toward Wolf Who Hunts Smiling. The wily brave's clever posturing at the council had once again revived the specter of Touch the Sky's supposed treachery. How much longer, he wondered bitterly, must he be punished for the crime of having been raised by whites?

All these thoughts and worries scurried through his head like frenzied insects as he dressed and painted for the Renewal. He had just donned the mountain-lion skin Arrow Keeper had given him when he heard his name called harshly outside of his tipi.

No mistaking that deep, sullen bark: Black Elk.

Touch the Sky threw aside the entrance flap.

"Your war leader would speak with you," said Black Elk's haughty voice.

The young warrior was resplendent in his battle finery of war bonnet, bone breastplate, and leggings reinforced with stiff collars of leather to protect from lance points and tomahawks. His coup stick was heavy with tufts from enemy scalps, died bright red and yellow. Black Elk's face was streaked red and black for battle. Again Touch the Sky felt a slight shiver move up his spine as he looked at the dead-leather flap of severed ear sewn back on to Black Elk's skull with buckskin thread.

"Then speak," said Touch the Sky curtly. He was in no mood to conciliate his enemies within the tribe. He had learned that conciliation was seen as weakness.

"I am your war chief! You will not use this tone with me."

"And *I* am a warrior who has counted coup and slain enemies in battle. I have killed whites, Pawnees, and Crows in defense of my tribe. The council has honored me for my bravery. You will not talk down to me as if I were a dog. This is my tipi. Speak your words and then leave."

"As you wish, *shaman*. I am here to say only this. You have used your black arts to beguile Honey Eater. You have cast some sort of spell over her and hold her enthralled. But she is *my* bride! Her clan accepted my gift of horses and vows have been exchanged.

"So know this, if I ever see you exchange even one word with her, I swear by this coup stick to finish what our chief's summons interrupted. My blade will open you from throat to rump and spill out your guts for the maggots!"

His threat still hung in the air like bitter smoke long after Black Elk had turned and left. Touch the Sky finished dressing and painting. Then he met Arrow Keeper in the clearing before the council lodge. The four sacred arrows in their coyote-fur pouch lay atop a wide stump.

First the warriors danced a war dance, kicking their knees high to the steady *"hi-ya hi-ya"* cadence.

Arrow Keeper prayed to Maiyun while Touch the Sky gave his prayer wings, scattering rich tobacco as an offering to the four directions of the wind. Then the warriors lined up for the solemn ritual of presenting an offering to the Medicine Arrows.

They left skins, weapons, favorite scalps, bright beads, shards of mirror, doeskin wallets and parfleches, quilled moccasins, beaded leggings, brightly dyed feathers, tobacco, long clay pipes. Black Elk carefully avoided Touch the Sky's eyes as he knelt to leave a handsome calico shirt before the stump—this near to the Arrows was no place for hostile thoughts.

Wolf Who Hunts Smiling, however, showed no such restraint. As he rose, after leaving a tow quiver, he whispered for Touch the Sky's ears alone:

"A powerful shaman indeed! Where was his strong medicine to free his faithful friend Little Horse? He is dead by now, medicine man, and all your prayers and incantations are useless!"

These words burned in Touch the Sky's mind like glowing embers, refusing to go out. They still plagued him as the war party, in two long columns singing their battle songs, finally rode out.

The war party rode hard, constantly keeping flankers and point riders out. They all reported the same thing: There was evidence of many shod horses, but no sign of militiamen. Touch the Sky feared this could mean only one thing, that the mercenaries had been summoned to the *Sioux Princess* in expectation of a hard battle.

For two sleeps they rode hard. Touch the Sky had chosen his spirited dun mare, a present from Arrow Keeper. Cheyennes fasted before battle, and now they only gnawed on strips of venison as they rode, swallowing only the juice. They stopped twice to water their horses and sleep for short periods. When they finally crested the last long rise before the Tongue River valley, Touch the Sky's fear became reality.

Far below, still toy-sized in the waning sunlight, was the heavily armed keelboat. And surrounding it was the harrowing sight of a virtual army, dug in for heavy fighting. Scores of militiamen swarmed behind solid breastworks of pointed logs. The boatmen had been ordered to remain in their usual camp on the far bank, armed with carbines as a rearguard force. At this distance Touch the Sky could make out no signs of Little Horse or Old Knobby.

"Brothers, hear me well!" said Black Elk as they camped that night below the crest.

It was a cold camp by strict order, and sentries had been sent out. As was the custom, the attack would commence at dawn and they would attack out of the sun.

"The hair-faces have put up a mighty show of defense. But tomorrow the green grass beside that river will flow red with hair-face blood! They are fighting for nothing but money; *we* fight for the red homeland! Apaches are better fighters than these men. Yet did I not rout the Apache leader Sky Walker and thirty followers from breastworks?"

Several warriors had been at that battle, when Black Elk had only 18 winters behind him. Now one of them said, "You did, Black Elk, I was there!"

Wolf Who Hunts Smiling rose beside his cousin and addressed himself to the junior warriors whom he had recently trained.

"Little brothers, some of you too have seen your fathers and mothers slain by white devils as I have!

Tomorrow you give your enemies a war face. If you must die, and some *will* die, know it will be the glorious death! And when you fall, fall on the bones of a white dog! These are the murderers who exterminate the red man! Little brothers, at first light show the blooded warriors among us that you are eager! I want to see my warriors racing to count first coup!"

Wolf Who Hunts Smiling's eyes had held Touch the Sky's as he said this, issuing a challenge. Touch the Sky held his face impassive, but gave a slight nod—the challenge had been accepted.

Though few would sleep soundly that night, the warriors drank much water as was the custom. Thus, aching bladders would waken them early for the attack. Well before dawn, Touch the Sky was running his weapons and equipment through one final check. Then, as the newborn sun streaked pink the horizon, he rode his dun to the long, curved battle line forming just below the crest.

His last act, as he waited, was to don his magic mountain-lion skin.

The junior warriors were nervous, eager to prove themselves, and more experienced braves held them in check with stern glances and remarks. *Wait for the signal* was the command passed up and down the line.

Black Elk took in a mighty breath, ready to scream the war cry that would signal the attack.

Wolf Who Hunts Smiling met Touch the Sky's glance, his quick eyes mocking the tall brave. Then, before Black Elk could signal, Wolf Who Hunts Smiling dug his knees into the flanks of his pure black pony. His mount leaped forward, already a half-dozen paces downhill when Black Elk's shrill "*Hi-ya hi-i-i-ya!*" sounded.

The curved line surged forward, the war cry filling the air. Their enemy had been prepared for attack for two days. Now the best sharpshooters knelt out front of the others, waiting for the Cheyennes to ride into maximum effective range.

The attackers knew that their best defense across open territory was the agility of the ponies. Riding in a straight line provided an easy target, as did predictable patterns. Now the lead warriors zigzagged in crazy patterns as they rode close enough to send in the first bullets and arrows.

The sharpshooters were amazed—the Cheyennes were so skilled as riders they seemed an extension of their ponies. They bounced with perilous ease, seeming always on the verge of flying off the horse, as they strung their bows or reloaded their rifles. Several sharpshooters fell in that first volley, yet only one Cheyenne pony was hit. The rider leaped up behind another warrior and they escaped.

The success of the first wave heartened the second. While the scattered marksmen were hurrying back further behind their breastworks, the fighting Cheyennes rode close and fired a second fatal volley.

So far, though, no attacker had penetrated the breastworks to count the first coup of the battle. Despite his lead in the attack, Wolf Who Hunts Smiling had been kept busy outriding bullets. Now, as the second wave of Cheyennes fired into the whites, he and Touch the Sky both urged their ponies closer to their enemies.

An opening appeared between the points of two breastworks and Touch the Sky spotted the deck of the keelboat. And his heart leaped into his throat with sudden hope: He couldn't tell if they were dead or alive, but two figures lay staked out on the deck near the plank cabin.

Then his attention returned to the breastworks closer at hand. At the same moment he and Wolf Who Hunts Smiling watched Sam Meeks, the Bluecoat deserter whose testimony had sealed their fate, leap from a rifle pit. He fired at a junior Cheyenne warrior, knocking him from his pony with a fatal hit to the chest.

Touch the Sky dug heels into his pony and leaped over the pointed breastworks from the left; Wolf Who Hunts Smiling kicked his pony into motion and sailed in from the right. The dun was quicker, and Touch the Sky brought his lance down hard on Meeks just a moment before Wolf Who Hunts Smiling tapped him with his rifle.

It was Wolf Who Hunts Smiling who got the kill on his second pass, firing point-blank to avenge their fallen comrade. But as Touch the Sky raced on, toward the *Sioux Princess*, he exulted in the knowledge that Black Elk and others had seen him count first coup.

Behind him, as he deserted his pony now and moved forward from tree to tree on foot, the Cheyenne warriors covered their tribe with glory. Wave after wave assaulted the breastworks now, emboldened by the success of the first attacks. Several more warriors lay dead or dying, but even more white militiamen had been sent under, and more were dying in the unexpectedly fierce attack.

A group had been held in reserve to fight from the keelboat. Touch the Sky couldn't spot Munro, but there was Hays Jackson and Fargo Danford and Heck Nash. All crouched behind barrels and crates, their weapons at the ready.

In the corner of his eye, Touch the Sky saw Wolf Who Hunts Smiling sneak up to a tree beside him. Heck Nash, his attention distracted by the main battle at the breastworks, did not notice the Cheyennes closer at hand. He moved from behind cover to see better.

Wolf Who Hunts Smiling unlashed the throwing tomahawk secured to his legging sash. He had been waiting for this opportunity to avenge himself on the white dog who had made water in his face. He stepped from behind his tree and threw his tomahawk hard. It caught Nash high in the chest and brought him down hard, still alive but blood spurting high from his wound.

"Behind the trees!" shouted Fargo Danford, snapping off a round at Wolf Who Hunts Smiling. But a moment later Danford's hands flew to the hole Black Elk, just now charging the keelboat with several warriors at his heels, shot through his forehead.

Under cover of Black Elk's charge, Touch the Sky and Wolf Who Hunts Smiling also charged the boat. Touch the Sky sent a bullet from his Sharps into the face of a militiaman, then tossed his rifle aside and strung his bow, dropping a second mercenary. He and Wolf Who Hunts Smiling reached the boat at the same time. As Touch the Sky leaped aboard, Wolf paused to scalp Heck Nash while the wounded man, still alive, screamed hideously.

More Cheyenne attackers leaped aboard, and screams filled the air as the bloody fight was reduced to knives and tomahawks. Slashing furiously, his face and hands covered with enemy blood, Touch the Sky fought his way toward the two prisoners staked out on the deck on the far side of the cabin.

He reached them and felt a tight bubble of joy rise into his throat—they were both alive. Battered and bruised and filthy, but alive.

"The hell took you, sprout?" demanded Knobby in a show of bravado. "This deck plays hell on my rheumatic!"

Touch the Sky knelt and sliced through their bonds. But neither one moved at first, muscles locked into position.

"Where's Munro?" Touch the Sky asked Little Horse.

"Hiding in the cabin with his pistols and his talking papers!"

With a mighty victory cry, the Cheyennes at the main battle had routed the last of the militiamen. These were fording the river in retreat. But now a surprise lay in store for them: At a command from Etienne, who until now had kept his men out of the battle, the rearguard of Creole voyageurs was cutting the mercenaries down.

Knobby and Little Horse were finally sitting up, making their first efforts to stand and find better cover. Touch the Sky, intent on reaching the cabin, didn't notice when Hays Jackson suddenly swung one of the swivel-mounted blunderbusses full around and aimed it at him point-blank.

"Brother!" screamed Little Horse, but he was too late. With a deafening roar the blunderbuss fired its eight-ounce ball.

Only Little Horse and Jackson saw a hole appear in the plank wall of the cabin behind Touch the Sky. But instead of falling to the deck, a hole punched through him, Touch the Sky only stared in bewilderment at his unharmed mountain-lion skin—the same skin which Arrow Keeper assured him had strong medicine.

Jackson's jaw fell open in astonishment, and for a fatal moment he was surprised into immobility. The ball couldn't have passed through the Indian; his aim had to have been off.

Little Horse, limping badly on the leg Jackson had ruined with the belaying pin, hobbled to another blunderbuss. Knobby joined him and put a sulphur match to the touch hole. The gun spat fire, and there was a sound like a water bag bursting as the ball tore out Jackson's ample stomach. For a moment he stood rooted, the river behind him visible through the hole in his body, before his ruined carcass collapsed.

Wolf Who Hunts Smiling had already approached the cabin and been sent sprawling by a near-fatal blast from one of the dueling pistols. Now, with the last of the militiamen dead or routed, Touch the Sky called out, "Hold! The white dog cannot go anywhere."

The horses and mules had already been moved to a safe spot downriver. Using hand signals, Touch the Sky cleared everyone off the boat, helping Little Horse ashore. The last thing he did was smash a coal-oil lamp and trail the flammable oil in a line from the boarding ramp to the powder cache just aft of the cabin.

Knobby struck a match with his fingernail and flipped it in the oil. A fast, snaking trail of flame covered the deck, reached the cache, fizzled for a moment. A heartbeat later a deafening explosion obliterated the deck and the cabin, sending planks and ropes and tattered pieces of canvas sail—and fluttering sheets of "private treaties"—sailing off high into the sky.

* * *

The Cheyennes held an impromptu scalp dance that night beside the river, thanking Maiyun for this important victory. Only four Cheyenne braves had died, while five times that number of enemies had been slain. Tomorrow they would spend the day helping the Creoles, now their unlikely battle allies, build a crude flatboat so they could return to New Orleans. For their part in helping the Cheyennes, they were given a share of the captured horse herds in addition to their weapons.

Touch the Sky was elated with the victory. But while he was still rejoicing, watching the last smoldering embers of the *Sioux Princess* sink into the river, he was momentarily sobered. As this battle proved, their homeland had been permanently invaded. And as his vision at Medicine Lake had so painfully made real, for the red man, the fighting had just begun. Word of this Tongue River battle would eventually reach the Great White Council and their blue-bloused soldiers. Each victory spawned more bloody battles.

Nor were his personal battles within the tribe over. It wasn't enough for Black Elk that he swore to respect his marriage vows. The war chief also insisted that Touch the Sky somehow give up his love for Honey Eater. That would never happen. Nor would Wolf Who Hunts Smiling be content until one of them crossed over. So let the battles come, he was ready.

Arrow Keeper had spoken the straight word: Touch the Sky would face many trials and much suffering before he raised high the lance of leadership. But Arrow Keeper had also said he was the son of a great Cheyenne chief. That it was his destiny to find greatness just as his father had.

A shadow limped across from the dancers circling the huge victory fire. Touch the Sky turned to his friend.

"Come dance for me, brother," Little Horse said. His leg had been splinted, and he used a hickory-limb crutch. "I would dance with the tribe, but I cannot. I need your legs."

Touch the Sky knew what his friend was doing. He was telling him that it was the white man's way to brood after a great victory. A Cheyenne celebrated with his people.

"Then let us dance, brother!" Touch the Sky said. A moment later a tall Cheyenne warrior took his place among the dancers kicking high about the fire. The others made room as was his due. Something about his manner suggested that none had better challenge him. And none did.

For they had seen him count first coup in the day's great battle, and though he was clearly marked for trouble, all agreed that Touch the Sky was no warrior to trifle with.

COMANCHE RAID

Prologue

In 1840 Running Antelope and his Northern Cheyenne band were massacred by blue-bloused pony soldiers. The only survivor was his infant son.

His Cheyenne name lost forever, the boy was adopted by John and Sarah Hanchon and raised in the Wyoming Territory settlement of Bighorn Falls. They named him Matthew and loved him as if he were their own blood.

For a long time their love was enough to protect him from the hatred other settlers felt for a full-blooded Indian in their midst. But then he turned 16 and fell in love with Kristen Steele, who returned his love. Her father had the youth viciously beaten. Knowing he was as good as dead unless he left her alone, Kristen lied and told

Matthew she didn't want to see him anymore.

Then a young cavalry officer named Seth Carlson, who planned to marry Kristen, threatened to ruin John and Sarah Hanchon's mercantile business unless Matthew cleared out for good. Forsaken in love, driven from the white man's world to save his parents, he fled north to the Powder River and Cheyenne country.

He was suspected of being a spy, and the Cheyenne nearly killed him. He was considered no better than a white man's dog by most of Chief Yellow Bear's tribe. But Arrow Keeper, the tribe shaman, had recently experienced a powerful medicine vision. This tall youth was marked by destiny to become a great warrior and leader of his people, though much suffering must come first.

Though Matthew was renamed Touch the Sky and began to learn the Cheyenne Way, his enemies were many. The fierce young warrior Black Elk hated him instantly when he saw that Chief Yellow Bear's daughter, Honey Eater, was captivated by the tall stranger. And Black Elk's younger cousin, Wolf Who Hunts Smiling, openly announced his intention to kill the suspected spy.

After helping to save his tribe from annihilation by Pawnees, Touch the Sky earned some respect and trust from the Headmen. But his enemies hated him even more for this recognition. Then Henri Lagace and his whiskey traders invaded Indian country, kidnapping Honey Eater when Chief Yellow Bear's tribe painted for war against them. Touch the Sky killed Lagace and freed Honey Eater. But now, after hearing Honey Eater swear her love for Touch the Sky, Black Elk hated him more than ever.

The tribe's suspicions against him only deepened when Touch the Sky rushed back to the river-bend settlement of Bighorn Falls to help his white parents. Hiram Steele and Lieutenant Seth Carlson had already ruined the Hanchons' mercantile trade; now they had launched a bloody campaign to drive them from their new mustang spread.

Assisted by his friend Little Horse, Touch the Sky defeated hs parents' enemies. But his tragic plight worsened when he returned to the Cheyenne camp. Chief Yellow Bear had died, forcing Honey Eater to marry Black Elk. Worse, spies watched Touch the Sky during his absence. They mistook his meetings with the sympathetic cavalry officer Tom Riley as proof the Cheyenne was a traitor to his people.

Old Arrow Keeper used his power as acting chief to save the youth. He announced that Touch the Sky would be trained in the shaman arts. He sent the young buck to sacred Medicine Lake in the Black Hills, to seek the same vision that Arrow Keeper had originally experienced. Touch the Sky received the images and secrets of the Vision Path, and saw his destiny as a great warrior who would someday lead the Shaiyena people in one last great victory.

But he knew he must face many dangers before that time arrived. Shortly after his key vision at Medicine Lake, the chief-renewal ceremony was held, and Gray Thunder was selected to replace the dead Chief Yellow Bear.

During the festivities, a keelboat called the *Sioux Princess* sailed into camp. The skipper, Wes Munro, claimed to be on a "goodwill" trip through Indian country, distributing gifts from the Indian Bureau. In fact, he was signing illegal "private treaties" with renegade subchiefs, swindling the tribes out of their best land so he could start a transcontinental wagon road.

Chief Gray Thunder sent Touch the Sky, Little Horse, and their enemy Wolf Who Hunts Smiling to join the crew of the *Sioux Princess* as replacements for boatmen killed in a Mandan raid. They learned of Munro's plans, and worked secretly to thwart him. Captured and brutally tortured, they escaped and brought word to their tribe.

Touch the Sky counted first coup in the climactic battle against Munro's mercenaries. But the jealous Black Elk hated him more than ever after catching Honey Eater crying in fear for Touch the Sky's safety on the keelboat. And the ambitious Wolf Who Hunts Smiling, who dreamed of leading the tribe in a war against the Bluecoat pony soldiers, had warned Touch the Sky that one of them must die.

Chapter 1

In the Moon When the Ponies Shed, Chief Gray Thunder of the Northern Cheyenne sent out scouts to locate buffalo trails. The cold moons had been long and hard, and the tribe badly needed fresh meat.

The scouts returned with welcome news. The fresh trail of a huge herd had been spotted in the Valley of the Greasy Grass, near the Little Bighorn. It led due south toward the Colorado Plains.

The Cheyenne Hunt Law was strict on the matter of buffalo hunting. Because buffalo were so essential to Cheyenne survival, and because everyone was needed if waste was to be avoided, the entire tribe must take part in the annual buffalo hunts.

The unusually harsh winter had kept most of the tribe huddled around the firepits in their tipis. Now, with the new grass well up and the mountain runoff swelling the rivers and creeks, the entire tribe was ready for the welcome activity of the hunt. The Headmen did not even bother to count stones when they voted on Gray Thunder's proposal to head south in pursuit of the buffalo.

Touch the Sky was even more excited than most of the others. Though he had been on several hunts since joining the tribe nearly four winters ago, in the year white men called 1856, this was the first time the trail had led so far south. They would be traveling to the lands of tribes he had seldom seen—not only their brothers, the Southern Cheyennes, and their allies, the Southern Arapahos, but enemy tribes too, as Arrow Keeper reminded him.

"The new soldiertowns erected by the Bluecoats," the old shaman explained, "have sent up the white man's stink, frightening the herds and turning them far to the south. Now we must approach the valleys and peaks of the Kiowa and their loyal battle companions, the Comanches."

Touch the Sky listened eagerly as he lashed tipi covers to a packhorse. He and the elder were standing just inside a huge corral formed by buffalo-hair ropes snubbed around cottonwood trees. It was the custom for every member of the tribe past infancy to perform work related to the hunt. But since Touch the Sky had no official clan to designate his task, Arrow Keeper had assigned this one. No one questioned this openly, since Arrow Keeper was the most respected elder in the tribe. And Touch the Sky was, after all, his apprentice in the shaman arts—a fact which caused several to remark privately that old Arrow Keeper had gone soft in his brain.

"The Kiowa," Arrow Keeper said, "are the envy of the red nations, for their pony herds are the finest. Better even than our Shaiyena ponies, and where is the Bluecoat horse that can match ours? But it is the fierce Comanche who truly become one with a horse! I swear by the sun and the earth I live on—there are no finer horsemen anywhere."

Touch the Sky nodded as he used rawhide thongs to secure the buffalo-hide tipi covers. He had nearly 20 winters behind him and was tall and broad-shouldered for a Cheyenne. The days had warmed since the spring melt, and now he wore only a clout, buckskin leggings, and elkskin moccasins. He had a strong, hawk nose, and his thick black locks were shaggy and long except over his brow. There they had been cropped short to leave his vision unobstructed.

"I have seen Comanches when their ponies are shot out from under them," Arrow Keeper said. "They are bowlegged and oddly built, and on foot the most awkward creatures I have ever seen. It is said they lose their courage too when not on horseback. But when riding in battle, there is not a coward among them."

"Father!" a mounted warrior shouted from the clearing in front of the council lodge. "Gray Thunder sent me to ask you. Should the soldier societies prepare for the Animal Dance tonight?"

Arrow Keeper nodded. The young warrior, a member of the Cheyenne military society known as the Bowstrings, raced off to find the camp crier so the word could be spread. Touch the Sky watched the brightly dyed feathers tied to the tail of the warrior's horse. These marked him as a member of a military society, or soldier troop, which had been selected to enforce the rigid Hunt Law between the day of the Animal Dance and the final slaughter of the hunt.

By now Touch the Sky had learned how the various soldier troops differed from each other. The Bowstrings were the favorites because of their belief that negotiating was the best way to end a confrontation. The Bull Whips, in contrast, were quick to resort to their highly feared knotted-thong whips.

Arrow Keeper saw Touch the Sky staring at the dyed feathers.

"Soon, little brother," he said, "you must consider which society you wish to join. I suggest the Bowstrings. Their leader is Spotted Tail of the Eagle Clan. He has courage, but also the good sense to look before he wades in. I cannot say the same for Lone Bear, who heads the Bull Whips."

Touch the Sky nodded. "Little Horse tells me that Wolf Who Hunts Smiling has brought a gift of arrows to Lone Bear. That he wishes to join their society."

"Your friend Little Horse speaks the straight word," Arrow Keeper said. "I am not surprised. Wolf Who Hunts Smiling is hot-tempered and quick to rise up on his hind legs. He will make a good Bull Whip. They are becoming more and more like the Dog Men of the Southern Cheyenne who ride under the leader War Horse. True, they are fearsome warriors to be respected. But they openly defy their Headmen and the chief."

"Will his gift be accepted?" Touch the Sky said. "Will he be initiated?"

Arrow Keeper shrugged. Despite the warming weather, he was still wrapped snugly in his red blanket. His long hair was much thinner than Touch the Sky's, silver and brittle with age.

"He is young, younger even than you. Normally a Cheyenne buck does not go to war before he has sixteen winters behind him. Before he approaches the soldier societies, he should have at least four winters behind him as a warrior. But Wolf Who Hunts Smiling was blooded early, like his cousin Black Elk. He can easily defeat any two Bull Whips, and Lone Bear knows this."

Touch the Sky finished his task in disheartened silence. Wolf Who Hunts Smiling was already doing a good job of keeping many in the tribe suspicious of Touch the Sky. How arrogant and influential would he be once initiated into the fierce Bull Whip Society?

Arrow Keeper reminded Touch the Sky that he would be needed to assist at the Animal Dance later. When the old shaman returned to his tipi to rest, Touch the Sky took a break from his boring labors to check on his ponies.

While he headed toward the far end of the corral, threading his way through the grazing ponies, he thought again of the upcoming hunt. Despite the dangers of entering enemy territory, the risk must be taken. Gray Thunder's Cheyenne people needed much more from the buffalo than just fresh and jerked meat. They were critically short on hides for tipi covers, on warm fur sleeping robes and winter leggings. Cups would be made from the horns, belts and ropes from the hair, thread from the sinews, water bags from the bladders.

Touch the Sky paused to watch a mare frisking with her new foal. Overhead, a red-tailed hawk circled against a seamless blue sky. Down by the river, a badger was digging its burrow. Wildflowers were ablaze further out on the prairie, and the rivers and creeks were swollen with snow runoff. The snowcapped mountain peaks on the horizon glittered white in the bright sunlight.

One of Touch the Sky's earliest lessons among the Cheyennes was to talk and think less and observe more. And lately, at Arrow Keeper's quiet but steady urging, his young shaman apprentice was developing the habit of reading the secret language of nature. This very morning, Arrow Keeper had shown him how to examine a spider's web and predict whether the warm moons would be rainy or dry—long, thin threads meant dry weather, short and fat meant rainy. This particular web had foretold a rainy summer, good news since it meant the buffalo grass would be high and the herds fat.

Touch the Sky spotted a beautiful gray pony with a thick white mane, stamping her feet in irritation at pesky flies. He cut her from the herd. She nuzzled his shoulder, glad to see him again. He had stolen her from a Crow warrior after beating Wolf Who Hunts Smiling at counting first coup on him.

Touch the Sky grabbed a handful of mane. He was about to swing up onto his pony when a familiar voice abruptly caught his attention. Clearly the speaker was infuriated.

"You make me a squaw in front of my clan brothers! I have warned you before about doing your duty!"

Black Elk! Touch the Sky peered over his pony's withers. The river was close by, and the grass dipped sharply to form its bank. So at first he spotted only Black Elk's muscle-corded back. The young war chief was speaking to someone further down the bank, out of sight.

"This is proof you do not carry my son in your womb! Why do you not bathe with the others? It is because your belly-mouth bleeds the unclean blood!"

Suddenly Touch the Sky understood he must be speaking to Honey Eater. Cheyenne women were required to bathe separately when their bleeding time came.

"You make me a squaw!" he repeated angrily. "The others are joking behind my back, saying that perhaps a Pawneee must be brought into my tipi to make a son for me!"

His threatening tone alerted Touch the Sky. The young brave swung under the corral ropes and headed slowly toward the river. Every instinct warned him not to interfere with the fierce Black Elk. Yet those same instincts drew him to protect Honey Eater from his wrath. Now Touch the Sky could hear her speaking.

"I do my duty and submit. You have your pleasure at night. Would you fault me because Maiyun has not chosen to make me a mother yet?"

"I am a warrior, I do not quarrel with women! When I speak, you listen! It is common knowledge that, if a squaw hardens her heart toward her buck, his seed will not fertilize. You have turned your heart to stone against me. Thus, you deny me my son!"

"Has Black Elk been visiting the Peyote Soldiers? This is wild nonsense."

"The cow does not bellow to the bull! I swear by the four directions, I will *shame* you into your duty, wife!"

Touch the Sky broke into a run, fear icing his veins, when he saw Black Elk grab his knife from its beaded sheath and leap down the bank. There was a sharp cry of protest from Honey Eater, a snarl of rage from Black Elk. By the time Touch the Sky reached the edge of the bank and peered down, the damage had been done.

Honey Eater was still damp from her bath, and her doeskin dress clung to the soft curves of her body. Sunlight gleamed off the bone choker around her neck. A sob hitched in her chest when Black Elk threw the long, beautiful braid he had just cut off into the churning water of the Powder River.

Rage warred with pity in Touch the Sky's breast. Honey Eater's long, thick hair had been her pride. Every day she picked fresh columbine petals to braid into it. She looked lost and vulnerable now without it, her once-beautiful hair now a mass of jagged locks over her nape. Worse, Touch the Sky knew that cutting off a squaw's braid was a public mark of shame. Black Elk had announced that she was failing to do her duty as a Cheyenne wife. He was calling on public censure by the tribe to force her to her senses.

"Leave me alone!" Honey Eater said bitterly. "I cannot bear to look at your arrogant, accusing face. If I *can* prevent your child from growing in my womb, I surely will. Once I thought you were a hard man, but a fair one. I was wrong, you are only hard."

Black Elk's rage was instant. He lifted his hand to hit her.

Touch the Sky drew his knife and shouted, "Touch her again, and I swear by my medicine bundle I will send you under!"

Black Elk whirled and looked up the bank. Honey Eater too stared at him. Her shame at the public mark of dishonor was evident immediately in the deep flush which turned even her earlobes red.

Black Elk watched the two of them drinking each other in with their eyes. Disgust filled his voice when he said, "Moon Calf and his bitch-in-rut! Did you come down here, Woman Face, hoping to bull my squaw?"

"Only to save her from murder," the tall youth retorted. "The heathen Comanches, Arrow Keeper says, can kill their wives and it is not murder. But the Cheyenne Way does not permit wife-slaughter."

"No, *shaman,*" Black Elk said, his tone ominously low with rage, "but it does permit a war leader to take his wife's braid. This is the second time you have pulled your knife and spoken the he-bear talk to me. I *trained* you, buck!"

"And I learned my lessons. Remember this when you lift your hand to strike Honey Eater."

"I will remember it *now,* squaw stealer, and gut you like a rabbit!"

Black Elk unsheathed his knife again, his eyes dark and dangerous. His war face was made even more hideous by the dead, leathery flap where part of an ear had been severed by a Bluecoat saber, then later sewn back on with buckskin thread. Again Black Elk thought of the time he had caught Honey Eater kneeling before Touch the Sky's empty tipi, crying in fear for his safety aboard the white men's keelboat.

Touch the Sky made no move to leap down the bank, though his weapon was still in his hand. Black Elk was halfway up the bank when a shout from camp made both braves look that way.

Touch the Sky's drawn knife had earned the attention of a vigilant Bowstring named Tangle Hair. With the hunt preparations underway, they were patrolling the camp.

Tangle Hair raced over on his jet-black mustang.

"Black Elk! Touch the Sky! Would you sully the Arrows even as your tribe prepares for the hunt?"

Despite their anger, Tangle Hair's words shamed both warriors. According to the Cheyenne Way, the four sacred Medicine Arrows, always protected by Arrow Keeper, must be kept forever sweet and clean. The bloodshed of any Cheyenne stained the Arrows, and thus the entire tribe. When violent emotions were brewing, the thought of the Arrows prevented many fights. It would be an especially serious wrong to the tribe to sully them as a hunt was beginning, thus creating bad medicine to scare off the herds.

Tangle Hair nodded toward Touch the Sky. "I am not surprised to see *this* one brandishing his knife as the hunt begins. He was raised among hair faces and it is said he does not truly respect the red man's ways. But you, Black Elk! You are my war leader! For this very reason, you should be the last to risk bloodshed now!"

His words flew straight-arrow. Even the proud Black Elk, who brooked censure from few men, nodded to admit their truth. Still, his anger at Touch the Sky's interference was great.

"This spy for the long knives has been working his trade again," the war chief said, "only now he spies on me as I discipline my squaw."

"I was not spying," Touch the Sky said hotly. "I saw this brave warrior beating a defenseless woman, and I interfered as any warrior is required to do. The Cheyenne Way does not permit the beating of our women."

By now several more Bowstring soldiers had ridden over to see what was wrong. They conferred among themselves for some time in low voices. This was an awkward matter. The tall youth was right. Yet few Cheyenne braves did not occasionally beat their women. It was a private matter. Still, all could see that Black Elk had cut off Honey Eater's beautiful hair. This was a severe punishment for a girl well liked by everyone in the tribe, the daughter of the great Chief Yellow Bear.

The Bowstrings now demonstrated their tact once again. Clearly, Black Elk's pride had been offended, his manhood challenged publicly by

Touch the Sky's interference. Yet they grudgingly agreed among themselves that the youth had been right to do so.

"Black Elk," said Tangle Hair. "Help us have a good hunt! It has been decided that you should ride over with us now to our troop's pony herd. Select two of our finest ponies and add them to your string. A warrior with so many feathers in his bonnet should have the pick of the best."

The last thing Black Elk needed was more ponies. But Tangle Hair's gesture allowed him to save face without risking the severe stigma of murder. Black Elk nodded. Then he fixed his stone-eyed stare on Touch the Sky and said, "I have no desire to sully the Arrows. But Bowstrings, during this hunt watch this white man's dog close and keep him far from me, or I swear his gut will string my next bow!"

Chapter 2

The Kiowa leader named Hairy Wolf halted his band at the rim of Blanco Canyon.

All around the warrior as far as his eyes could see stretched the vast Llano Estacado, the Staked Plain—a land of endless, barren desert plains divided by sterile mountains and bone-dry arroyos. This remote wilderness, covering much of the Texas Panhandle and eastern New Mexico Territory, was an unsettled, almost treeless wasteland seldom visited by the hair-face whites. It was inhabited by buffalo, antelope, wolves, coyotes, jackrabbits, prairie dogs, rattlesnakes—and the Kiowas' closest allies, the Comanches.

The Llano's searing sunshine and chalky alkali dust made their enemies reluctant to go in pursuit of them—thus it had become the Comanches' favorite haunt. Blanco Canyon, the largest single break dividing the Staked Plain, was now home to Iron Eyes and his Quohada, or Antelope Eater, band of Comanche. Hairy Wolf had led his Kiowa warriors from Medicine Lodge Creek in Oklahoma for this important council.

Longtime friends, hunting partners, and battle allies, the Kiowas and Comanches were even closer than the Cheyennes and their Lakota Sioux cousins. Many found this close alliance odd, since the towering, broad-shouldered Kiowa warriors were considered a strikingly handsome tribe; the Comanches, in contrast, were small and bandy-legged and considered homely. Yet in fierce temper and love of battle the two tribes were twins. Both tribes were fluent in Kiowa, Comanche, and Spanish, and used all three languages interchangeably, especially to fool their enemies.

"Painted Lips," Hairy Wolf called to a nearby warrior, "bring me the war pipe."

Painted Lips owned a fine hand-tooled saddle captured during a raid on Mexican soldiers in the Superstition Mountains. He reached into a saddlebag and removed a long clay pipe painted in bright crimson and black. He nudged his pony closer and handed it to his war chief.

Hairy Wolf undid the thongs of a rawhide pouch. He removed a generous pinch of rich white man's tobacco. He stuffed it into the pipe, ready to present to his friend Iron Eyes. It was the custom to always arrive with a pipe filled when recruiting braves for a raid.

"Look!" Painted Lips pointed below into the canyon.

Hairy Wolf watched a magnificent herd of ponies suddenly round a sandstone shoulder. The Comanches, like the Kiowas, were rich in horses—indeed, much of their constant fighting with other tribes was to protect, or get back, their herds.

Below, a Comanche herd guard had spotted the Kiowas. He raised his skull-cracker—the stone war club so deadly in the hands of a mounted Comanche—in greeting.

Hairy Wolf lifted his streamered lance high overhead to return the greeting. The Kiowa leader wore captured Bluecoat trousers and boots. He was bare from the waist up except for a bone breastplate. He was huge—well over six feet—and thickly muscled, with an aquiline nose and long, flowing black hair that fell well below his waist. Now it was matted from exposure to pale alkali dust.

Hairy Wolf led his band down the narrow and rock-strewn trail which descended into the canyon. As they drew closer to the bottom, the well-disguised camp began to emerge from its natural camouflage. Unlike the tipis preferred by the northern Plains tribes, Iron Eyes' Comanches lived in one-room, mesquite-branch huts called jacals and in even cruder wickiups—curved-brush shelters which withstood the strong wind and dust storms of the Llano better than tipis.

Iron Eyes had already stepped out of his lodge to meet his Kiowa brothers. Hairy Wolf dismounted and greeted him with a strong bear hug, lifting the smaller Comanche clear off the ground.

Then, still without speaking a word, he solemnly offered Iron Eyes the filled pipe.

The Quohada leader stared at the pipe with the deep-brown eyes characteristic of his people. He had a sun-darkened, oval face. His hair was shorter than Hairy Wolf's, parted exactly in the center and just long enough to brush behind his ears.

"So," Iron Eyes said at last, speaking in the Kiowa tongue, "you are riding into battle. Hair faces?"

Hairy Wolf shook his head as the rest of his warriors dismounted and greeted old friends with their hearty bear hugs.

"Cheyennes," he said.

A look of satisfaction settled on Iron Eyes' weather-seamed but still-youthful face. The Cheyenne tribe had long been bitterly hated by the Kiowas and Comanches. More than 20 winters earlier, the Cheyennes had met their southern enemies in a major battle at Wolf Creek. The Cheyennes had not only possessed muskets and outnumbered their opponents, but had stunned them with their reckless bravery. On that fateful day scores of good Kiowa and Comanche warriors had been sent to the Land Beyond the Sun forever. Even today the words "Remember Wolf Creek!" were a Kiowa-Comanche battle cry which inspired heroism.

Iron Eyes reached out and accepted the pipe. "It was the Cheyenne who sent out the first warrior," he said. "We only sent out the second. Since Wolf Creek, they have constantly stolen our ponies, and for camp fires they have burned our lodges. I hate them almost as much as I hate the hair-mouthed Texans who are stealing our best lands. Come inside and let us smoke this good tobacco while you speak more on this thing."

The inside of the jacal was more spacious than the other lodges. The mesquite-branch walls were chinked with red clay. The skin of a roadrunner, the good luck charm of the Comanches, hung from the ceiling. Dangling all around it were enemy scalps. These had been cured and painted bright colors, the hair dyed in bright greens and yellows.

Iron Eyes waited respectfully until Hairy Wolf had seated himself first on a stack of coyote furs. After all, the Kiowa was a member of his tribe's most elite warrior society, the Kaitsenko—the ten bravest warriors of the Kiowa Nation.

They smoked, filling the jacal with the rich smell of the tobacco. Then Hairy Wolf laid the pipe down between them.

"You know," he said, "that the Northern Cheyenne have chosen a brave named Gray Thunder as their new chief?"

Iron Eyes nodded. "He is a good warrior, not so old as their former chief, Yellow Bear."

"He is leading his tribe on the spring hunt. We know this thing because buffalo scouts from his tribe have followed the herds south, close to our ranges. This can only mean they are leaving soon for the annual hunt."

Again Iron Eyes nodded, waiting for more. Outside the hut, a pistol shot, followed by a woman's scream, suddenly rose above the hubbub of voices. Both leaders calmly ignored it. The scream was followed by a loud chorus of laughter.

"You know," Hairy Wolf said, "that Cheyenne Hunt Law requires them to hunt the buffalo as an entire tribe?"

Iron Eyes began to see which direction his friend was grazing. His thin lips eased into a smile. "Of course. They are a people ruled by many strict and foolish laws."

"Yes—and a people whose beautiful women and children command a good price in Santa Fe."

Iron Eyes liked the sound of this. His tribe, like Hairy Wolf's, needed whiskey and new rifles. Both tribes were active in the Comanchero trade conducted with New Mexicans and Mexicans, supplying Indian captives as slaves in exchange for firearms and alcohol. It was illegal, as was slavery itself in both Mexico and the New Mexico Territory. But a constant market for cheap labor and prostitutes made it very profitable—much more so than selling hides or even fine horses. Hides and horses required much time and work, and besides, who wanted to part with a good pony once it was broken right?

"They are too strong in their camp," Hairy Wolf said. "But the tribe will be vulnerable on the move. Especially in a region less familiar to them."

"How far south must they come?"

"Well below the Smoky Hill River. That is the soonest they could catch the herds. We would not have far to ride."

"We can attack," Iron Eyes said, "while the braves are engaged in the hunt. The women and children will be alone at the hunt camp behind the herds."

Again outside there were more sharp cracks from a pistol, and again a woman's scream was followed by a loud ripple of laughter. Again the two war leaders ignored it.

"Brother," Iron Eyes added, "you saw me smoke your pipe. My lips touched it. You are a member of the Kaitsenko, honored by my tribe fully as much as yours. And we Comanche, are we not called the Red Raiders of the Plains? Again our two tribes will ride to battle as one, and the Cheyenne will pay dearly for their victory dance after Wolf Creek."

Hairy Wolf nodded. "We can expect a bloody fight if we do not strike quickly. Their war chief is a young buck named Black Elk, whose coup feathers trail to the ground. He is no warrior to take lightly."

"There is another," Iron Eyes said. "He is even younger. A tall one whom the Pawnee speak of with fear in their voices. They say his medicine is strong, his war lance unerring. They say he can summon insane white men from the forests, conjure up the angry silvertip bear to save himself."

"The Pawnee!" Hairy Wolf said scornfully. "They are fierce warriors, true. But brother, their superstition knows no bounds. Let him summon a crazy white—Hairy Wolf will scalp a soft-brain as quickly as any other hair face!"

"Well said, Kaitsenko! Then we ride north! Human flesh is not only valuable—it need not be broken like horses."

From outside, more pistols shots, more screams.

This time Iron Eyes smiled as he caught his companion's eye. "The ones we plan to *sell* need not be broken," he corrected himself.

Outside the jacal, while the two leaders planned their strike against Gray Thunder's Cheyennes, the braves from both tribes had gathered for the usual festivities when meeting after a long separation.

Whiskey was in short supply. But the Comanches had learned how to make corn beer from the Navajos to the west. There had been the usual competition in riding skills, won, as always, by the Comanches. A brave named Big Tree won shouts of approval from both tribes when he shot 20 arrows and rode 300 yards in the time it took a Kiowa to reload and fire a carbine twice.

But the real entertainment was provided by an Apache squaw the Comanches had captured during a raid into Sonora.

The Comanches prided themselves on having killed more white settlers than any other tribe. Like the Pawnee, they were fond of attacking at night. They excelled at stealth, and were fonder than most tribes of taking captives. And like their battle brothers, the Kiowa, they enjoyed torture—especially of women.

Two Comanche braves named Dog Fat and Standing Feather were in charge of the entertainment. This Apache squaw was too old to fetch much at the auction block and too ugly for the braves to bother rutting on. She was good only for fun.

They had tied a plaited thong around her arms and drawn her hands behind her. They had tied them so tight they turned purple. Then they had tied another thong around her ankles and drawn her feet and hands together. They then had flipped her on her face so she was unable to move, and begun beating on her head with their bows.

Her screams were piteous. To add to the torment, they laid their pistols right up against her skull and fired them. The caps and powder flew into her face and hair, producing bruises and powder burns until she was sorely disfigured.

This went on for hours, well into the evening. Now and then someone would throw a rock at her, cracking a rib or fracturing a facial bone. Finally, they grew tired of their sport and wandered off to eat, then sleep.

But the old squaw was still conscious, still begging them to kill her and end the pain. It was Dog Fat who returned, holding a lethally honed bone-handle knife. Casually, he wrenched the Apache's mouth open and reached far into her throat, slicing her tongue out at the very root. He left it lying in the dirt in front of her so she could see it.

She could no longer scream—she was too busy gagging in her body's reflexive effort not to drown in her own blood. This went on for nearly an hour longer before she finally lost the struggle and died.

Chapter 3

"Brother," Little Horse said, "I have heard a thing."

Touch the Sky looked up from the elkskin moccasins he was stitching with a bone awl and sinew thread. He sat beside the cooking tripod outside his tipi. Lost deep in thoughts about the upcoming hunt, he had not heard his friend approaching. All around the two braves, young boys fashioned travois out of limbs and vines, anticipating huge loads of fresh buffalo meat and hides.

"Sit and speak this thing," Touch the Sky told his friend.

Little Horse still moved a bit stiffly as a result of a leg injury inflicted when he was a prisoner aboard the white men's keelboat. He sat beside his friend.

"You know that Wolf Who Hunts Smiling wishes to be initiated as a Bull Whip?"

Touch the Sky nodded. His mouth was a grim, determined slit. That was one of the things he had been thinking about when Little Horse walked up. "I know that he has taken the gift of arrows to their leader, Lone Bear."

"He has," Little Horse said. "But do you also know that Black Elk is changing over to the Bull Whips?"

"But he is a Bowstring!"

"Lately he has told certain braves that he is not happy with Spotted Tail and his Bowstring troop. He claims that the Bowstrings settle things too much like women, that they are afraid to punish those who violate the Cheyenne Way. Also, Spotted Tail preaches cooperation with the palefaces who can be trusted. Lone Bear is for the warpath against all of them. Black Elk has ears for such talk."

"Yes," Touch the Sky said, "like his cousin, Wolf Who Hunts Smiling."

Touch the Sky said nothing about the incident earlier when Black Elk had cut off Honey Eater's braid. But Black Elk had accepted the Bowstrings' ponies, and now he had openly turned his back on them! Touch the Sky knew full well the reason behind Black Elk's hardening of heart. It was the fact that Honey Eater loved *him,* a Cheyenne who had been raised by whites, instead of Black Elk.

"Hearing this hurt my ears," Little Horse said. "The Bull Whips have many enemies among the tribe, those who believe in ways besides harsh punishment to settle disputes. Black Elk is a respected warrior, chosen battle chief over many older braves. By joining Lone Bear's troop, he lends the strength of his many coups to the name and beliefs of the Bull Whips."

"And the strength of his coups to Wolf Who Hunts Smiling's request to be admitted," Touch the Sky added. "They are both cousins, both of the Panther Clan. Lone Bear will surely accept him now."

Little Horse said something else, but Touch the Sky missed it—he had just spotted Honey Eater, returning from the river with a clay jar full of fresh water.

For a moment he stared at the crude mess Black Elk had left of her hair, so jaggedly cut over her neck it looked as if fire had gnawed away at it. Proudly, defiantly, she had taken no pains to disguise her husband's public mark of shame. Instead of casting her eyes down, as Cheyenne women often did when marked for censure, she boldly met all comers in the eye. Touch the Sky knew she was rebelling against Black Elk's tyranny. He was proud of her spirit, but afraid it would only lead to more trouble for her.

"Black Elk should *receive* the bull whip, not become one," Little Horse said with anger in his voice as he watched Honey Eater cross to her tipi. "Everyone in camp knows he has cut off Honey Eater's braid. Many are angry at this, although some of the warriors say it is Black Elk's business, that it may spoil the hunt to stir up trouble now."

Touch the Sky dropped his glance before Honey Eater could meet it. Not only did he wish to spare her feelings, but he felt that Black Elk was lurking somewhere nearby, watching as usual. Lately, because Black Elk's jealousy had become crazy-dangerous, Touch the Sky went out of his way to avoid chance meetings with or even glances at Honey Eater.

But this only served to charge their occasional accidental meetings with even more meaning. By now it was common knowledge in the clan circles that the two loved each other. The story was told clearly in the way they carefully avoided each other. On occasions when they were forced to be in the same vicinity, they both acted nervous, ill at ease.

One old squaw in the Sky Walker Clan, known as a visionary and a singer, had sung their love in a tragic song. The song did not say their names but was clearly about them. Now all the younger girls were singing it in their sewing lodge. Secretly, they hoped this love would somehow become a marriage.

"Look, buck!" Little Horse nodded across the central camp clearing, toward the hide-covered council lodge.

As if to grimly confirm what they had been talking about, Black Elk, his younger cousin Wolf Who Hunts Smiling, and Lone Bear, head of the Bull Whip soldier society, were conferring together. Now and then one of them glanced across the clearing toward Touch the Sky.

"They are plotting against you," Little Horse said with conviction. "I suspect they have some plan for the Animal Dance this night."

Touch the Sky said nothing, though he feared his friend was right. The Animal Dance was also known as the Crazy Dance or the Buffalo Dance, because it was always given on the night before the tribe left en masse for the hunt. Unlike most of the solemn Cheyenne ceremonies, it was known for its foolish mimicry of animals and sly ridicule of tribe members, which often left many of the observers rolling on the ground in gales of laughter.

Arrow Keeper stepped out from his tipi, which occupied a lone hummock beside Touch the Sky's. He crossed to speak to his apprentice.

"Are you prepared to assist at the dance?" he said.

Touch the Sky nodded. His nervousness was less now that he had successfully assisted the old medicine man at the Spring Dance during the chief-renewal one winter ago. Again Arrow Keeper had carefully rehearsed his part with him.

Now the old shaman too glanced across the clearing toward the trio of braves in front of the council lodge. Like Little Horse, he quickly guessed this signaled new trouble for Touch the Sky.

He pulled his red Hudson's Bay blanket tighter around his shoulders. The lines in his face were deep, like the cracks of a dried-up riverbed. But though the furrow between his eyes was deep in wrinkled folds, the eyes themselves were clear and bright and observed everything.

"Be ready, little brother, for some things we did not practice. I fear your enemies plan to use the dance against you."

Touch the Sky looked at him, waiting for more. But as if he had already said too much, Arrow Keeper changed the subject.

"I have had a medicine dream, and it told me the hunt will go well. Our travois will be heaped with tender hump steaks."

"Then we are fortunate," Little Horse said. "Each year, thanks to the white hunters and their long-killing rifles, we have fewer and fewer herds. Now look how far south we must ride. As young as I am, I recall a time when the buffalo came to us. Now we chase them into enemy lands."

"You speak straight-arrow, Cheyenne," Arrow Keeper said. "More and more white men, even some in the Great Council, are defending the slaughter of the buffalo as the best way to eliminate the red man. And in this thing they are right, for if they take our food and our clothing and our shelters, what is left to live with?"

"Truly," Little Horse said. "I hate the horse-eating Apaches. But in killing the white man's cattle and throat-slashing his ponies, they do right. Only then do the hairy faces know how *we* feel!"

Touch the Sky remained quiet at this, guilt lancing him inside as he recalled his own life among the white men in the river-bend settlement of Bighorn Falls. A buffalo hide was worth about three dollars on the Eastern market. He and his friend Corey Robinson had once laid eager plans to someday make their fortune slaughtering the great shaggy beasts—and never once, in their dream of riches, had they worried about the red man's fate.

Arrow Keeper saw clearly that his young helper was troubled. The old shaman knew full well what had happened to Honey Eater, knew that an innocent girl had been wronged. He also knew how Touch the Sky felt about that girl. The youth had had enough on his mind since Wolf Who Hunts Smiling had spoken against him at council, after the two had returned from the expedition on Wes Munro's keelboat. Cleverly, without actually inventing complete lies, Wolf Who Hunts Smiling had managed to cast suspicion about Touch the Sky's loyalty to the tribe and the Cheyenne Way. Now many still felt he was a white man's dog, not straight-arrow Cheyenne.

For these reasons, Arrow Keeper decided not to mention the rest of his medicine dream.

Yes, the hunt would go well. They would kill and distribute much meat. But in his vision, Arrow Keeper had also seen the four sacred Medicine Arrows which symbolized the fate of his people, and they were drenched in blood.

That night a huge ceremonial fire was lit in the vast square at the center of camp. Everyone attended the Animal Dance except the sentries and the herd guard sent out to protect the ponies grazing farthest from camp.

From the beginning Touch the Sky faced tense moments. Arrow Keeper had surprised his young apprentice by selecting him, before the entire tribe, to be Crooked Pipe Man for the ceremony. This prized role always went to a brave warrior. Many had expected Black Elk to be selected. But in selecting Touch the Sky, Arrow Keeper had reminded the tribe that the youth counted first coup in the critical Tongue River Battle—the great Cheyenne victory against land-grabber Wes Munro and his murderous militiamen.

Black Elk stood close enough, when this announcement came, for Touch the Sky to watch jealous anger spark in his fierce eyes, which were like black agates. In the shifting orange spears of firelight, Touch the Sky stared with grim fascination at the leathery flap where part of Black Elk's ear had been severed by a Bluecoat saber. The warrior had calmly picked up his detached ear, killed the soldier, then later sewn his own ear back on with buckskin thread.

But now Black Elk's anger did not last long. Touch the Sky watched him exchange conspiring glances with Lone Bear, his cousin Wolf Who Hunts Smiling, and Swift Canoe, who like Wolf Who Hunts Smiling had sworn to someday kill Touch the Sky. Black Elk's satisfied grin again reminded Touch the Sky to be prepared.

Though Honey Eater hid it well, Touch the Sky saw pride rise into her face for a moment when Arrow Keeper selected him as Crooked Pipe Man. Her approval heartened Touch the Sky. But truly, he thought with another pang of angry hate toward Black Elk, it is hard for her to face the tribe like this—her hair a ragged clump like a prairie chicken's tail. Yet it could do nothing to mar the flawless amber skin, the beautifully sculpted cheekbones, the slender, shapely body clinging to her buckskin dress.

The Animal Dance was a relaxed entertainment, not a formal ceremony. Touch the Sky wore no ceremonial finery except his mountain-lion skin, a gift from Arrow Keeper blessed with his big medicine. The warriors had left their war bonnets and scalp-laden coup sticks behind. Black Elk wore a fine new leather shirt adorned with beadwork so beautiful that even warriors—who seldom deigned to remark on women's work—openly complimented it.

Touch the Sky knew it was the handiwork of Honey Eater. Her skill was unmatched among Cheyenne women, whose beadwork was easily the finest of all the Plains tribes. Again, despite his vows not to torment himself, Touch the Sky heard the words of his crucial vision at Medicine Lake—the dead Chief Yellow Bear's words, spoken from the Land of Ghosts:

I have seen you bounce your son on your knee, just as I have seen you shed blood for that son and his mother.

But Yellow Bear had not spoken the mother's name. And Honey Eater was married to Black Elk. Why, Touch the Sky rebuked himself as he waited for the signal to take his place, could he not let this thing alone? Why could he not begin to look at other women in the tribe? Certainly, many of them looked at *him*.

All of this just made him miserable. He gave thanks to Maiyun, the Good Supernatural, when Arrow Keeper told the braves who were playing the part of the Four Directions to take their places.

Touch the Sky went to Crooked Pipe Man's place of honor in the dance square, the northeast corner. This was symbolic of the northern lights—a holy place called Where the Food Comes From, the spiritual home of the Big Holy Ones who first taught the Cheyennes their sacred myths and the secret of the Medicine Arrows.

Little Horse had been selected to be Spirit Who Rules the Summer; a brave named Eagle on His Journey was Spirit Who Gives Good Health; and Wolf Who Hunts Smiling was Spirit Who Rules the Ages. As the braves took their places on all four points of the square, Wolf Who Hunts Smiling passed close to Touch the Sky.

The young brave had only eighteen winters behind him, but was already respected as a fierce warrior. He had a wily, cunning face befitting his name and sharp eyes that seemed to dart everywhere at once. Now those eyes mocked his enemy, Touch the Sky, whom he would never forgive for growing up among the hair-face whites who killed Wolf Who Hunts Smiling's father.

The four braves selected to represent the directions danced in tight circles at their stations, knees kicking high as the tribe chanted *"Hi-ya, hi-ya!"*

"Now let the animals talk to us!" shouted Arrow Keeper, the signal for the comic mimicry to begin.

Touch the Sky had wondered why Swift Canoe had disappeared behind the council lodge. Now, as the costumed brave leaped suddenly into the firelight, he realized why.

The tribe burst into a collective roar of laughter as Touch the Sky felt heat creep into his face.

Swift Canoe's hair was greased with kidney fat and stacked on top of his head in the style of the whites. He wore a white man's shirt and trousers and heavy cowhide boots, captured in the Tongue River battle. The boots, especially, drew many stares and shouts of laughter. Clearly he was mocking Touch the Sky's appearance in the early days of his arrival, when he was called White Man's Shoes.

But the most humiliating part of his costume, to Touch the Sky, was the lace shawl he had wrapped about his shoulders. There was no greater insult to a warrior's manhood than to dress him in woman's clothing. To emphasize the point, Swift Canoe made exaggerated shows of emotion with his face—recalling another name, Woman Face, from the days when Touch the Sky had not yet overcome his white man's habit of showing his feelings in his face.

A young brave from the Shield Clan dashed out with a whiskey bottle. It had been filled with dark yarrow tea to resemble the white man's devil water. This brave too wore white man's clothing—a floppy plainsman's hat and a captured Bluecoat blouse, complete with shiny medals. He and Swift Canoe made an exaggerated show of shaking hands, a white man's custom which Indians found hilarious. Again the rest of the tribe burst into wild laughter and shouts of encouragement.

The two then took turns drinking from the bottle. This drew less laughter from the crowd, and more heat into Touch the Sky's face, as the tribe recognized a thinly veiled charge that Touch the Sky was a white man's dog, possibly even a Bluecoat spy.

But the mirth began anew as several young boys burst out from the surrounding trees, hunched under buffalo hides. They played the part of buffalo and charged all around Swift Canoe. He pretended great fear and clumsiness, tripping over the unlaced boots in his drunkenness and ignorance. Swift Canoe was mocking Touch the Sky's mistake, during his warrior training, of getting downwind of the buffalo and ruining hours of work for the hunters by scattering the herd.

The buffalos finally chased Swift Canoe off into the forest, his face twisted in exaggerated fear.

The tribe roared its collective appreciation when the capering buffalos returned to the square and performed a scalp dance to celebrate their victory over the white dog. The final touch, which sent even the most straight-faced soldiers of the Bull Whip troop double with mirth, came when the buffalos built a fire and roasted one of the white man's boots, just as a Cheyenne might roast a hump steak.

Honey Eater and Arrow Keeper did not laugh. The cruelty of this drama was not in keeping with the Cheyenne Way, and others besides Little Horse protested by turning their backs. The soldiers would not permit talking during the animal mimicry. Otherwise, Little Horse told himself hotly, he would have remined the troublemaker Swift Canoe that Touch the Sky had saved the tribe more than once to prove he was true Cheyenne.

Touch the Sky now gave his enemies no fuel for more ridicule. His face was alert but impassive, giving not the slightest clue to whatever feelings he held down inside. If his enemies expected him to be broken by this, he thought, they knew little about the courage of blooded warriors.

Black Elk, Lone Bear, and Wolf Who Hunts Smiling all stared at him with mocking eyes, waiting for his anger and humiliation to show.

Arrow Keeper caught his eyes and did something Indians rarely did. He winked at his apprentice.

Touch the Sky was at first confused. Then he understood the subtle hint. Suddenly the blank mask disappeared from his face, replaced by a smile.

The smile broadened, turned to laughter. The laughter bubbled in his chest, grew louder. Touch the Sky doubled over, his body spasming with uncontrollable hilarity.

At first the rest of the tribe was startled. Then their blank expressions turned to amusement and admiration. They too began laughing anew, this time led by their baffling new shaman apprentice. Soon stern warriors rolled on the ground like children, howling at the moon. The whole tribe was involved, led by the tall warrior Touch the Sky's infectious laughter.

The buffalos, totally ignored now, sneaked back into the trees, dragging their hides behind them. Black Elk scowled, embarrassed to have the thunder stolen from his act. He slipped past the soldiers and returned to his tipi, dragging Honey Eater with him.

Arrow Keeper grinned foolishly himself as he watched his young assistant reduce an entire tribe to hysterical giggles. He nodded his approval. It was good that this was happening, that they were laughing. Because soon they not only rode off to a good hunt—they also rode into the teeth of their enemies.

He had seen the blood on the Arrows, and Arrow Keeper knew that laughter, while necessary, always gave way to tears.

Chapter 4

Swift Canoe said, "Congratulations, brother! I see from your pony's tail that you are a Bull Whip now."

Wolf Who Hunts Smiling held his face proudly impassive. The men in his Panther Clan, which included Black Elk, took great pride in showing little concern for the praise of others. But the young brave was fully aware of the new streamers of red and black flannel tied to his pony's tail—the badge of the Bull Whip Society.

All around the two braves, Gray Thunder's people were preparing to move out in a long column behind the hunters. Most of the adults and children old enough to ride were mounted, some using stuffed buffalo-hide saddles, most just blankets. The infants and elderly would ride on travois. Young boys led packhorses tied to lead lines. Black Elk had already sent out flankers to protect the main column on the move. The women, well practiced, were taking down the tipis in minutes. But they would take much longer to erect again.

"What about the initiation?" Swift Canoe said. "When Blue Robe joined the Whips, they tied him up for one entire sleep with a huge rock on his chest."

Wolf Who Hunts Smiling shook his head in scorn. "Lone Bear knew that such children's games were useless in my case. He saw me fight at the Tongue River Battle, saw me kill the first enemy. He said the initiation would not be necessary for a warrior such as I."

Swift Canoe wisely said nothing. But he was thinking that it also didn't hurt that Black Elk was his cousin. Everyone in camp knew by now that Black Elk too had recently tied the Bull Whip streamers to his pony.

"So now you will ride as one of the Hunt Law enforcers," Swift Canoe said, admiration clear in his voice. "Perhaps you can speak for me in one more winter, when I send Lone Bear the gift of arrows?"

"Perhaps," Wolf Who Hunts Smiling said vaguely. Swift Canoe was his fawning imitator and often got on his nerves. He was a capable enough warrior and certainly no coward, though like most in his Wolverine Clan, he was a complainer and often shirked his duties. But he was also a loyal follower, and Wolf Who Hunts Smiling harbored secret plans of ambition, for which he would need loyal followers. For this reason he tolerated Swift Canoe—this, and the fact that

Swift Canoe hated Touch the Sky nearly as much as he did, blaming him for the death of his twin brother, True Son.

The two young braves were rigging their ponies for the hunt. Now Swift Canoe said, "Black Elk has blood in his eye over the incident last night. He was sullen with me, as if *I* had anything to do with Touch the Sky's clever victory during the Animal Dance. I played my part well."

"Woman Face will pay dearly for his short moment of glory," Wolf Who Hunts Smiling said. "Black Elk and I are both Hunt Soldiers, and we will be watching him closely. He will taste our whips before the meat is piled on our racks."

Despite Touch the Sky's improved standing among many in the tribe, Wolf Who Hunts Smiling was content. The young brave was as wily as his name. He knew full well that, despite all of Black Elk's courage and skill, he was a child in his feelings. Black Elk used to try to be fair toward the tall newcomer. But his increasing jealousy over Honey Eater had caused him to abandon his usual code of honor.

Once already he had sent Swift Canoe and Wolf Who Hunts Smiling to kill the young buck. They had failed, even after successfully luring a grizzly to his cave at Medicine Lake. But Wolf Who Hunts Smiling felt no shame in this failure—Touch the Sky was a true and mighty warrior. It simply was not possible for Wolf Who Hunts Smiling to achieve his plans if both of them lived.

And judging from the look on Black Elk's sullen face, he thought, Touch the Sky would confront more than the threat of bull whips on this hunt.

* * *

Once Gray Thunder raised his lance high, signaling the beginning of the hunt, the long column moved out quickly.

It was necessary to move fast because the buffalo moved fast. The great, shaggy beasts always moved at a stampede, stopping only to graze before stampeding on again. The sick, lame, and lazy were forced to the front. Any who stumbled would end up in the bellies of the wolves who worried the fringes of the herds.

Constantly Black Elk kept warriors riding on the flanks. They were in frequent communication with the main body thanks to the efforts of young runners who had been selected because of their swift ponies. Black Elk himself rode point, with the best scouts well out ahead of him. The pace was grueling.

They made good time, but not without mishaps. They were forced to use a bad ford when crossing the Shoshone River. Some tipi covers and poles were lost to the runoff-swollen current. A child nearly drowned when it fell off a pony, but was snatched out of the water by an alert old grandmother.

One sleep into their journey, they passed the awesome Black Hills. The Bowstring and Bull Whip soldiers rode up and down the column, enforcing silence while the sacred center of the Cheyenne world remained in sight.

Touch the Sky marveled again at the Black Hills' beauty. They stretched from the northeastern Wyoming Territory into the Dakota country, a series of rocky, craggy heights rising above the semiarid plain that surrounded them. Lush, dark green forests stood out against barren backgrounds of shale, sandstone, and limestone.

Streams tumbled everywhere.

When the Black Hills were well behind them, and they were approaching the Platte River, Little Horse rode up beside his companion.

"Brother," he said, "I hope you are keeping eyes in the back of your head."

It wasn't necessary to say more—Touch the Sky knew what he meant. Wolf Who Hunts Smiling had made a point of letting him know he was watching him intently. The other Bull Whips too made contemptuous faces when they passed him in the column.

"I am," he replied. "The arrogant Wolf Who Hunts Smiling is waiting to pounce on me at my first mistake. He knows that resisting a hunt soldier is a dangerous business. I cannot even fight back."

"This thing is wrong," Little Horse said. "Arrow Keeper tells me the soldiers were originally limited to making sure no hunter attacked the herds too early once the buffalo were spotted. Now the Bull Whips freely beat anyone at any time during the hunt."

Little Horse looked over his shoulder to make sure a Bull Whip was not riding close.

"Consider the last hunt, what the Whips did to Black Robe of the Root Eaters Clan. He fired on a buffalo before the command was given. The Whips threw him on the ground and beat him until he could not stand. They broke up his weapons. They cut his blankets, moccasins, and kit to shreds. When they had finished, they took all of his food and went off with his horse. They left him alone on the prairie, sore and bleeding, too weak and hurt to move. And the Hunt Law would not permit anyone to help him."

Touch the Sky nodded grimly. "Wolf Who Hunts Smiling has picked a troop to his liking."

"Truly, brother. Hold that thought close to your heart, especially after making a fool of Black Elk and Swift Canoe at the Animal Dance. They are *for* you, buck!"

The Kiowa scout named Stone Mountain peered out past the rimrock, watching the long Cheyenne column advance below on the plain.

He and his Comanche companion, Kicking Bird, had been camped for many sleeps here in the steep hills just north of the Smoky Hill River, well south of the Wyoming-Colorado border. Stone Mountain was aptly named. The huge Kiowa was even taller than his leader, Hairy Wolf, and his shoulders were so massive he had been forced to cut a slit across the back of his captured Bluecoat blouse in order to put it on. His thick black hair fell past the base of his spine.

"Maldita sea," Kicking Bird cursed in Spanish. "Now we must finally leave this fine camp."

Stone Mountain nodded glumly. He had been glad to leave the hot, dry ravines and canyons and arroyos of the Staked Plain behind them. They had found this place and used it as a base camp when spying on the Cheyenne's advance scouts. But now the tribe had finally reached this far south, and he and Kicking Bird would have to give up this safe, snug place with its good hunting and clear, cold water. It was time to head back now and alert the main band.

True, there were far more blue-dressed soldiers

up north. But the two Indians were so used to finding cover in the desert that they could move with ease up here. Even when trees were scarce, one could hunker down in the waist-tall buffalo grass.

Stone Mountain left a little leather pouch with a few beads inside under a rock in the center of the camp—it was the Kiowa way to leave a gift to a place that had been good to them.

"Watching the Cheyenne tribe on the move is a child's job," Kicking Bird said. "But I would rather sneak into a bear's den than spy on their camps. Their dogs are many and raise a clamor at the first smell of an enemy."

Stone Mountain nodded. Dogs were also likely to make a racket at the wrong time. For this reason the Cheyennes left them behind when riding into battle or the hunt.

"It was the Cheyenne," he said, "fighting beside their cousins the Sioux and their allies the Arapaho who first drove the Kiowa out of this fine land. At one time we shared the Kansas and Nebraska ranges with the Pawnee. This green land is our rightful homeland. Now look how they fly right into our faces again! Will they not be content until we are camped in Sonora?"

The two scouts had moved down below the rimrock to untether their ponies. Kicking Bird, who craved tobacco badly, paused to split his wooden pipe open with a rock. Eagerly, he sucked at the brown gum inside it.

"Take heart, brother," Stone Mountain said as he swung his huge bulk onto the back of his sturdy buckskin pony. "You saw the women and children just now. Prices are good in Santa Fe.

There will be no shortage of fine tobacco if this raid goes as planned!"

Three sleeps into the hunt journey, Gray Thunder's Cheyennes sighted the Arkansas River. The largest and most treacherous of all the rivers on the Southern Plains, it wound from the Colorado Rockies across the Plains to the huge river the Indians called Great Waters, the whites the Mississippi.

Fresh meat was needed for the trail. One of the braves who had lived in this area with the Southern Cheyennes recalled that a huge salt lick, which attracted game, was located nearby. Gray Thunder called for volunteers to search for it.

Touch the Sky and Little Horse were among the braves who rode off from the main column. They all fanned out, dividing the river valley into sections for the search. Touch the Sky nudged his gray toward a stretch of thickets just past a huge bend in the river.

The salt licks were places where earth surrounded saline springs. The vast amount of salt which accumulated brought deer, elk, and antelope in fantastic numbers. Touch the Sky tethered his pony and entered the thickets on foot, searching for fresh game prints.

He searched the river bank in both directions, finding signs only of rabbits and other small game. He had returned to his pony, and was about to break out of the thickets onto the plain when, suddenly, he felt a sharp tug at his legging sash.

A sapling behind him suddenly split; a heartbeat later, the sharp crack of a rifle reached his ears. Only then did Touch the Sky realize that the tug was a bullet which had reached him before the sound of the rifle—he was being fired upon!

Instinctively, he leaped out of the line of fire. But he couldn't retreat deeper into the thickets while his pony was tethered in the open.

He leaped out of the thickets and raced toward his horse. But when he glanced out across the short-grass expanse, he spotted no enemies closing in—only Black Elk accompanied by two other riders. Touch the Sky waited for them to reach him.

"Do not stand there gaping as if you were beholding the Wendigo, mooncalf!" Black Elk said as he dismounted. He was accompanied by Tangle Hair, the Bowstring Soldier who had settled the dispute over Honey Eater's braid, and Lone Bear, the leader of the Bull Whip soldiers. "A wounded elk may be escaping. I shot at one just now. Help us find it."

"You have found your elk already," Touch the Sky said.

He grabbed his buckskin legging sash and twisted it until they could see the small hole where Black Elk's bullet had torn through.

Black Elk's face revealed nothing. There was silence for several heartbeats while Lone Bear exchanged a long glance with his troop's newest warrior. Touch the Sky watched both men carefully.

"Truly," Black Elk said, "from where I stood, I was shooting at an elk."

"It is common at such distances," Lone Bear said, "to mistake buckskin clothing for an elk's hide. Indeed, palefaces are always shooting each other this way. Do I speak straight-arrow, Tangle Hair?"

Tangle Hair was young, only a soldier and not head of a troop as Lone Bear was. Besides, why did this tall Cheyenne always manage to be in the middle of trouble? Nonetheless, Tangle Hair could not help admiring him. He was no brave to fool with. Besides, Tangle Hair had been patrolling the flanks of the column when Touch the Sky entered that thicket—and he could have sworn Black Elk too had seen him enter.

"You speak straight-arrow indeed," Tangle Hair finally replied. "It is a common mistake. Good thing for Touch the Sky that Black Elk's aim was not a cat's whisker better."

"Yes," Black Elk said, staring at Touch the Sky with the hint of a smile playing at his lips. "Good thing."

Chapter 5

Two sleeps passed after the incident in the thicket. Touch the Sky kept a wary eye on his enemies while the land all around him gradually changed as the tribe pushed further south, following the buffalo trail.

There was still enough grass, especially near the rivers, to support the buffalo herds. But more and more now Touch the Sky noticed flowering mescal, the white plumes of the tall, narrow cactus known as Spanish Bayonet, and the low-hanging pods of mesquite. Now they had to be careful to keep the horses and children from drinking bad alkali water.

Touch the Sky was riding by himself on flank guard when Spotted Tail, leader of the Bowstrings, rode out from the main column to join him.

"I would speak with you," Spotted Tail said, his pony falling into step beside Touch the Sky's. The brave had 30 winters behind him. But the white streaks in the back of his hair, which had earned him his name, had appeared in his youth.

"I always have ears for words spoken by the leader of the Bowstrings," Touch the Sky said with genuine respect.

"This is a delicate matter." Spotted Tail glanced out across the mesquite-pocked range, toward the main body. Touch the Sky knew he was watching for Bull Whip soldiers.

"I saw you count first coup at the Tongue River Battle," said Spotted Tail. "I have watched you since you arrived at our camp. I have heard the charges against you. Indeed, I was among those who voted for your execution when you were first charged as a spy for the blue blouses. I am glad now that old Arrow Keeper intervened to save you. After watching you fight at Tongue River, I will never question your loyalty to Gray Thunder's tribe. You are a warrior, buck, and straight-arrow Cheyenne all the way through!"

These were important words, coming from the leader of the tribe's most popular soldier society. But Touch the Sky held his face impassive, as warriors did. A man who knew he had earned praise never showed gratitude for it.

"However, many in the tribe—many in my own society—disagree with me. Some think that a Cheyenne who once wore white man's shoes and lived under a roof can never be a Cheyenne. For this reason I cannot follow my heart and invite you to undergo the initiation into the Bowstrings—not yet."

Touch the Sky nodded, understanding this thing. No Indian leader, be he a chief, a clan headman, or a military society leader, could dictate to his followers.

"However," said Spotted Tail, glancing again toward the main column, "that is not why I rode out here. I came to tell you that you better play the sharp-eyed hawk during this journey. Something is afoot with the Bull Whips. They have plans for you. In this they are spurred on by Black Elk and his hotheaded young cousin. Indeed, it was to make your life miserable, I believe, that Black Elk left the Bowstrings."

Touch the Sky nodded. "There was a time when he felt nothing but cold contempt for me. Now he hates me."

"Everyone knows why," Spotted Tail said, not bothering to elaborate. "Know this. I have told my Bowstrings, watch not only the people, but the Whips too. They are no men to fool with. Nor are many of them honorable—more than one has stolen meat from Bowstring racks.

"But though I have asked my troop to watch over you, some will refuse to help. Those who are opposed to you say it does not matter that you are brave and strong. They say you are still a lone coyote without a clan and therefore loyal only to yourself. So be wary like a fox. Do not give the Bull Whips the smallest reason for noticing you."

Touch the Sky nodded, thanking the warrior before Spotted Tail rode back to join the main column. His words left the tall brave apprehensive, but determined. He had sworn this thing to his friend Little Horse when Touch the Sky returned from Medicine Lake after his vision: He was home to stay. Anyone who planned to drive him out now would have to either kill him or die in the attempt.

As if to reassure himself, his hand dropped to the butt-plate of the percussion-action Sharps protruding from his scabbard. The weapon had been a gift from his white father in Bighorn Falls. But if the soldiers chose to invoke the strict Hunt Law, as an excuse for "punishing" him, he would not be free to fight back.

Despite these worries, the increasing excitement of the tribe, as they drew nearer to the buffalo, infected Touch the Sky too. Several of the hunters carried their specially blessed buffalo shields, depicting the tufted tails and woolly humps of the great shaggy creatures. In camp at night, the children who'd been on previous hunts lorded it over the younger ones and kept repeating, "Wait until you *see* them!" The braves said little. They smiled and looked away, embarrassed to admit that they too were affected by the excitement—though obviously they were.

They were fully aware that this mesa and ravine country was the home of their enemies, the Kiowa and Comanche. The far-flung flankers and scouts sent back word of any movements by red men or blue-bloused soldiers. Black Elk, reckless in battle, showed great prudence when responsible for the entire tribe—at the least sign of potential danger, he led the column wide around it. As was Cheyenne custom, they rode under a white truce flag to announce this was not a hostile movement.

They reached a series of sandstone rises between the Canadian River and the Red River. The spot offered plenty of water, good protection from the sand-laden winds, and plenty of drift cottonwood to make excellent fires. Black Elk called a halt for the day, giving the order to make camp.

Touch the Sky and Little Horse were ordered to backtrack some distance and make a "false camp." This consisted of building a few fires and leaving a few ponies tethered in the area. It would serve as a decoy. If attacked by Kiowa or Comanche, the racket would alert the real camp upriver.

By the time they returned to the main camp, Touch the Sky was famished. Little Horse joined his clan circle, and Touch the Sky crossed to Arrow Keeper's fire. As usual, the old shaman had cooked meat for him too, and prepared extra yarrow tea.

While he ate, Touch the Sky saw Honey Eater crossing to join the women of her clan. After the hunt, the hunters would congregate for hours and boast about their kills. But the hard work of skinning and butchering would fall to the women and children.

Touch the Sky carefully avoided looking at her. Black Elk's jealousy had softened the warrior's brain, and Touch the Sky knew he was on the feather-edge of killing both him and Honey Eater. He would do nothing to set the hot-tempered warrior off.

On the other hand, he was determined to keep as close an eye on Honey Eater as he possibly could. The murder stigma was strong, but Touch the Sky would sully the Arrows if necessary to protect the woman he loved with all his heart.

Arrow Keeper glanced at the youth's face and read some of these conflicting thoughts in the flickering firelight as they ate.

"Will you be riding herd guard again, little brother?" the shaman asked him.

Touch the Sky nodded. He had learned a valuable lesson from the hunt journey: When the tribe stopped for the day, always send the ponies out farther away from camp during the early part of the evening, under guard. That way they could graze until moved in closer during the late hours, yet there would still be grass left for them near camp.

"The duty is unpopular," Touch the Sky said. "But I volunteer because of your advice that a shaman should seek time alone. And truly, Father, I have come to enjoy the time spent with the ponies."

"This is a good thing. A shaman, like a chief, must love and serve his people. But he is not as afraid as most to spend time alone, meditating and observing. Only by listening closely to the language of Nature can you learn her secrets. Still . . ."

Arrow Keeper gazed beyond the circle of the fire, past Touch the Sky and off into the grainy twilight of the Southwestern Plains.

He was thinking of his medicine dream, his vision of blood staining the sacred arrows. And he was thinking of this feeling now, this premonition which stained the air. This was enemy territory, after all.

"Still," he repeated, "shaman or no, it is also a good thing to keep your weapons at hand."

* * *

Touch the Sky's gray was exhausted, so he let her rest. Instead, he cut a good little paint out of the herd and rode north of camp, toward the Red River, to guard the ponies grazing the bunchgrass farther out. Wolf Who Hunts Smiling and several other Bull Whips watched him closely. But Arrow Keeper too was watching, and they left him alone.

The sun had bled slowly out of the western sky, leaving a blue-black dome smattered with glittering stars. Spanish Bayonets rose tall and dark against the skyline. Now and then coyotes barked—a series of fast yelps ending in a long howl that made Touch the Sky's hackles rise.

The portion of the herd he was protecting was grazing close to the river. Touch the Sky gave the paint her head and let her wander and graze, only occasionally nudging her into movement to bunch the ponies a little tighter.

Finally they settled in one area. He dismounted and took up a position with his back against a cottonwood, his Sharps lying across his legs. From here he commanded a view of the long, moonlit rise which was the best line of attack.

Despite his vigilance, Touch the Sky was weary. He had been up with the sun, ridden guard on the flanks, then doubled back with Little Horse to set up the false camp. Now he would remain with the ponies until they were called in for the night.

For a time, despite his determination to the contrary, his mind was filled with thoughts and images of Honey Eater. But slowly, as his weary muscles began to grow slack, he pushed the thoughts aside and listened to nothing but the bubbling chuckle of the river, the eerie rhythm of cicadas, the occasional nickering or snorting or stamping of the horses.

Then, even those noises blended together, then faded. His eyes appeared glazed over, he sat absolutely motionless, and even his breathing seemed suspended.

Once again Touch the Sky saw images from his powerful vision at Medicine Lake, only they flew past like rapid birds and he glimpsed them only for a heartbeat. But when the words were spoken clearly inside his head, it was not the voices of the dead who had spoken in his vision—it was Arrow Keeper's:

Wake to the living world now, little brother, or sing your death song!

An instant later Touch the Sky blinked, and he stared into the war paint of a Comanche!

From the vivid descriptions given by Arrow Keeper and others, he knew immediately it was a Comanche, despite never having seen one close up. A large, cruel mouth was made even more ferocious with streaks of their brilliant green and yellow war paint. His ears were pierced with large brass hoops, and a bear-claw necklace dangled around his neck. His small but lethal skull-cracker was raised at the ready. Two more steps closer, and he would have dashed Touch the Sky's brains out against the tree.

Touch the Sky raised his rifle off his lap and slid his finger inside the trigger guard.

But when he aimed out into the darkness, the Comanche was gone.

For a long moment the dumbfounded Cheyenne simply sat there, stupidly aiming at nothing. Slowly, the muzzle of his rifle lowered, and he asked himself: Had the Comanche brave disappeared like a thing of smoke because he *was* a thing of smoke? A fancy coined by Touch the Sky's tired, overwrought brain?

But no! He had been so real Touch the Sky could count the quills in his moccasins. Their enemy was upon them!

Quickly he slipped the paint's hackamore back on, then rounded up the ponies and pointed them toward the main camp. It was nearly time to drive them in anyway, as he could see from the position of the Always Star to the north.

Touch the Sky had been filled with his news as he rounded up the ponies. And he had kept a sharp lookout for more Comanches. But now, as he added these ponies to the herd near camp, doubts again assailed him. True, the Comanches were famous for stealth. But how could *any* Indian simply be there one instant, gone the next?

By the time Touch the Sky returned to camp, few people were interested in his news. Scouts had just returned with news that the buffalo birds had been spotted! These were the parasites that traveled with the buffalo, living off the ticks in their hide. Whenever they were discovered, the herd was close by. Now the camp was buzzing with talk and preparations.

"Tomorrow, brother, we eat hot livers!" Little Horse greeted him triumphantly. "I will kill a huge bull and tie its beard to my pony's tail!"

Touch the Sky took his news to Spotted Tail of the Bowstrings. He listened closely. Then he said, "Black Elk has taken too many precautions, there could not be a large war party nearby. It was only a lone renegade, hoping to steal ponies. You scared him off."

Arrow Keeper said little when he told him the story. He only stared long into the fire, his eyes dark, glittering chips of obsidian. After a time, Touch the Sky thought he had fallen asleep. The old medicine man nodded off more and more now, seemed to tire more easily.

But he suddenly reached out and stirred the fire with a green stick. A column of sparks flew up with the smoke. Outside the warmth of the clan fires, another coyote howled.

"It hardly matters, little brother, whether the warrior you saw was real or not. Either way, you saw him. It is a warning. Gray Thunder's tribe is marked for grave danger."

Chapter 6

"Soon they will attack the herd," Hairy Wolf said. "So we must strike soon too."

He and the Comanche leader Iron Eyes sat their ponies where they had stopped their bands at a water hole in the Texas Panhandle. They were still south of the Cheyenne tribe. The land hereabouts was cracked and dried from the sere summer heat. The grass was thin and brittle, and the midday sunshine drew heavy sweat that mixed with the dust coating every Indian, forming a paste.

Their combined bands had ridden north from the Blanco Canyon camp after receiving favorable reports from the scouts Stone Mountain and Kicking Bird.

"Remember," said Iron Eyes, leader of the Quohada Comanches, "we must stay out of sight of the hunters. There are too many warriors for us to take on, especially now that they are keen for the hunt blood."

Iron Eyes truly respected the Cheyenne as warriors. But what kind of men permitted themselves only one wife? He himself currently had three, and if any one of them crossed him, he would simply kill her and take another as Comanche law allowed. Women were like horses, there were more to be had.

"Yes," Hairy Wolf agreed. "Our target is the hunt camp itself. It will be under light guard unless we are spotted."

The giant Kiowa leader was bigger than every member of his band except Stone Mountain. His rich black mane of hair flew out behind him now as a dust-laden wind kicked up. He was dressed in captured cavalry trousers and high-topped riding boots, and was bare from the waist up except for his sturdy bone breastplate.

"We hit fast," Iron Eyes said. "We lash the prisoners to the spare ponies; then we count on the superior speed of our horses to stay ahead of the Cheyenne if they come for us. They will never touch us in the Blanco."

Behind the two leaders, Painted Lips and some of the others towed extra mounts on lead lines. Big Tree, the Comanche who could shoot 20 arrows while an enemy fired and reloaded a rifle twice, had painted his face in vertical and horizontal stripes of black, the color of death.

"No," agreed Hairy Wolf, "once in the canyon the fight is ours to win. When it is safe, we will then mount an expedition to Santa Fe to meet the Comancheros. We will take no fat or ugly or old women, nor children still sucking at the dug—these are hard to sell."

"Straight words, Kaitsenko. And these are Cheyennes, so we must remember to get the knives which all the young girls wear around their necks. They will kill themselves if we do not."

"Then they are more vigilant than their savage lords," Hairy Wolf said scornfully. "Dog Fat claims he nearly walked up to a herd guard and brained him against a tree where he sat dreaming."

But despite these brave words, both leaders respected and feared the Cheyenne. This was clear as they set out again. Iron Eyes turned and started the word with Painted Lips: *Remember Wolf Creek!*

The rallying cry spread quickly through the ranks as the two bands moved north.

Early the next morning the hunters rode out. The buffalo birds had been spotted near enough by then that the Cheyenne decided against moving the hunt camp. It was necessary to keep the women and children close by for the skinning and butchering should the kill go well.

Black Elk naturally assumed that enemy scouts were in the area. But the reports from his own scouts strongly confirmed his own sense that no large deployment of warriors was in the vicinity. The hunt would be near enough to the camp, which would be safe under the protection of a few junior warriors-in-training.

Touch the Sky's strong feelings of anticipation affected his pony. It wanted to run, but he held her in. The hunters kept their horses to a walk, planning to unleash them only at the last moment, when the buffalo had sensed them and started their inevitable stampede.

These were the critical moments of the hunt, and the soldier societies were in full force. Despite the Cheyenne brave's respect for custom and the tribal law-ways, they were a warrior society—the traits needed in a good warrior were not always in harmony with those of a good tribe member. The rash, reckless, fearless bravery of individual effort was what decided Indian battles. The honor of counting first coup went to the warrior who moved first, acting on his own.

This strong tradition of individual effort meant that the hunters naturally got carried away in the competition to kill the first buffalo, a high honor indeed. But a herd warned too early could escape, and thus an entire people go hungry and poorly clothed because of one man's rashness. So the Bowstrings and the Bull Whips rode on either flank. They would not leave their vigilant guard positions, and join the hunt, until the hunt leader signaled the charge.

River of Winds had been selected as hunt leader. Talking would be permitted, in low voices, until he gave the command for silence. Little Horse nudged his pony up beside his friend.

"Brother," he said, "I have been thinking about Black Elk's shot into the thickets. Ride close to me during the hunt so no more 'accidents' like this happen."

Touch the Sky nodded, his lips pressed into their determined slit as he glanced to both sides of the wedge-shaped formation. Black Elk rode slightly ahead of him. Wolf Who Hunts Smiling rode directly across from him on the flank, in line with the other Bull Whips. Certainly another accident could happen easily.

"Once the hunt is underway," Touch the Sky said, "we will move well away from the others."

Further conversation ceased as River of Winds signaled the command for silence. They were approaching the last long rise before the spot where the scouts had last spotted the herd. And Touch the Sky could see the tiny buffalo birds flitting about, sure proof the buffalo were near.

The wind was favorable for the hunters, blowing hard into their faces. Buffalo were nearly blind, but possessed an extraordinary sense of smell. Touch the Sky could not help thinking about Swift Canoe's Animal Dance antics, heat rising into his face. Once before he had carelessly frightened off the herd by getting downwind of them.

But former disasters faded from his mind as he cautiously walked his horse up to the crest of the last rise overlooking the herd. He joined the long line of waiting hunters, getting his first glimpse of the beasts.

The sight made belly flies stir in his stomach.

The herd was grazing in a lush valley, bright with thick patches of golden crocuses growing against the deep green of the grass. From the rim of the canyon walls rising above them, giant stands of cactus stood like timeless sentinels.

Touch the Sky couldn't even estimate how many there were—so many they formed a great, shaggy carpet that seemed to cover the land as far as the eye could see, heaving and rolling like a giant wave.

More luck was with the hunters. Just past the neck of the valley, the herd's only escape route, was a series of steep-sided sand dunes. When the buffalo were chased into these, their hooves would flounder helplessly.

So far the men had escaped notice. Several ponies wanted to surge forward and were barely restrained by their riders. The desire to draw first hunt blood filled each Cheyenne and made his blood sing. When River of Winds finally dropped his streamered lance, and the line of hunters surged forward, their collective shout rose above the thundering of their ponies' hooves.

As they had agreed, Touch the Sky and Little Horse angled off from the other hunt groups, avoiding the Whips. Their ponies raced down the slope into the thick of the herd, which was only now coming to life as the dominant bulls bellowed the stampede call.

One moment Touch the Sky saw green grass racing below his feet; the next he was swept up in the stampede, and nothing was visible all around him but shaggy brown fur and dangerously sharp horns. The air was clamorous with the sound of hooves pounding, calves bawling, cows lowing, bulls roaring their angry roar. Sometimes the buffalo pressed in so tight his legs were trapped between them and his pony.

Bulls constantly tried to gore his pony. But the gray was too quick, nimbly lunging to safety each time. He saw Little Horse flashing in and out of the swirling dust, bouncing wildly on top his pony. Touch the Sky's Sharps was loaded and ready in his hand. But he knew it was suicide to simply shoot at a buffalo in the main part of a stampede like this—as it went down it could cause a choke-point, throwing the hunter to sure death by trampling.

It was the Cheyenne way to hunt buffalo by skillfully moving to isolate one portion of the vast herd. Then, turning it from the main body, they would close in on it tighter and tighter—much as they fought the white man's circular defense for wagons, attacking in an ever-tightening pattern.

Within a short time he and Little Horse had bunched a group off to the right of the main herd. They were adeptly pointing the stampeding animals toward the sand dunes, whistling, shouting their war cry. Abruptly, several of the biggest bulls veered sharply away from the buffalo they were pointing. Touch the Sky didn't even need to rein the gray—she leaped after the buffalos with a mind of her own.

A few heartbeats later, Touch the Sky's eyes widened in shock when the buffalos suddenly disappeared!

He realized why just in time to rein in his pony before she too plunged over the blind cliff which had just sent the buffalo to their death.

He turned to look behind him. Little Horse, intent on driving their bunch into the dunes, had missed all this. But someone else had seen it. And now, as he raced over to join Touch the Sky, the tall young brave stared with dread at the red and black streamers tied to his pony's tail.

"Woman Face!" Wolf Who Hunts Smiling shouted above the din of the hunt, receding now behind them. "Surrender your weapons! I command this in the name of the Hunt Soldiers!"

"Why?" the warrior demanded. "I have done nothing to violate the Hunt Law."

"Done nothing?" Wolf Who Hunts Smiling nodded behind him, in the direction of the cliff. "Hunting by yourself, you sent at least a dozen fine bulls over a cliff. The Hunt Law strictly forbids solitary kills—no hunter rode anywhere near you! Now these animals are contaminated and cannot be touched."

"I did not chase them over the cliff. They escaped in that direction. I did not know about the cliff until they went over."

"So you say. I saw it differently. Save it for my leader, Lone Bear. I said surrender your weapons!"

Wolf Who Hunts Smiling held his Colt rifle, which had belonged to Touch the Sky in the days when he was still called Matthew Hanchon, aimed at the brave. Reluctantly, Touch the Sky obeyed. As much as he despised Wolf Who Hunts Smiling, disobeying a Hunt Soldier was a serious offense.

His enemy's wily face was triumphant. The swift, furtive eyes mocked him. Clearly, this moment made up for the brief moment of glory when Touch the Sky had ruined Swift Canoe's Animal Dance mimicry.

"You have done it now, *shaman* who likes to laugh at his own unmanly mistakes! We shall see if the others laugh with you and roll upon the ground *now*!"

Wolf Who Hunts Smiling cracked his new, knotted-thong whip hard.

"You'll soon taste this. We'll see then how much laughing Woman Face does!"

Chapter 7

Soon the buffalo had thundered on toward the mountain peaks to the west, yellow-brown dust clouds boiling up behind them.

The kill had gone well and the hunters were exhilarated. They had already made the first cut of the butchering, to reach inside and dig out the still-warm livers. They ate them raw from their cupped hands, savoring the hot, tender mouthfuls.

At first they were busy exchanging excited comments about the hunt and the delicious hump steaks they would feast on later. They were slow to notice that the new Bull Whip soldier, Wolf Who Hunts Smiling, held Touch the Sky prisoner. Curiosity took over once they saw something was afoot—quickly they gathered around the pair.

Little Horse was less curious. He knew full well that his friend's enemies had managed to stir up some new trouble. The timing could not be worse for Touch the Sky. Arrow Keeper had ridden out to observe the hunt, as had Chief Gray Thunder. But by law the chief could not hunt, and Arrow Keeper had joked that he no longer had any desire to die anywhere but in his sleep. They had ridden back, after tasting warm liver with the hunters, to supervise the moving of camp. The rest of the tribe must be brought up to butcher the first day's kill.

That meant, Little Horse thought grimly as he joined the others, that by the Hunt Law a soldier troop's decision was final. Worse, the two military societies were independent of each other. Each must respect the other's decisions. And *this* was now a Bull Whip matter.

"What is the meaning of this?" Lone Bear demanded.

"This one," Wolf Who Hunts Smiling said, "deliberately hunted by himself and used a buffalo jump to kill many bulls! Look, below lies the proof!"

"He lives up to his name," Touch the Sky said, "by speaking in a wolf bark. I never saw this cliff. I was chasing buffalo that strayed from the group which Little Horse and I were driving toward the dunes."

"He speaks the straight word," Little Horse said. "We were hunting together. Nor did I see this cliff. Look here how it—"

"Silence!" Lone Bear commanded. "You jabber on like a squaw."

Touch the Sky's glance shifted from Wolf Who Hunts Smiling to Swift Canoe to Black Elk. All were gloating, enjoying it immensely as they anticipated the outcome. As if he couldn't hold off, Wolf Who Hunts Smiling kept flicking his whip.

Lone Bear stared at Touch the Sky where he stood beside his pony. "The Hunt Law is strict on the number of buffalo a tribe may kill. This is because Maiyun has ordered that we may take from this earth only what we require to live. Thus the buffalo jump may be used only when there are no horses for the chase, no weapons for the kill. Entire herds have gone over cliffs, dying and rotting in numbers too great to imagine. *You* could have caused it again today."

Touch the Sky tried to speak up, but Swift Canoe was first.

"This is our greatest complaint against the hair faces. We take only what is needed; *they* waste all they can. And here before us stands one of them."

"You swell up with righteousness," Touch the Sky said. "Why not also tell them, *noble warrior,* how you hid like a white-livered coward and tried to murder me at Medicine Lake, sullying our tribe's Sacred Arrows."

"This is not Medicine Lake," Lone Bear said, "and Swift Canoe has not been arrested by one of my soldiers—*you* have, buck! I have ears for Swift Canoe's words. *This*"—Lone Bear pointed over the cliff—"is just one more proof that you have little respect for the Cheyenne Way."

The rest of the hunters exchanged troubled, embarrassed glances. The hunt celebration had been on their minds until this. Only a few times in their memories had the hunt soldiers been forced to discipline a brave for a violation this serious. This Touch the Sky, he was a straight enough warrior. But how did he always manage to be where trouble was?

"Brothers!" Black Elk called out. "This could ruin the rest of the hunt! Our kill today was good, but we need much more meat for the cold moons. His presence may have put the stink upon us so the herds will smell us every time."

"This trail is taking a wrong turn," Little Horse said. "Lone Bear says I jabber on like a woman, but have I not slain our enemies and counted coup like a man? When did Little Horse ever hide behind a better fighter? I say Touch the Sky speaks straight-arrow. He did *not* chase the buffalo over the cliff. They led him toward it."

"True it is that Little Horse can fight. But everyone knows," Wolf Who Hunts Smiling said scornfully, "that he is quick to play the dog for this white man wrapped in a Cheyenne skin. My cousin Black Elk, our war leader, is right. The stink is on him, he will scatter the herds!"

The blood of Wolf Who Hunts Smiling was up now. He harbored great ambitions for tribal leadership. The others were listening respectfully to his words, which lent them a fiery eloquence.

"Red brothers! Only think on this thing. Brother Buffalo knows it is the white men who are exterminating him, not the Indian. And *this* make-believe Cheyenne carries the white smell on him.

"Brothers, have you never caught a skunk's spray direct on your clout or leggings? It *never* washes out. The same with the white man's stink. Black Elk has taught this one the warrior ways, and he does not lack courage. But he is a white man at heart, and his face will soon show his feelings for all to see."

As he finished speaking he cracked his knotted rawhide whip to emphasize his point. This oration stirred several others to approving nods.

"You puff yourself up like the white fools who jump on stumps to speak," Touch the Sky said defiantly. "Like their lies, yours are worth no more than a pig's afterbirth."

Wolf Who Hunts Smiling's sneer twisted into a snarl of rage. He raised his whip to strike, but Little Horse deftly swung his lance out to stop it. The gesture was useless, however, because Lone Bear now spoke up again.

"Enough of this quarreling! Are we women in their sewing lodge? The Hunt Law is clear on these matters. Now the whips will speak with much sharper tongues."

Lone Bear nodded once. The Bull Whips prepared to set upon Touch the Sky.

"Warriors! Hear my words!"

The speaker was Spotted Tail, leader of the Bowstrings.

"In the Bowstrings we require more proof than the word of one witness, an enemy of the accused man at that. Recall, Wolf Who Hunts Smiling now speaks against Touch the Sky after openly walking between him and the camp fire! Do we trust a witness who has thus threatened to kill the very buck he now accuses?"

Black Elk, sparks snapping in his fierce dark eyes, whirled toward the Bowstring leader.

"You have called my cousin a liar. Very well. Do you also call me a liar?"

Spotted Tail bit back his words. He was no coward, but Black Elk was certainly no warrior to provoke when he was keen for a fight as he clearly was now. Getting killed, Spotted Tail told himself, would not help Touch the Sky.

Thus seeing which way the wind must set for now, Spotted Tail called out, "Bowstrings! If you honor justice, turn your ponies!"

As one, the soldiers of the Bowstring troop joined their leader in turning their ponies around. By turning their backs, they protested the Bull Whip's actions; by remaining, they supported Cheyenne law. Several other hunters belonging to neither of the troops also joined the Bowstrings in turning their backs.

Touch the Sky refused to flinch back when the Bull Whips advanced upon him, Black Elk and Wolf Who Hunts Smiling riding at the head of the pack behind Lone Bear. It was the usual custom for the troop leader to strike the first blow. But now Lone Bear nudged his pony to one side, letting the other two advance first.

Black Elk and his younger cousin exchanged a quick glance. Wolf Who Hunts Smiling nodded slightly, also dropping back. Black Elk rode forward, turned his pony, and raised his whip. His hate-glazed eyes met Touch the Sky's, and his words proved it was Honey Eater on his mind, not violations of Hunt Law.

"You squaw-stealing dog," he said in a voice meant just for Touch the Sky's ears. "Your hot blood will cool once it drips into the Plains!"

The corded muscles of his shoulders bunched tightly as he lashed out savagely with the knotted rawhide, expertly cracking it across Touch the Sky's chest and ripping open a burning line of flesh. The incredible pain jolted Touch the Sky, but though he winced he refused to cry out or show the pain in his face.

Again and again Black Elk brought his whip down, ripping, tearing, opening up lacerations all over Touch the Sky's body. Only when Black Elk's arm began to tire did the rest set upon him.

Now, despite all his efforts, Touch the Sky was driven to his knees by the sheer force of the pain. Little Horse made as if to leap from his pony, but the braves on either side restrained him.

The whips hissed and cracked, and Touch the Sky's blood flowed in scarlet ribbons into the ground. Every nerve ending in his body seemed to have been stripped raw and held up to a flame. But though he was on the ground now, he refused to cry out or show anything but defiance in his face.

"Cry, Woman Face!" Wolf Who Hunts Smiling taunted him, breathing heavily from his exertions with the whip. "Twist up your face like the newborns do and make your chin quiver!"

A moment later Wolf Who Hunts Smiling leaped back in rage when Touch the Sky hawked up a wad of phlegm and spat it into his face. This made Wolf Who Hunts Smiling strike even harder, but Touch the Sky still refused to cry out—even though now he was so bloody the soil clung to him like brown bark.

In a fury of sudden strength, Little Horse broke free of the braves restraining him and leaped from his pony. Screaming the war cry, he waded among the flailing whips, catching them, tangling them, jerking one from its owner's hand, taking the lashes meant for his friend. One hand flew to his beaded sheath and removed his knife.

"Hold! The first Bull Whip who comes close enough dies a hard death!"

The Bull Whip soldiers stopped, looking to Lone Bear for their instructions. Lone Bear considered carefully. He knew that his troop was not eager to flog Little Horse—a brave honored in council for his fighting courage when he had only 15 winters behind him. Yet the leader of the Bull Whips was no man to trifle with.

"Black Elk!" he called out. "What do you counsel?"

Black Elk's blood was still up from the beating. Now his nostrils flared wide with his hard breathing.

"Little Horse is too much influenced by Touch the Sky. But he is a warrior unlikely to die in his sleep."

"I have seen him fight like five men," another Bull Whip said.

"Brothers! These things are straight enough," Wolf Who Hunts Smiling said. "But only think on this! He plays the dog for one who openly drinks strong water with the hair faces, one who leaves messages in the forks of trees for Bluecoat soldier chiefs. *I* have not forgotten the sight when Bluecoat canister shot butchered my father as surely as our women will soon butcher these buffalo! Now Little Horse has brazenly defied Cheyenne law by interfering with a soldier troop! Whip him too!"

Lone Bear nodded slowly, still considering how to handle this thing. He was not known for fairness, and now he was leaning toward Wolf Who Hunts Smiling's suggestion.

Now Spotted Tail too spoke up.

"Dismiss your troop, Lone Bear, or I swear I'll go to the Star Chamber!"

This was the final Cheyenne court of appeal, made up of six Headmen whose identities were known only to Chief Gray Thunder. They met in secret at the emergency request of respected war leaders. Their judgments outranked any others.

Lone Bear did not fear such an action. But it was clear that his men, with the exception of Wolf Who Hunts Smiling, were not eager to draw more blood from either Cheyenne.

"The punishment is terminated," he announced. "As for Little Horse, I have ears for those who plead his case. He will not be held in violation of the Hunt Law. But he and all others must remember—the law is strict on this point, that none may assist Touch the Sky. He has set himself outside of the tribe by his actions. Now he must suffer alone."

The braves were beginning to scatter when Touch the Sky's voice rang out. It was weak, strained from the injuries he'd received. But the words were clear enough even though spoken past bloodied, cut, and swollen lips.

"Wolf Who Hunts Smiling! After I saved you from the Pawnee, you vowed never to attempt to kill me again. But I would respect you more for killing me than for *this* cowardly sport! And so I warn you, best to kill me now, buck, or I will turn your guts into worm fodder."

Now Touch the Sky looked at Black Elk.

"And you, war leader! I used to call you my better. No more. Never mind what you have done here today to me! A man who would hit a woman, especially when she has done nothing to merit it, is merely a killer, not a true warrior.

"You once had honor, and I respected you for that. You no longer have it. And I warn you as I just warned your cousin, best to kill me now and have done with it. For truly I speak only one way, and I say this for all to know now. My father was a greater Cheyenne warrior than any man's here, and on his honor I swear it, both of you will pay for this."

A surprised silence greeted this announcement. This was the first time anyone, besides Arrow Keeper, had known anything about this supposed warrior father.

Black Elk, however, was enraged that this meddling squaw-stealer had publicly talked about his disciplining of his own wife!

"My father," he said, making the cutoff sign as one did when speaking of the dead, "died the glorious death at Wolf Creek. But only after he had smeared enemy blood over his entire body."

"And *my* father," Wolf Who Hunts Smiling said, "was killed by the paleface devils whose ways are in your blood."

"Both of us," Black Elk said, "have their weapons, their war bonnets, their enemy scalps on our lodgepoles. Can you produce these things that once belonged to your famous warrior father?"

This was greeted with laughter from the others. Soon everyone was mounting.

Touch the Sky spoke his final words on this matter. Little Horse could not believe his friend was still conscious after all this blood loss.

"I am not a sweet-talking Ponca who forgives his enemies. I tell you again, Black Elk and Wolf Who Hunts Smiling. Kill me now or sing the death song because I am *for* you!"

Chapter 8

While Touch the Sky lay helpless, the women and children moved the hunt camp to the dead buffalo. It was their job to do the bloody skinning and butchering.

The new temporary camp was a festive and noisy place. Hunters called out to each other, bragging, congratulating each other, acting out scenes from their kills. The women and children, lugging empty travois, were led to the animals killed by hunters in their clan.

The hides were stripped from head to buttocks. Then they were staked out flat to dry. Knives and stone chisels were used to scrape off every last bit of fat or flesh. Later, back at their permanent summer camp, the hides would be smoked over sweet grass to take out the smell.

The butchering was a bloody mess, and soon all the women, Honey Eater included, were covered with sticky blood from their hair to their moccasins. Drying racks had already been made out of mesquite branches. The women sliced most of the meat as thin as paper. Hung on the racks, it would be quickly dried by the Southwest sun and wind. It would remain edible for many moons.

Nothing was wasted. Other parts were set aside for the feast tonight at the dance of thanks for the good hunt. Blood and brains would be boiled together with rose hips to provide a true delicacy; the delicious tongues would be roasted so tender they would fall apart without chewing; the curdled, partially digested milk in the stomachs of the young buffalo calves was a treat many Indians dreamed about during the cold moons.

Everything they weren't consuming tonight would be piled onto the travois. Bones would yield tasty marrow; the horns of the bulls would provide cups; ropes and belts would be woven from the hair. Guts would soon string new bows; the kidney fat was stored in clay jars for cooking.

When the main job of butchering was finished, the hunt distribution was held.

This ancient Cheyenne custom ensured that sufficient fresh meat and delicacies would go to the elders and the poorest members of the tribe. The women of each clan had started a pile in a conspicuous place, contributing some of their clan's kill. When Chief Gray Thunder saw the pile, he ordered the soldier chiefs to take charge of the distribution.

Those who needed meat were already on hand. The soldiers set the meat up in equal piles. Then Spotted Tail of the Bowstrings selected River of Winds, known for his fair dealing, to inspect each pile and make sure they were equal. Then River of Winds made sure that no one was overlooked.

The soldiers were forced to turn away a woman from Swift Canoe's Wolverine Clan, though she protested loudly—she had already sent her daughter for a ration of meat, hiding it and getting in line herself.

Only after the soldiers reported the distribution complete did Gray Thunder order the dance of thanks to begin. Tonight they would feast; soon, when the meat was dried, they would move on after the herds. At least one more good kill was needed to see them through the cold moons.

Little Horse, like all the hunters, celebrated with his clan. But constantly he worried about Touch the Sky. However, the Bull Whips were making sure that no one went anywhere near the hunt transgressor. Hunt Law was strict on this point. Wolf Who Hunts Smiling especially kept his furtive, mocking eyes on Little Horse, daring him to violate the Hunt Law by helping his friend.

While the rest gorged themselves on fresh buffalo meat, many eating until they vomited, then eating more, Little Horse thought again with wonder of the thing Touch the Sky had claimed—that he was the son of a great Cheyenne warrior. This was the first Little Horse had heard of such a thing. He knew his friend too well by now to ever doubt his word.

Besides, Little Horse had glimpsed the mulberry-colored birthmark just past Touch the Sky's hairline, the perfect arrowhead shape. The traditional symbol of the warrior.

Earlier, Honey Eater had been clearly distraught when the women and children had been brought up to the site of the kill and she had realized Touch the Sky was not among the hunters. Little Horse, knowing he had to get word to her before she spotted the injured brave and rushed to him, took a great risk. He managed to get her aside for a moment, without being spotted by Black Elk, and explain the situation.

"How badly is he hurt?" she asked, alarm tightening her voice. She was kneeling over a hide, scraping fat away from it with a sharp-pointed stone chisel.

Little Horse, glancing around again to make sure Black Elk wasn't near, said, "He has been badly beaten, but he is strong. He has endured greater pain than this. He will survive. But it will be some time before he is able to move on his own."

"And Black Elk?" she said, her dark eyes snapping sparks. "Did he play the leader in this too?"

Little Horse glanced away, his silence answering her question for her.

"You say he has endured greater pain than this," Honey Eater said bitterly. "You speak true. Pain is all he has known since he joined our tribe. I am glad you are his friend, Little Horse."

"I am his friend until death, sister. But I can do nothing for him now."

Even covered head to toe with blood, her hair a ragged mass where Black Elk had cut her braid off, Honey Eater was pretty. Little Horse thought again how natural it was that Touch the Sky would love her and she him. But the Cheyenne law-ways had forced her into a loveless marriage. And now Black Elk was making both of them suffer for their love.

They could risk no further conversation. Wolf Who Hunts Smiling was already riding over to see what was happening. Little Horse turned to leave. But Honey Eater called out his name. He turned back around.

Keeping her head down, continuing to scrape away at the staked-out hide, she said, "You know that I love him?"

"Yes. And I know that he loves you."

"Please do not let his enemies kill him!"

Wolf Who Hunts Smiling was almost upon them now, his knotted-thong whip cracking.

"If they do kill him," Little Horse vowed just before he left, "I swear by the four directions of the wind that my blood will run with his."

Touch the Sky lay where he had fallen beaten, unable to move, an outcast until he could ride on his own to camp. His weapons had been left alone, and his obedient pony grazed nearby without benefit of a tether.

For a long time—while his sister the sun slid across the sky—he lay dazed. His body alternated between dull throbbing and fiery pain. Awareness had become a narrow place surrounded by patches of dense fog. His mind passed from fog to clarity and back in an endless pattern. The skinning and butchering and feasting had gone on nearby with all the usual clamor. But to him it was all a dream, a thing of smoke.

His uncle the moon took over the sky, the long night passed, and the tribe moved out just after sunup of the new day. But Touch the Sky lay in utter exhaustion caused from enduring massive pain. However, even though the pain lanced deep into his flesh, his mind was freed as it had been on the Spirit Path at Medicine Lake. And once again images from his past were sprung from memory.

He glimpsed the unshaven, long-jawed face of Hiram Steele's wrangler Boone Wilson, again saw him unsheathing his Bowie knife while Steele's daughter Kristen screamed. He flexed another memory muscle, and now he saw the smug, overbearing sneer of Seth Carlson, the Bluecoat lieutenant who had helped Steele destroy the Hanchons' mercantile business.

There was more, images flying past like quick geese in a windstorm: He saw his own people torturing him over fire; saw the white whiskey trader again slaughtering white trappers and making the killings look "Indian"; saw himself counting coup on Seth Carlson when the officer tried to torch the Hanchon spread; saw the terrified Pawnees fleeing from Medicine Lake when he summoned a ferocious grizzly; saw the keelboat called the *Sioux Princess* exploding into splinters as he led his people to victory over the land-grabber Wes Munro during the already-famous Tongue River Battle.

And mixed in with all the fragments from his past were glimpses from his vision quest at Medicine Lake, glances stolen from the future: He saw his people freezing far to the north in the Land of the Grandmother, saw Cheyenne blood staining the snow. The screams of the dying ponies were even more hideous than the death cries of the Cheyenne.

It all led to one huge battle. And then the warrior leading the entire Cheyenne nation in its last great stand turned to utter the war cry, and Touch the Sky recognized the face under the long war bonnet as himself.

When all seems lost, Chief Yellow Bear's voice said to him again from the Land of Ghosts, *become your enemy!*

When he finally left the Spirit Path and woke to the life of the little day, the morning was well advanced. And now he felt the pain so intensely that he dared not move—every effort to do so sent a white-hot jolt through him and left him gasping.

The unjust beating had not left him humiliated. He had not been in the wrong. And did he not suffer in silence like a true warrior, only speaking to give his tormentors insults to answer their insults?

No, he told himself, his mouth a grim, determined slit against the pain, this was a matter of just revenge, not humiliation. He had meant what he told Black Elk and Wolf Who Hunts Smiling. Their lives were now forfeit. It was not just a matter of his own safety. Black Elk's jealousy was a worm cankering in his brain. In his insane rage, Black Elk would eventually do more to Honey Eater than cut off her braid.

Despite the sure knowledge that these things he was thinking were true things, Touch the Sky felt some sharp doubts pricking at him. The buffalo hunt was at the very core of the Cheyenne way, the basis for their very existence. Yet was this not twice now that he had failed the hunt in some way—his fault or not?

Had he not, after all, violated Hunt Law and wasted good meat? Never mind the reasons and excuses—the results could not be denied.

He knew that by now the tribe was moving on, trailing the herd for the next kill. If—

Touch the Sky abruptly saw a harrowing sight that scattered his thoughts like chaff in the wind.

Fear moved up his spine in a cool tickle. Cresting the hills on the horizon, many riders strong, was a large war party. Touch the Sky was too far distant to make out their style of hair, by which tribes could always be identified. But almost surely in this area they would be Kiowa or Comanche, probably both given their closeness when it came to treading the warpath.

And these riders were definitely riding the warpath—so many streamered lances, easy to make out in silhouette, could signify nothing else.

He clenched his jaw in frustrated helplessness when he again tried to move. The effort made his vision go dim with overwhelming pain.

And then the truth struck him with the force of a blow. He was trapped, unable to even crawl into hiding. If the war party kept advancing, they would probably spot him and enjoy a bit of unscheduled torture before they killed him.

Then they would move against the new hunt camp, wherever it was established. Caught flush in their hunt, the Cheyenne warriors, though numerous, would be unpainted for battle, their bonnets and shields unblessed. They would have no time to renew the Medicine Arrows for battle.

He recalled Arrow Keeper telling him the Kiowa and Comanche were zealous slave traders—especially in women and children. And he thought of Honey Eater and the suicide knife under her dress.

He was their only hope of an advance warning. Again, desperation warring with the pain, he tried to sit up. But his tortured flesh seemed to scream its pain, and his mind shut down to darkness.

Chapter 9

Hairy Wolf halted the column of warriors in the lee of a long ridge.

"We camp here," the big Kiowa told Iron Eyes.

His Comanche friend nodded. "This is a good place. We can make small fires, and if they send scouts behind to check on their back trail, we will not be spotted."

Hairy Wolf reined his pony around. His bone breastplate gleamed brightly in the late afternoon sun. He signaled for the best scouts, Stone Mountain and Kicking Bird, to ride forward.

"Ride on ahead," he told them, "and discover where the next hunt camp is located. As soon as you know when the hunters will be going out again, race back with the word."

"Move like coyotes through prairie chickens," Iron Eyes added. "They must *not* spot you. We want the women and children left alone in camp."

While the scouts rode out, the Comanche named Dog Fat returned from a quick check just forward of their present position.

"The Cheyenne are long gone. But there is a fine gray pony grazing by itself, untethered, near the sight of their first butchering. I want to ride closer and see if it is for the taking."

Dog Fat had not noticed the injured Cheyenne brave lying in the knee-deep buffalo grass not far from the pony.

Iron Eyes considered his request. "You are sure it is not simply another one of their clever false camps?"

"No one would leave this fine pony in a false camp as a lure," Dog Fat said with conviction. "And it is rigged for riding. I think something happened to its rider, and it is for the taking."

Iron Eyes looked at Hairy Wolf. His friend nodded once. Dog Fat, known for his love of torturing captives, was also a capable buck with a reputation for superior stealth. It might be useful to have a look around the area of the Cheyenne's last camp.

"Go then," Iron Eyes said. "But be all eyes and ears."

Dog Fat loosened the lead line tied to his buffalo-hide saddle. Then he brandished his stone skull-cracker. "If I set eyes on a Cheyenne, he will never make another track."

* * *

Touch the Sky felt like he was floating up toward the surface of a river, rising faster and faster like an air bubble. Then suddenly he broke surface, and his eyes snapped open.

The afternoon sunlight was hot on his face. For a moment he remembered nothing, did not know where he was or how he got there. Then he tried to sit up. The abrupt jolt of pain brought him back to the present, and he remembered the war party.

This time he did manage to sit up, though the pain made his eyes water. He could move a little easier now. But why was he even still alive? The war party surely could not have missed him when it passed by.

But they must have. Somehow, though he was stiff and bloodied and raw from his beating, he had to race on and warn the tribe. By now they were almost a full sleep's ride ahead of him.

He had just screwed up his courage to attempt rising from the ground when he glimpsed a lone rider approaching from the ridge on the horizon. He lowered himself again into the waving buffalo grass. Spotting the gray made him realize that the war party could not have ridden past. Even if they had missed him, quite possible in the grass, they would not have left his pony.

In fact, clearly it was his pony this lone brave was interested in now.

His curiosity was mixed with a feeling of sick dread. What did this enemy have planned? If they meant to engage Cheyenne warriors in a fight, why halt their advance now so early? The Comanche especially were known for attacking at night. So why weren't they following the tribe, moving into position to strike?

Unless they had something else in mind—some opportunity they planned to seize when the Cheyenne braves were all distracted by the hunt.

Some opportunity which these infamous slave-takers would seize in the hunt camp itself, not on the battlefield.

But now there was no more time to speculate. The rider was close enough for Touch the Sky to recognize that he was definitely Comanche. He was heavy but strong, a roll of fat hanging over the top of a pair of filthy Army trousers with yellow piping down the sides. His hair was parted exactly in the center and tucked back behind his ears. He carried a stone war club resting across one thigh.

And he was definitely intent on capturing the gray. As he drew closer, he looked cautiously all around. Touch the Sky, wincing at the movement, ducked even lower.

His rifle was still in the scabbard sewn to his horse blanket. His lance and throwing ax too were lashed to his pony. The only weapon left to him was the obsidian knife in his beaded sheath. He slid it out now, even that simple movement sending hot explosions of pain into his limbs.

The Comanche halted his buckskin pony and dismounted, uncoiling the lead line as he moved closer to the gray. The gray shied and nickered, moving off a few paces.

Touch the Sky's brain raced, searching for a way out of this threatened loss of his horse. He himself was safe for now, but what good was safety on the Plains without a horse? In his condition, he was as good as dead.

The fat Comanche moved in again. Again the gray nickered and trotted off. But the Comanche obviously had experience with horses. He continued speaking to it gently as he moved in, soothing it.

The brave wasn't looking in his direction now. Touch the Sky rose to his knees again, pain screaming from every pore of his whip-lashed body. The Comanche was actually singing to the gray now, a low, soothing song in words Touch the Sky couldn't understand. But the song had a lulling effect on the pony. She finally stood still as the Comanche moved in close enough to slip the lead line through her hackamore.

Trembling with the effort, Touch the Sky drew his right hand back behind his head. As the intruder began to lead his pony back to his own mount, Touch the Sky threw the knife in a fast overhand throw. The exertion made him gasp with pain.

But his aim was true. The knife punched into the Comanche's back just behind the heart, dropping him to his knees. A moment later he dropped forward onto his face, legs twitching in death agony.

Touch the Sky set his lips in a grim, determined slit and rose shakily to his feet. It cost a great effort, but he managed to cross to the dead Comanche and jerk his knife from his back. He wiped the blade in the grass and slid the weapon back into its sheath.

The gray nuzzled his shoulder, glad to see him on his feet again. It made hot red waves of pain wash over him, but in a few moments he was mounted. He glanced once toward the long ridge behind him, then stared out across the parched expanse in the direction his people had ridden. It was a vast vista of redrock canyons and arroyos, of steep mesas and buttes and sandstone rises.

Reading their trail would be no challenge, not with all those travois heavily laden with meat. But was there time to catch them and warn them? If Kiowas or Comanches on their notoriously fleet-footed ponies spotted him, he knew he could never outrun them—certainly not in his present condition.

But he had no choice. It was either do it or don't do it. And if he didn't do it, Gray Thunder's tribe was surely in great danger. This Comanche was no lone spy sent to gather information. He was part of a powerful war party.

Nor could Touch the Sky be sure he would ride out of this place alive. He had no exact idea where the rest of the enemy might be camped. Perhaps they were keeping an eye on him at this very moment.

Trying not to glance at his blood-encrusted wounds, Touch the Sky nudged his pony's flanks and set out in search of his tribe.

When Dog Fat did not return in a reasonable time, his friend Standing Feather accompanied Iron Eyes and Hairy Wolf to learn what had delayed him.

He was still barely breathing when they found him, bloody foam bubbling on his lips. Even as

Standing Feather turned him onto his back, the death rattle rose in his throat with a noise like pebbles shaken in a shaman's dried gourd.

His face grim, Standing Feather performed the Comanche death ritual. "Father in heaven," he intoned, "this, our brother, is coming." Then, embracing the dying man, he flapped his hands behind him like wings while he imitated an eagle's call. Thus Dog Fat's soul would be flown to heaven.

While Standing Feather lashed his dead companion to his horse, Hairy Wolf gazed off in the direction Touch the Sky had recently ridden out. The Kiowa chief looked for a long time, as if reading some clue on the distant horizon. His eyes squeezed to slits as they stared into the setting sun.

Iron Eyes knew perfectly well what he was thinking. After all, it was the Comanches who had perfected the tactic of attacking out of the sun.

"I do not relish riding into the sun," Hairy Wolf finally said. "But neither can we stay. Surely it was a Cheyenne who killed Dog Fat. He could not have much of a lead. Never mind our fine camp. I say we ride now and reach the Cheyenne before this dog's barking alerts his fellow warriors."

"Tienes razon," Iron Eyes said in Spanish. "You are right. And when we catch him, we will feed his own eyes to him."

By nightfall Touch the Sky realized his enemies were closing in on him.

The gray was well rested from her long graze. But Touch the Sky could not constantly hold a fast pace. The jarring and bouncing felt like more whips—dozens of them—flailing him raw all over again.

Each time he crested a ridge, he glanced back and spotted his dogged pursuers closing the gap. Clearly there would not be enough time to warn the tribe.

Fear and frustration vied with the excruciating pain of bouncing on his pony. Several of the deeper whip cuts were bleeding afresh, and occasionally he tasted blood running into his mouth or was forced to swipe at his eyes to clear his vision.

As he clung to his mount, trying to place the pain outside of himself as Arrow Keeper had taught him to do, he thought of a desperate plan. It might well get him killed. But otherwise, Gray Thunder's tribe was in serious trouble.

Touch the Sky knew his trail was being lost in the much larger path left by his tribe. When he reached an arroyo that ran at right angles to the trail, he leaped the obedient gray into it and doubled back around. Riding behind a huge, sloping rise, he hurried into position behind the war party.

As he had hoped they would, the combined band of Kiowa and Comanche warriors made a brief stop to eat and water their ponies in a clear tributary of the Brazos River. While they prepared their meals of parched corn and a thick soup made from the paste of crushed insects, their ponies were hobbled in a group at the water's edge.

Touch the Sky rode his own pony as close as he dared. Then, grimacing at the throbbing pain, he dismounted and tethered his gray behind a thick stand of Spanish Bayonet. It was nearly dark now. But he knew darkness would not deter either tribe from moving and attacking. The pain making his entire body protest, he leapfrogged from cottonwood to cottonwood, from prickly pear to prickly pear, moving ever closer to the hobbled ponies.

Small groups of braves were scattered about everywhere, cooking over small fires. At times Touch the Sky could find no cover. Then he was forced to simply crawl along the ground and pray to Maiyun that he would not be spotted. Sweat broke out all over his body and streamed into his cuts, causing a fiery, itching sting.

Finally he reached the horses.

Moving quickly despite the pain, he began untying the short rawhide hobbles. He prayed that none of the horses would move enough to capture enemy attention, at least not before he had freed plenty of them.

This night Maiyun was with him. He had untied nearly half of the horses before any of them began moving very far. Knowing he had reached the most dangerous moment of his plan, he abruptly shouted the shrill Cheyenne war cry as he slapped the nearest ponies on the flanks.

"Hi-ya, hii-ya!"

Only a few heartbeats later the frightened mounts were scattering across the shallow tributary and out onto the flat.

In the confusion he was able to slip away and return to his pony. Cutting well around the tumult of the campsite, he urged the gray onward. He knew his enemies would lose valuable time recovering their ponies. But would it be enough time? he wondered.

And even as he asked the question, he also answered it: He had done all he could. It would *have* to be enough time.

Chapter 10

All through the night Touch the Sky pushed his horse as hard as he possibly could, stopping only to make sure he was still on the trail of Gray Thunder's tribe.

He was numb now to the pain. After his sister the sun had gone to her resting place, the night air had cooled considerably and soothed his pain-ravaged skin. A three-quarter moon and a star-shot sky made visibility good and fast riding easy.

He ate while he rode, chewing on the pemmican and dried plums in his legging sash. Each time he stopped to verify the trail, he knelt and placed his ear close to the ground, listening for sounds of pursuit. He heard nothing, but this hardly reassured him. The Kiowas and

Comanches were famous for their stealth—often, only one scout would actually follow behind an enemy, the rest riding well to the flanks and using lone riders to stay in touch with him. This way their quarry might relax and easily be taken by surprise. Every Cheyenne knew the famous stories about Comanches stealing up to sleeping couples so quietly they could kidnap the wife without waking the husband or her.

So Touch the Sky did not relax his vigilance. He was still riding hard when dawn finally painted the eastern sky in roseate hues.

Despite his pain and fear for the tribe, Touch the Sky could not help being filled with wonder at the grand beauty of this Southwest canyon country. Mountains never seemed close, yet in every direction he looked they raised their white-capped peaks into the sky above the distant horizons. Startled roadrunners scurried in front of his horse, and huge tumbleweeds bounced and hopped and rolled with incredible speed. Everywhere majestic cactus formations stood out against the sky. Some bore uncanny resemblance to human figures.

Grass was not as plentiful as it was on the Plains to the north. But neither were white hunters, blue-dressed soldiers, and paleface work crews stringing the talking wires which carried words through the air like bolts of lightning. As a result, game had become more plentiful in this semiarid country. Toward mid-morning Touch the Sky glimpsed a herd of antelope, their white-spotted flanks flashing in the sun.

In daylight the churned-up earth caused by the buffalo herd was easier to follow than a paleface wagon road. It was shedding season; occasionally, near water, he would encounter cottonwood trees, their thick-ridged bark covered with woolly hair where the buffalos had backed against them to scratch themselves.

Finally, riding up out of a shallow red-dirt ravine, he spotted the conical tipis of the temporary Cheyenne hunt camp.

He saw at his very first glance that the men were gone. Clearly they had already ridden further forward for the next kill. This troubled Touch the Sky. Had Arrow Keeper and Gray Thunder and the rest been present, he could have warned them that an enemy war party was near, probably approaching.

Now he would almost surely have to convince whoever was in charge of the hunt camp to pack it up and go forward, joining the hunters for safety even earlier than Hunt Law dictated. This could jeopardize the hunt by frightening off the buffalo. But if they were indeed in danger of attack, his action would not cause him trouble with the headmen. However, if enemy pursuers failed to show up, he would be in trouble yet again.

Still, he thought, thinking of Honey Eater, the risk was worth it.

Then, as he topped the last long rise before entering camp, he realized there would be no chance to join the hunters. He had turned to look behind him one last time. And there, on the distant horizon, he saw a brown cloud of dust swirling above the ground—riders approaching fast. The attack was coming.

How many? he wondered. Could they have captured their horses so quickly they were able to catch him like this? It didn't seem likely, as hard as he had been riding. More likely, they had sent a smaller force on the horses Touch the Sky had not been able to scatter. He hoped this last was the case.

And now his suspicions became a certainty: This was not strictly a war party, but a slave-taking mission. The Kiowas and their Comanche allies were especially fond of the Cheyennes because the Beautiful People brought a good price in guns and bullets and alcohol and the white man's rich tobacco. And Honey Eater might very well end up in one of Santa Fe's or Chihuahua's stinking bordellos.

As he entered the camp, the women and children and elders eyed him curiously. They knew he had been punished by the Bull Whips. Yet very few respected the Whips, so their eyes were sympathetic when they saw his wounds. The warriors-in-training, who had between 12 and 15 winters behind them, had been left in charge of the camp. They too eyed him curiously, many with open respect—though he was called a troublemaker and a white man's dog, all knew of his feats as a warrior. They had counted the coup feathers in his war bonnet, remarked on the mass of scars covering his chest and back.

"Little Brother!" Touch the Sky called out to a junior warrior named Stump Horn. "Who is in charge?"

"Two Twists," the youth replied.

"Run quickly and get him. You are about to taste your first fight!"

The youth's dark eyes widened at this news. He tore off to find Two Twists. Meantime, drawn out of her tipi by the sound of his voice, Honey Eater crossed quickly toward Touch the Sky as he dismounted.

She stopped dead in her tracks, however, when she saw what the savage whipping had done to his flesh. Before she spoke even a word, her eyes filmed with tears.

"Is this what my husband the Bull Whip has done to you? *This?* Little Horse told me they hurt you, but this!"

The words choked her throat and she turned her head away, tears now openly streaming down her cheeks.

"It was not enough," she added bitterly, "that they beat you this way. Black Elk and Wolf Who Hunts Smiling are also saying things. They say you should not be allowed on this or any other hunt because your smell is scaring away the herds."

"To you I will say nothing against your husband," Touch the Sky said. "I will settle with him and his lying cousin, all in good time. For now, little Honey Eater, dry your tears and draw on your courage as a Cheyenne woman—an attack is coming!"

At this news the sadness left her face, replaced by the same grim determination that now marked his scarred features. Now Two Twists was rapidly approaching from the opposite end of camp.

As they waited for the youth, Touch the Sky hungrily drank in a long glance at the woman he loved with all his soul. Rarely did he get an opportunity to be this close to her without having to worry about Black Elk's jealous eyes.

She flushed under his stare, turning her face away. "I am ashamed to have you see me like this."

He knew she was talking about her mangled hair.

"A beautiful oak," he said, "is the same tree even after its leaves blow away during the cold moons. And soon, the new leaves grow back."

Despite the danger approaching, his words brought a brief smile to her face. But now Two Twists had arrived.

"Little brother," Touch the Sky said, "how long would it take to move the women and children to the hunt?"

"Perhaps half a morning's ride."

This news made Touch the Sky frown.

"Then we must stand and hold," Touch the Sky said. "Kiowas and Comanches are approaching even now and will catch us if we try to flee. Gather all your warriors, buck."

Two Twists, who had earned his name from his preference for wearing his hair in two braids instead of just one, which was the usual custom, swelled with importance at these words. He nodded and raced off to gather the bucks.

"Honey Eater," Touch the Sky added, "gather the women and elders. We must make our battle plan, and quickly. I fear these red devils are not coming simply to fight. They plan to steal women and children as slaves!"

Touch the Sky knew their enemy was approaching rapidly, so the impromptu council was brief.

As always when the tribe was traveling, the women had brought along their stone-bladed hoes which they used to dig up wild turnips and onions. At Touch the Sky's instructions, they went to work digging shallow rifle pits in the loose soil. He had come up with a reckless plan which might well get him killed. But Touch the Sky knew full well it was their only chance.

The young warriors had no time to paint or dress for battle. Unlike some tribes, which rode into battle on a moment's notice, the Cheyenne tribe always painted their faces and donned special battle garb. This was considered so important that, often, courageous warriors fled from a fight if they could not thus prepare.

But fleeing, and deserting the women and children, was out of the question now. So Two Twists went around to all the junior warriors, quickly marking their faces with black charcoal—the symbol of joy in the death of an enemy.

Then, while Honey Eater and the other young women gathered up all the children, Touch the Sky addressed Two Twists and the rest of the youths.

"Little brothers! Hear my words and place them in your sashes. Soon the war cry will sound, and blood will stain the earth. True it is you are young. But every great warrior was once young. I watched my brother Little Horse wade into the midst of frenzied Pawnees when he had only fifteen winters behind him, like Two Twists here. And I swear by the earth we live on, my brother greased their bones with his war paint!

"Little brothers! Of course you feel fear at this moment. So do I, and have you counted my scalps? There is nothing unmanly in feeling fear. It is staying and doing that counts! We are the fighting Cheyenne! Remember this, you do not fight for glory or for scalps or for the right to stand in the doorway of the clan lodges and make brags. You fight to save your mothers, your grandparents, the little ones who are the future of the Cheyenne people."

The youths were stone silent, stone still, absorbing every word. This Touch the Sky, had he not counted first coup at the famous Tongue River Battle which saved their homeland from greedy whites?

It was a rare mark of distinction for a warrior such as this to address them as fighters, as brothers. Yes, they were afraid. But their games from infancy on had all centered around mock battles, taking scalps, and counting coups. Two of them had even lost an eye from "toy" arrows fired from miniature bows in battle. They were afraid, but they were keen to prove themselves.

"Bucks, this day you will cover your tribe in glory! If you fall, fall on the bones of a Kiowa or Comanche. If their blood be rain, cause a flash flood! The Cheyenne tribe defeated them at Wolf Creek. Some of your fathers were in that battle when they were barely older than you are today. What Cheyennes have done, Cheyennes will do!"

Now Touch the Sky thrust his war lance over his head.

"Hi-ya!" he screamed. *"Hii-ya!"*

As one, the junior warriors repeated the war cry.

"One bullet!" Touch the Sky shouted.

"One enemy!" the warriors responded.

"One bullet!"

"One enemy!"

They were worked up to a frenzy, their eyes blazing.

"Quickly now," Touch the Sky said. "Make ready your battle rigs. And never forget, the fight is not over until the last Cheyenne buck is dead. I have spoken and can say no more. From this moment forth, let deeds speak for words. Two Twists, take command of your warriors."

Hurriedly, Two Twists began issuing orders while Touch the Sky headed quickly to a spot just north of camp. It had caught his eye because of a series of small humps on the ground, humps that could not be seen easily from horseback.

Sure enough, it turned out to be an area pocked with holes left by prairie dogs. Touch the Sky saw that he could stand behind it and still be close enough to call out commands to the warriors in the rifle pits just to his right and behind him. He would be completely exposed, but that was part of the plan.

The dust cloud on the eastern horizon was beginning to take shape now. Touch the Sky gave thanks to the four directions and to Maiyun, the Good Supernatural, when he realized this force was only about half the size of the original war party he had spotted—meaning that only those whose horses he had not scattered had come after him.

Still, even so, there were at least three Comanche and Kiowa attackers for every young Cheyenne defender. It was not just a brave rallying cry—it really *would* have to be one bullet, one enemy, or they would be overrun in mere moments.

Before he walked back to the main camp, he dropped to his knees and briefly offered a battle prayer. Already, he could hear Two Twists leading the youths in a Cheyenne battle song to fortify their courage.

Now it was time to return and give them their final instructions.

By now Honey Eater and the others had gathered the children and elderly behind a hastily erected breastwork. She knew by now that the attackers were Kiowa and Comanche—and she also knew what that meant.

Unaware that he was observing her, Honey Eater's right hand rose to touch the rawhide thong of the suicide knife hidden under the neck of her doeskin dress. If the attack went badly, he knew the women would try to kill the children and themselves before they allowed the slave-takers to grab them.

Then Honey Eater saw him watching her.

She lifted both hands and crossed her wrists in front of her heart—Cheyenne sign talk for love.

Out on the horizon, the boiling, yellow-brown dust cloud drew closer and closer.

Chapter 11

Two Twists and the other junior warriors had settled into the rifle pits and readied their weapons. Fortunately, the Cheyenne beaver traps had yielded a good supply of pelts this season, and the tribe was well equipped with rifles, ball, and black powder.

Touch the Sky walked up and down among the pits, calming the youths, inspecting weapons, repeating his instructions over and over. He knew that, caught flush in the heat of battle, the brain could sometimes shut down completely and cause serious mistakes.

His plan revolved around the words Arrow Keeper had spoken to him before the hunt:

I have seen Comanches when their ponies are shot out from under them. It is said they lose their courage when not on horseback.

The fierce warriors *must* be separated from their mounts. The number-one priority this time was neither counting coup nor even killing their enemies—they must simply prevent them from ever getting past the line of defenders. A thin line made up of Touch the Sky and a dozen or so unblooded warriors was all that protected the women and children and elders.

Touch the Sky had already borrowed Two Twist's war shield made from the sturdy wood of an osage tree. It would stop arrows, but not bullets. He could only hope the attackers were not rich in firearms and bullets, for his part in the plan would call for constant exposure to the attackers.

For this reason, he also removed the mountain-lion skin tucked into the pannier sewn to his horse blanket. Arrow Keeper had given it to him, assuring him it was blessed with strong medicine. Little Horse swore that, while he was wearing it during the Tongue River Battle, it had made a load of musket balls fired from a blunderbuss miss him at point-blank range. Touch the Sky donned it now, not sure if he believed or not. But he did believe in Arrow Keeper's magic—had in fact witnessed it numerous times.

By now the hollow thundering of hooves clearly reached the camp as the attackers drew ever closer. Touch the Sky returned to his position just to the left, and in front of, the rifle pits and the camp.

"Stay out of sight!" he called out again to the junior warriors when one of them peeked anxiously over the top of his pit. "I will be your eyes.

They must not see you. If they do, they will go into a circular attack, and then all is lost."

In fact, Touch the Sky feared this might happen anyway. If it did, his plan to use himself as a lure would be useless. It was necessary to convince the attackers that he was the only defender and trick them into a direct assault. He knew the Kiowa and Comanche would prefer this, not wishing to give the Cheyenne women time to use their suicide knives.

"Steady, little brothers!" he called out again. "Heads down! You know what you must do. We are the fighting Cheyenne!"

He was forced to speak even louder now above the noise of the ponies and the shrill war cries of the Comanche and Kiowa. He could make them out clearly now, racing through the flowering mescal and low-hanging pods of mesquite. Their leader was a huge Kiowa with a bone breastplate and a flowing black mane of hair streaming behind him.

"Two Twists!" Touch the Sky shouted above the din.

"Yes!"

"A pure black with white forelegs, bearing straight down on you. It is their war leader's pony."

"I am *for* him!"

The first sharp cracks of the attackers' rifles sounded. Bullets whipped past Touch the Sky's ears with a sound like angry hornets. Holding the shield in his left hand, Touch the Sky lifted his Sharps into the socket of his right shoulder and snapped off a round. As he had hoped, this seemed to focus the attackers' attention squarely on him.

"Walking Coyote!"

"I hear you, Touch the Sky!"

"A buckskin, bearing down just to my left! Wait for the command."

"Already dead!" the youth shouted back.

More rifles cracked, a chip flew from Touch the Sky's shield. The first arrows had already embedded themselves in the sturdy wood.

"Stump Horn!"

"Here, brother!"

"A small chestnut on the far right flank!"

"My aim will be true!" the youth replied.

Now the attackers were closing fast. More chips flew from the war shield, and an arrow flew past his exposed right leg so close that the fletching burned his skin. Touch the Sky could clearly make out the painted horses, distinguish the oval-faced Comanches with their green and yellow war paint from the Kiowa faces painted in garish greens and yellows and reds.

"Young Two Moons!"

"I have ears!"

"A pure ginger with a tan mane!"

"I will leave it for the Apaches to eat!"

And thus it went, Touch the Sky calling out the junior warriors' names one by one, calming them while also telling them exactly which horse was their target so that each shot might count.

The arrows were coming in with more accuracy now, and Touch the Sky tried to hunch himself into a smaller target behind the shield. A bullet ripped through the parfleche on his sash. Despite the danger now pressing down on him, Touch the

Sky could not help admiring the skill of the riders. The Comanches especially seemed to blend with their horses. They did not even bother to hold on—they strung arrows and reloaded their rifles, which thankfully were not as plentiful as bows, as easily as if they were sitting on the ground.

A bullet pierced the shield and almost knocked it from Touch the Sky's hand. Now the enemy was so close he could see the blood lust in their eyes.

"Steady, little brothers! Steady! One shot, and you must make it count."

The Comanches liked to capture Bluecoat bugles in battles with the pony soldiers, then blow them to mock their enemies. Now, celebrating what was clearly about to be an easy victory, one of them sounded a bad version of "Boots and Saddles."

A flurry of arrows rattled into the shield and were shot between his legs. Another corner of the shield was chipped away.

"NOW, Cheyennes!" Touch the Sky bellowed above the din.

As one man, the dozen young warriors rose from their rifle pits and fired together. Immediately, at least ten ponies collapsed. This took the thunder out of the enemy war cries and silenced the bugler, who found himself bruised and shaken on the ground with many of his comrades.

But though the attack was considerably slowed, the rest continued charging toward Touch the Sky. However, he had timed his command to come just before the survivors would reach the stretch of ground pocked with prairie-dog holes. They entered it now, and several ponies tripped hard, throwing their whooping riders earthward.

One pony, ridden by a Comanche on a captured cavalry saddle, quickly struggled back up and bolted off to the right. The rider was trapped with one foot twisted in the stirrup. The panicked mount raced directly through a patch of sturdy, sharp-needled prickly-pear cactus, dragging the rider behind. The Comanche's screams were hideous as the needles turned him into a raw, red, glistening mess, literally skinning him alive.

His screaming death agony finally unnerved the attackers. Stopping only long enough to let their brothers whose horses had been shot leap up behind them, they retreated.

A triumphant victory cry rose from the young warriors in the rifle pits, and was taken up by the noncombatants huddled behind the breastworks.

But Touch the Sky, though elated by this temporary victory, was not lulled into a sense of security. Of all the tribes whose treachery could not be predicted, Arrow Keeper had often told him, the Kiowa and Comanche were the most dangerous.

There was no time for a celebration. This was only half of the combined enemy force. And only one had died here today. This was their homeland, and fresh remounts would not be far off.

Another attack, a far bigger one, would soon be coming.

Touch the Sky, assisted by Two Twists, supervised the move as the camp was once again dismantled to join the hunters. He had no idea when the next attack was coming. But he feared it would be soon. Although the strict Hunt Law required the camp to wait until it was summoned, the delay couldn't be risked.

Tipi covers and poles, cooking utensils, drying racks, and other possessions were lashed to travois along with the dried meat and other parts of the buffalo already killed. Thus weighted down, the camp could not make such good time as the unencumbered hunters had. As always, flankers were sent out, selected from the junior warriors, as well as a guard to ride behind in case the attacking band should decide on an immediate second strike.

Touch the Sky's numerous cuts had finally scabbed over, a dull itching replacing the burning pain. Still, he was nearly exhausted from the ordeal of his beating and the all-night ride to warn the camp in time. Only the thought that Honey Eater and the rest depended on him kept him going. So far, not one drop of Cheyenne blood had been spilled. It was his responsibility, as the only full warrior in the group, to make sure that none was.

He was proud of Two Twists and his warriors. The youths had played their parts well, had followed orders exactly. So he wisely held silent now as they puffed themselves up with pride, boasting to each other as warriors will do. Around the women and children, however, they showed the taciturn reserve of the older Cheyenne braves—after all, had they not fired upon an enemy in battle? It was no longer acceptable to act like children.

And they looked toward Touch the Sky with a new respect in their eyes. Each of them had watched him stand and hold in an uncovered position while enemy arrows and bullets rained down upon him. The elders and the women smiled shyly each time he met their eyes, admiration clear in their manner. Touch the Sky did not know it yet, but the same old squaw of the Sky Walker Clan who had sung the song about his love for Honey Eater was already composing another about his bravery this day. Soon it too would be sung in the clan circles and lodges and become part of the history of the Cheyenne people.

But wisely, Touch the Sky now kept his distance from Honey Eater as they rode. The two could not be near each other without showing their powerful love. And despite Touch the Sky's bravery, Black Elk's friends and informers were numerous.

The sun was a flaming red ball balanced on the western horizon by the time they reached the spot where the hunters had congregated. The hunters spotted them as they emerged over a long ridge. The herd could be seen far below in a grassy valley of the Red River. Clearly the kill had not yet taken place. No doubt, thought Touch the Sky, it was planned for sunrise.

Although they were approaching against the wind, Touch the Sky halted his column well back from the hunters and waited for a delegation to approach.

Their faces incredulous at this clear violation of Hunt Law, the Bull Whips raced out ahead of Chief Gray Thunder and Arrow Keeper. They were led by Lone Bear and Black Elk, Wolf Who Hunts Smiling close on their heels.

"You!" Lone Bear said. "What is the meaning of this outrage? You know full well the people must

be left behind until after the kill or the herd may be scared off."

Touch the Sky was about to speak when Two Twists rode boldly forward.

"Fathers! I am young, but today I fought in my first battle. Please have ears for my words. Touch the Sky has the courage of ten warriors! This day he saved Gray Thunder's tribe from a terrible tragedy."

Clearly, emboldened by his part in the fight, Two Twists narrated the events of the attack. Gray Thunder and Arrow Keeper rode up as he told the story and listened attentively. Some of the women and elders crowded closer as Two Twists spoke, nodding excitedly. "Yes, this is surely true!" they said, or, "Yes, I saw him do that!"

By the time Two Twists finished and fell silent, Gray Thunder was staring at Touch the Sky with respect clear in his eyes. Old Arrow Keeper too gazed at the youth fondly, nodding his head as if this were to be expected from a youth who carried the mark of the warrior on his scalp. Little Horse, his face proud, glanced around at the others as if to say: *Do you mark this? This is my brother, the warrior!*

Black Elk, Lone Bear, and Wolf Who Hunts Smiling, however, exchanged troubled glances.

"Father," Touch the Sky said to Gray Thunder, "I took it upon myself to move the camp early because I am convinced our enemies plan another strike, a bigger strike with many more warriors. It is only a matter of time."

Gray Thunder nodded. "You were right to do so."

Now the chief glanced with disapproval at Lone Bear and Black Elk. "It was the responsibility of our soldier societies and our battle chief to make sure our women and children and elders were better protected. Fortunately, our young calves turned into raging bulls under Touch the Sky's brave example."

Lone Bear, Black Elk, and Wolf Who Hunts Smiling chaffed under this criticism.

"But Father!" Wolf Who Hunts Smiling protested. "Touch the Sky ruined the first hunt. He has the stink on him. He should leave before the herds smell him."

"He will stay," Gray Thunder said firmly, brooking no argument. "Every instinct now tells me he was unfairly accused and whipped. I know that Hunt Law leaves this matter up to Lone Bear and Spotted Tail, leaders of the soldier troops who police the hunts. But I swear by my medicine bundle, I will convene the Star Chamber and override them if they fight me on this point!"

Neither troop leader spoke up to object. A Cheyenne chief could not dictate to his people—he was the voice of the tribe, not its will. But Gray Thunder was still, in his fortieth winter, a vigorous warrior and highly respected for the eagle feathers in his war bonnet.

"We will post guards all about," the chief continued, "and we will renew the Medicine Arrows for battle just in case Touch the Sky is right and the attack is coming. But tomorrow the hunt goes on as we planned. It is too important to our tribe. Shaman!"

He turned to Arrow Keeper.

"Prepare the Sacred Arrows. Tonight the warriors will make their offerings. Then, tomorrow, they will paint and dress before the kill. Thus we will be ready if the attack comes to us."

Gray Thunder looked at Two Twists, a smile touching his stern features. "And tomorrow, Two Twists and the junior warriors who saved our people will ride in the hunt with the blooded warriors."

A cheer rose from the warriors-in-training. But Touch the Sky watched Black Elk and Wolf Who Hunts Smiling exchange a long, conspiratorial look, and he knew that more trouble was in the wind.

Chapter 12

Hairy Wolf finished smoking and laid the long clay pipe on the ground between himself and Iron Eyes. This signified that he was now ready to speak.

"They shot my best pony out from under me," he said with bitter humiliation. "All of our warriors witnessed it. Those were *children* who made a brave warrior, a member of the Kaitsenko, show the white feather and flee! Am I a Kiowa, or a cowardly Ponca who grows gardens and preaches peace?"

He and Iron Eyes sat apart from the rest of their band, faces grim and hatchet-sharp in profile in the flickering orange flames of a small camp fire.

"I hear this, Kaitsenko," Iron Eyes said. "When

they first drove us Comanches to this land, there were no buffalo herds here. The hair mouths had not yet diverted the herds south. We were finally forced to kill and eat our dogs, then our ponies. This thing today, it will not stand."

"It will not," Hairy Wolf agreed. "The runners report that our braves who were delayed capturing their ponies will soon arrive. And I have already sent a loaded pipe to He Bear and his band. Count upon it, he will respond quickly. No man alive has more reason to hate the Shaiyena than He Bear. True it is, we will be forced to split with him the goods we receive from the slave sale. But the price is well worth it."

Just south of their present camp lived the Kiowa Apaches, close kin to the Kiowa, under their war leader He Bear. Each fall, during the Deer-rutting Moon, various tribes of the Southern Plains assembled in conclave at Medicine Lodge Creek in the heartland of the Kiowas. Almost all of these tribes had been driven from the north by combined Cheyenne-Sioux might. Thus the Cheyennes had become their hereditary enemies.

"This year," Hairy Wolf said, "at Medicine Lodge Creek, He Bear complained bitterly about Cheyennes raiding on his pony herds. But his band is too small to attack in revenge. This will be a perfect chance to exact blood justice against them. Our three tribes will raise our battle-axes as one."

All evening both leaders had carefully avoided mentioning a certain name which was much on their minds. The Comanche killed in that prickly pear patch had been Painted Lips, one of the favorites of both bands. But by Comanche custom, a warrior whose body had not been recovered could never be mentioned again.

"Yes," Iron Eyes said, "we will attack as one. I like this. It is worth surrendering some of our profits from the slaves. Because now we can do more than simply sneak up and steal women and children—we will also annihilate their warriors!"

"Brother," Little Horse said, "I am proud of you. Do you know that old Sweet Medicine of the Sky Walker Clan has composed a song honoring your bravery? All of the young warriors are singing your praise, telling how a lone Cheyenne brave stood before an entire band of Kiowa and Comanches and never once flinched at their arrows and bullets."

"I flinched, brother," Touch the Sky said, though indeed he was proud to hear such words from Little Horse, his best friend and the warrior he admired most in his tribe. "It was our tribe behind me which held me fast, not my contempt for death."

"I have no ears for this. But bend words anyway you wish. Deeds hold only one shape, and your deeds today have the shape of courage. My young sisters and brothers were among those children, my uncles and aunts and grandparents among the elders. We are warriors, and I will not embarrass you by dwelling upon this thing longer. So brother, I say it once and then put it away: You are the bravest warrior I know, and I thank you with my life."

Touch the Sky might have reminded Little Horse that, more than once, the sturdy young brave had placed his life on the line to save *him,* had stuck by him when very few others in the tribe besides Arrow Keeper or Honey Eater cared if he lived or died. But it was not the Cheyenne way to dwell on such things. Both youths knew, without words, that anyone who meant to kill one of them would have to kill both.

The camp had been reestablished well below the long ridge which separated them from the herd below. The buffalo were content to graze the lush bunchgrass of the river valley. The wind continued steadily to blow from the west, posing no threat of carrying their human smell to the buffalos and scattering the animals before the strike tomorrow.

Little Horse had killed a plump rabbit and dressed it out, and now they were building a fire to cook it. Touch the Sky, finally able to move without wincing at the pain, squatted to build a small bed of punk or dried, decayed wood. When it was finished he removed the flint and steel from the chamois pouch on his sash. A slicing blow with the steel against the small piece of flint sent a shower of sparks downward. The heat of the sparks soon caused some of the fine fibers of punk to smolder.

Carefully, Touch the Sky blew on the punk until he had coaxed it into flames. Then he piled on more substantial materials—dry wood shavings, fine splinters of wood, dry leaves and grass, then small sticks—to kindle a bigger fire.

"Word of what you did," Little Horse said, "has flown through the camp. Now there is much remorse over the beating you suffered. Even some of the Bull Whips who flogged you now say they did wrong. But when you whirl the water in the pool, you also stir up the mud. Your enemies are speaking against you. Keep your back to a tree."

Little Horse used the same arrow which had killed the rabbit as a spit, skewering it from throat to rump. He jabbed two forked sticks into the ground on both sides of the fire and placed the rabbit over the growing flames.

"Black Elk, Swift Canoe, and Wolf Who Hunts Smiling have put their heads together again. They are going among the Bull Whips, saying that once again you used white man's tactics, not the Cheyenne way. They tell all who will listen—and many still do—that you employ tricks learned from the blue-dressed soldiers who take our best hunting grounds.

"Just now, as I crossed camp, I heard Wolf Who Hunts Smiling speaking to his fawning admirers. 'Every time this make-believe Cheyenne earns the praise of the Headmen,' he told them, 'it is by some cunning piece of paleface trickery—where is the *Cheyenne* in him?' "

"All in good time," Touch the Sky said, "Wolf Who Hunts Smiling will die the dog's death he deserves. I am loathe to sully the Arrows by killing a Cheyenne. Only this has kept me from spilling his blood out onto the ground. But the reckoning is coming."

"Something is afoot," Little Horse said. "Count on it. They are determined to keep you from the hunt tomorrow."

Touch the Sky nodded. Later this night he would assist Arrow Keeper in the Renewal of the Sacred Arrows, an important rite before possible battle. And the "hidden eye" which Arrow Keeper was teaching him to develop as a shaman already told him there would be trouble during the ceremony.

Black Elk had noticed Honey Eater's sullen silence ever since she had arrived with the rest. He knew it was because she had seen the marks of the beating he and the other Bull Whips had inflicted on Touch the Sky.

Her silence infuriated him. What right did a squaw have to approve or disapprove of a war leader's actions? Though she was careful to avoid any open flaunting of her love for the tall youth, it was there for all to see.

Back at the permanent camp, he had passed the entrance of the women's sewing lodge and heard them at their song. And although it mentioned no names, it was clear enough whose love they sang about. Now the tribe was singing another song about Touch the Sky's bravery—as if no other warrior could violate Hunt Law and lead women and children around.

Now, as she served him a juicy hump steak on a thick piece of bark, he said, "I would speak with you."

Honey Eater had already turned away and started to leave. She stopped, waiting.

"Look at your husband!" he commanded her. "Your war leader is speaking!"

She finally turned, but kept her eyes cast downward.

"Honey Eater, I do not like your manner with me."

"What would you have of me?"

"I would have you remember that I am your husband!"

"Truly," she said bitterly, "I cannot forget this."

He suddenly threw the steak down on the ground. His breathing grew so fierce with anger that his nostrils flared.

"You will not take this tone with me! I could have had my pick of any woman in the tribe."

Honey Eater feared Black Elk's rage. But ever since seeing what he and the other Bull Whips had done to Touch the Sky, her own anger was deep and strong. Now she could not bite back her words as she usually did.

"Would that you had picked another! If you are not satisfied with the wife you have, you may sing the Throw-away Song and divorce me on the drum. *I* will shed no tears."

"No, you would not, for you are too eager to rut with your tall white man's dog! You call yourself a Cheyenne maiden? Where is your virtue, your modesty?"

"They are in the same place where you left behind your manly courage and fairness!"

Rage actually paralyzed him for a moment. "What do you mean by these words?" he demanded.

"I mean that I have seen what you, your hateful cousin Wolf Who Hunts Smiling, and the other 'courageous' Bull Whips have done to Touch the Sky."

"You she-bitch, hold your tongue! We have done what men will do when the Hunt Law must be upheld. I do not quarrel with women!

What right have you to question the actions of men?"

"I have eyes to see, ears to hear. And I do not think these were the actions of men, but the actions of cowards!"

This was incredible. Black Elk was so shocked at her insolence that he merely stared at her, his mouth gaping. The dancing firelight failed to soften his stern features, his fierce black eyes, the leathery hunk of dead ear he had sewn back on himself with buckskin thread after a Bluecoat saber had severed it in battle.

"You bitch in heat! You will not give your war leader a son, but you will pine away for *him,* a white man's dog who arrived among us wearing shoes and offering his hand to shake like the blue-bloused liars who shake our hands before they kill us! You *hope* that I will divorce you on the drum. But I swear by the sun, the moon, and the directions of the wind that I will take you out on the Plains if you do not learn to be a good Cheyenne wife!"

Now it was Honey Eater's turn to fill with hot rage. "Taking a woman out on the Plains" was the most severe punishment a Cheyenne man could inflict on a wife, and could not be done without clear proof that she had lain with another man. It had never, to her knowledge, been done in their tribe, though she had heard stories of it in other tribes. The man deserted his wife out in the wilderness and announced that she was available to any man in the tribe who wanted to rut on her. Though the woman was not banished, her shame afterward was so great that she was expected to kill herself. In reality, a man who did such a thing, no matter for what cause, could never be respected again.

"You speak this way to me," she said, "and call yourself a warrior? I am the daughter of the great Chief Yellow Bear. I will not be threatened like this! You already went too far when you cut my braid. Do not forget that a Cheyenne woman too can petition the Star Chamber for a divorce."

But she had pushed Black Elk too far with these words. A moment later she cried out in shock when the powerful brave brought the side of his fist against her face hard, knocking her down.

"Place my words in your pockets," he told her in a cold, dangerously low voice. "I swear I will kill you *and* him before I let that false Cheyenne mount you! Do you have ears for this?"

But Honey Eater was beyond words now. She held her already swelling face, great sobs hitching in her chest.

"Prepare my clothing and war bonnet for the Medicine Arrows ceremony," he said. "And pray that your tall buck does not cross me, or I swear I will turn him into worm fodder!"

Chapter 13

The buffalo herd on their left flank provided a natural defense against any Kiowa-Comanche attack launched from that direction. Likewise, the Red River protected the northern approach, and a series of deep redrock canyons the southern approach.

The only vulnerable spot was their right flank, and Black Elk had already ordered a strong guard to protect it. The hunt would go on as planned tomorrow. But the hunters would be in constant communication with the sentries by way of signals flashed with fragments of mirrors. At the first sign of attack, they would rush back toward the camp and head it off before it reached the women and children and elders.

Touch the Sky belonged to no clan. But Arrow

Keeper, as always, had instructed the women of his Owl Clan to erect the young brave's tipi. The youth was crossing the central clearing, heading toward his tipi to prepare for the Medicine Arrows ceremony, when he spotted Honey Eater.

She carried her curved skinning knife, blood pail, and other equipment. He knew she was probably on her way to join the other women in her clan, making preparations for the skinning and butchering tomorrow after the kill. Fires had been kept to a minimum, and he couldn't tell if Black Elk was lurking nearby. Playing it safe, he started to veer wide around the girl.

A moment later, however, she passed close to the small fire under the cooking tripod outside Arrow Keeper's tipi. Though she turned her face hastily away, Touch the Sky spotted the nasty, swollen bruise covering nearly half of one side of her face.

Black Elk's handiwork! The jealous, hotheaded warrior had beaten her.

Touch the Sky's anger was sudden and deep. For a moment he almost ran after her to catch her and question her. But he decided against this—there was no question as to what had happened.

The only question now, he told himself, is what am I going to do about it?

He had warned Black Elk before to keep his hands off her. Warnings had clearly had no effect. Now it was time to give up on words and do as Black Elk himself often preached—let deeds speak for words.

He went to Black Elk's tipi and found the war leader seated before the entrance flap, sharpening his knife on a whetstone.

Keeping all emotion out of his voice, Touch the Sky said, "Black Elk, I would speak with you."

Black Elk glanced up at him, immediately wary. "I have nothing to say to you, make-believe Cheyenne."

"No," Touch the Sky agreed, "I have something to say to you."

"Whatever it may be, I have no ears for it."

"If you value life itself, you will find ears for it."

Black Elk scowled. "Do you threaten me?"

"I have had done with threats. Now, I swear by Maiyun, you will listen! You and your worthless cousin call me a white man's dog until I am weary of hearing it. Then so it is. This white man's dog *did* learn some tricks from the hair faces, Black Elk. Let me teach you one of them."

Without another word, Touch the Sky reached down and plucked the warrior's bone-handle knife from his hand and threw it into the surrounding bushes.

For a long moment Black Elk's face looked as surprised as it had when Honey Eater called him a coward. Then, suddenly, he was on his feet.

"Clearly," he said, "you are looking for your own grave."

"Not at all," Touch the Sky said. "I am here to show you what I learned from the palefaces. See, now you stand without a weapon to hand. Let me show you a trick."

A heartbeat later he delivered a powerful uppercut to the point of Black Elk's chin. It was a smashing right fist, exactly like the blow which Hiram Steele's wrangler Boone Wilson had given Touch the Sky when the Cheyenne was caught with Steele's daughter Kristen.

Black Elk staggered back hard, almost falling.

Touch the Sky waded in quickly before the brave could recover his balance.

"See, Black Elk? This is how white dogs are taught to fight—with their paws curled into fists. Here is some more."

He brought a hard right to Black Elk's stomach, a left jab to the war leader's face. The blows were powerful, backed by hard muscle and deep wrath. Black Elk, like most Indians, knew little of boxing. Without a weapon, all he knew to do was wrestle. But the quick flurry of blows had left him stunned.

"How do you like it, Panther Clan? Now you know what it is like for Honey Eater when you strike her."

A final hard right to the jaw dropped Black Elk where he stood.

"Now you *will* have ears for my words," Touch the Sky said.

He removed his own knife from its beaded sheath and suddenly slashed his own inner left arm, drawing a scarlet ribbon of blood to trail into the ground at Black Elk's feet.

"Now I make this blood vow, Black Elk. The next time I see or learn of you hurting her, I swear by the sun and the earth that I live on you *will* die a hard death! I will send you under and sully the Sacred Arrows. I do not care if it means my banishment. I am alone anyway, thanks to you and your cousin."

Black Elk was too stunned to get back up immediately. But as Touch the Sky started to walk away, he called out.

"You might as well sing the death song now, White Man's Shoes! Everyone in the tribe knows that you long to put on the old moccasin." To a Cheyenne, "putting on the old moccasin" was a reference to a single man who wanted to marry a one-time married woman. "But you will have to kill me first!"

Touch the Sky turned back around.

"All in good time, Dead Ear. I have glanced the other way when you tried to murder me. When you played the white-livered coward and sent your cousin and Swift Canoe to kill me at Medicine Lake. When you fired at an 'elk' that turned out to be me instead. I am done trying to make peace with low-crawling cowards who speak in a wolf bark and beat women.

"I say it again, and you had best place these words next to your heart. Hurt Honey Eater one more time and this white man's dog will feed your liver to the carrion birds."

While Touch the Sky was setting Black Elk on the ground, Wolf Who Hunts Smiling was up to his own tricks.

The young warrior was extremely ambitious and harbored secret dreams of someday leading the Cheyenne Nation in a war of extermination against the whites. Like most Indians, he had no actual concept of their numbers. But his hatred for white men had festered inside him like a poisonous canker ever since he had stood by, horrified, when blue-bloused soldiers turned his father into stew meat with a double charge of canister shot. And this Touch the Sky, had he not lived among the paleface devils so long that he permanently carried their stink?

He was also a serious obstacle to his plans. Clearly, old Arrow Keeper, perhaps the most respected elder among all the Shayiena people, favored the pretend Cheyenne. Selecting him to train as a shaman was a great honor. A tribal medicine man, in his own way, could wield as much power and influence as a chief—even more, since the Cheyenne faith in the supernatural was strong.

Wolf Who Hunts Smiling was no fool. He had seen how strong his people's faith in visions and medicine dreams was. And he also knew that this Touch the Sky supposedly possessed the gift of visions. He was not sure how much he himself believed in visions, but he was certain that Touch the Sky was a liar. Clearly, the white man's dog was cleverly pretending to walk the Spirit Path. He knew full well that Arrow Keeper, who had begun to dote and drool in his frosted years, and some of the others would be impressed.

So now it was time to trap the fox in his own den.

With Swift Canoe at his side, he was paying a secret visit to an old squaw named Calf Woman of the Root Eaters Clan. Calf Woman had at least 70 winters behind her and was generally considered to be a soft-brain. However, it was common knowledge that visions were often received by the sick, dying, and mentally infirm. And Calf Woman had a certain reputation for pronouncing visions which had come true.

She also had a reputation for her love of white man's coffee and sugar. And in his legging sash

Wolf Who Hunts Smiling carried a little of both. He and Swift Canoe had obtained these at the trading post in Red Shale in exchange for pelts and furs.

Fortunately, it was dark around her tipi and no one would see them paying this visit. The two youths found the old woman sitting before the raised entrance flap, sipping yarrow tea from a buffalo-horn cup.

"Good evening, Grandmother," Wolf Who Hunts Smiling greeted her respectfully.

She peered up curiously at the two new arrivals, trying to make out their faces in the grainy twilight.

"Is that you, Half Bear?"

Swift Canoe dug an elbow into Wolf Who Hunts Smiling's ribs. Half Bear was the old woman's son, but he had died many winters ago during the battle with the Pawnee at Beaver Creek.

"Brother," Swift Canoe whispered, "this old hag has been struck by lightning. Best to leave it alone."

Wolf Who Hunts Smiling shook him off and said patiently, "No, Grandmother. It is Wolf Who Hunts Smiling of the Panther Clan and Swift Canoe of the Wolverine Clan. We have come to see how you are getting along."

The old woman vaguely recognized the clan names and their faces. But both names were unknown to her addled brain. Still, it was a fine thing for such young men to come visit an old woman like this. She smiled her toothless smile and bade them sit down beside her.

"Here, Grandmother," Wolf Who Hunts Smiling said, "let me put some sugar in your tea."

"Sugar?"

"Yes, Grandmother, not honey. Fine white man's sugar."

The old woman gripped her cup eagerly with both hands and drank the tea down quickly. She smacked her lips together appreciatively, glancing with longing at the drawstring pouch in the boy's hand. Purposely, Wolf Who Hunts Smiling dangled it as he spoke.

"I have heard a thing, Grandmother. I have heard that you are blessed with visions."

She nodded, still watching the pouch. "Sometimes Maiyun opens the hidden eye for me, yes."

"What sorts of things do you then see, old one?"

At a sign from Wolf Who Hunts Smiling, Swift Canoe stirred up the dying embers of the old woman's fire. Now they could see the deep lines and crags of her face, the scrawny shoulders hunched under her red blanket.

Swift Canoe dumped the last of the tea out of her baked-clay kettle and added more water from the bladder bag nearby. He threw a little coffee in to boil. Despite her advanced age, Calf Woman smelled it instantly.

"Is that coffee?" she asked eagerly.

"Yes, indeed," Wolf Who Hunts Smiling said. "Fine white man's coffee, not the bitter brew which our Southern kin acquire from the Mexicans. It will be very tasty with sugar in it."

"May I have some?"

"Have some? Grandmother, we are preparing it for you."

She smiled happily. Wolf Who Hunts Smiling repeated his question. "What do you see in your visions, Grandmother?"

"I see many things, child. I have seen revelations, and I have seen curses. When War Bonnet was killed by Pawnees, I saw it happen while he still lay sleeping in his tipi. When Sun Road lost the sacred Medicine Hat, a vision told me where to find it."

The coffee was boiling now, the deep, rich aroma wafting into the old woman's nostrils.

"These are fine things indeed," Wolf Who Hunts Smiling said. He handed the horn cup to Swift Canoe, who poured some coffee into it. Wolf Who Hunts Smiling added a few generous pinches of sugar and handed it to Calf Woman.

She sipped at it. *"Ipewa,"* she said in Cheyenne. "Good."

"Tell me, Grandmother," Wolf Who Hunts Smiling said. "Have you never had a vision concerning this Touch the Sky?"

She glanced up from the cup. "Touch the Sky?"

"The tall youth who arrived in our camp four winters ago dressed in white man's clothing?"

She shook her head. "I think not."

"Are you sure, Grandmother?" Wolf Who Hunts Smiling added another pinch of sugar to her coffee. His furtive eyes never left the old woman. "Perhaps if you could recall a vision about him, there would be more coffee and sugar in it for you."

"More coffee and sugar?"

"All of this," Wolf Who Hunts Smiling assured the confused old woman, proffering the packets.

The old woman stared at them covetously. Coffee and sugar were fine things indeed. And truly, she had had many visions in her time.

"Perhaps," Wolf Who Hunts Smiling suggested,

reading the look on her face, "you have simply forgotten it?"

"Perhaps," she agreed.

Wolf Who Hunts Smiling shared a victorious glance with Swift Canoe.

"Let us see," the youth said, tucking the coffee and sugar into her sash, "if we can refresh your memory."

Chapter 14

Soon after Wolf Who Hunts Smiling and Swift Canoe visited old Calf Woman, the Renewal of the Medicine Arrows ceremony was held. Once again Touch the Sky would serve as assistant to Arrow Keeper.

The entire tribe began to gather in the middle of their temporary camp, although this time only the warriors would actually participate in leaving gifts for the Arrows. The Renewal was held annually, and before battle, and after some serious crime such as murder had sullied the entire people.

The Kiowa and Comanche had no taboo against attacking by night. So all the warriors had their battle rigs ready and to hand. Women and older children had all armed themselves with knives, clubs, and spiked tomahawks. Sentries had been posted, and would be relieved later to make their sacrifices to the Arrows.

Touch the Sky donned his mountain lion skin, again wondering for a moment—had its big medicine protected him from bullets and arrows during the attack on the hunt camp, or had he just been fortunate? He braided his long, loose locks and then wrapped them with strips of red-painted buckskin.

Two Twists and the other junior warriors were especially proud. As recognition of their bravery during the attack, they would be participating in the Renewal for the first time. Tomorrow, during the hunt, they would serve as the all-important guard on the tribe's vulnerable east flank—in the direction of the rising sun, out of which the Kiowa and Comanche often chose to attack.

For a moment, before he left his tipi and joined the gathering clans, Touch the Sky stared off into the darkness which surrounded the camp.

He heard nothing to cause fear: only the occasional bellowing of a buffalo bull in the nearby valley, or the staccato barking of coyotes. But although the sentries had not raised the wolf howl of alarm, he sensed the presence of their enemy nearby.

Nor were all his enemies outside the clan circles. Again he heard Little Horse's warning: *Keep your back to a tree.*

His beating of Black Elk earlier had marked a new stage in their mutual hatred. For the first time he had gone on the offensive and whipped his enemy into temporary submission. But he knew Black Elk would never brook such treatment. And Wolf Who Hunts Smiling had been convinced, after the Bull Whips flogged him during the hunt, that Touch the Sky would again be clearly marked as an outsider. He had been seething ever since his enemy's rescue of the noncombatants had again restored Touch the Sky to a position of some respect in the eyes of the others.

However, there was no time now to dwell on such thoughts. He heard the rhythmic drumming start as young women began the dance beat, pounding on hollow logs and shaking gourds filled with pebbles.

Many had gathered by the time he joined Arrow Keeper in front of a cottonwood stump. A huge ceremonial fire illuminated the clearing and the coyote-fur pouch atop the stump, which held the four sacred Medicine Arrows that symbolized the fate of the tribe.

Touch the Sky spotted Black Elk in his best war bonnet, coup feathers trailing the ground behind him. Many stared curiously at the dark bruises discoloring his face, knowing full well how he must have gotten them.

But when Honey Eater stepped into the firelight, Touch the Sky had eyes for no one else. Indeed, everyone in the tribe stared in awe.

She had never looked this beautiful. She wore her finest doeskin dress with a tasseled belt of buffalo hair. The dress was adorned with dyed elk teeth, gold coins, brightly dyed feathers. She had donned new quilled moccasins and her finest bone choker. No attempt had been made to disguise her mutilated hair. It was as if she wore

Black Elk's unjust punishment as a badge of honor.

Touch the Sky also spotted Wolf Who Hunts Smiling and Swift Canoe when they exchanged conspiratorial glances. Some new trouble was in the wind, and Touch the Sky expected it to blow his way.

Arrow Keeper opened the ceremony with a prayer of praise and thanks to Maiyun, the Great Medicine Man. Then, one after another, the painted warriors began dancing around the fire, kicking their knees high and shouting *"Hi-ya, hi-ya!"* over and over in time to the pounding rhythms. Since a possible battle loomed, they would fast from now until the danger was over. Although this sometimes weakened them, it also created the lightheaded trance which encouraged brave deeds—and immunity to pain—in battle.

At a signal from Arrow Keeper, Touch the Sky stepped behind the stump. He scattered rich tobacco as an offering to the four directions, the sun, and the moon. Then, his face solemn with pride, he carefully unwrapped the four Sacred Arrows.

An absolute hush fell over the entire gathering. Not even a child coughed. One by one, the noncombatants filed by for a rare peek at the prize which old Arrow Keeper had sworn to protect with his life. Touch the Sky had lain two of them horizontally, the other two across them vertically. They were striped in bright blue and yellow, tipped with chipped stone, fletched with scarlet-dyed feathers.

After the rest had glimpsed the Arrows which must be kept forever sweet and clean, Arrow

Keeper called out to the warriors to offer their gifts to the Arrows.

Valuable items were soon heaped before the stump as, one by one, the braves filed by: new bows, a handsome parfleche with intricate beadwork, a fine tow wallet, enemy scalps, wool blankets, clay pipes, brand-new moccasins and leggings, a lace shawl, a leather shirt, a foxskin quiver, an obsidian knife with moonstones laid into its bone handle. It cost Touch the Sky extra effort not to smile when Two Twists and the warriors-in-training filed by last, their faces sternly proud at this important rite of passage to manhood.

When the last gift was piled on the heap, Arrow Keeper declared the Arrows renewed and chanted the closing prayer. But before the people could scatter to their clan circles, old Calf Woman boldly stepped into the flickering circle of the firelight and made a startling announcement.

"Hear an old woman's words! I have had an important vision concerning the tribe."

The first reaction was one of collective shock. Cheyenne women never put themselves forward in tribal ceremonies. But a vision was an important thing, and Calf Woman was said to possess the gift of visions.

Everyone, including Chief Gray Thunder, looked to Arrow Keeper.

"Speak this thing you have seen," Arrow Keeper told her.

"There is to be a battle soon," she said. "Very soon, before the hunt is over. We have just renewed the Arrows. So, it is good. But in my vision, there was blood on the Sacred Arrows."

A low murmur erupted. Blood on the Arrows meant blood on the tribe. Much blood.

"This blood," she continued, "was caused by a reckless youth who violated the sacred Hunt Law. The Great Medicine Man is angry, the buffalo are angry. The generous gifts of Maiyun were carelessly squandered when buffalo were sent over a cliff to die. Now many, many Cheyenne people must die to atone—not just our warriors, but our women and children and the old ones."

Her words struck Touch the Sky with the force of a battle lance. Every head turned to stare at him. Warm blood crept up the back of his neck and into his face. He knew Calf Woman on sight, of course, but had never spoken to her—though her Root Eaters Clan was well respected. Clearly, however, she could be talking of no one else but him.

Arrow Keeper was troubled. Frowning, he said, "Calf Woman, are you sure this thing was a vision and not just *odjib,* a thing of smoke? You have seen many winters, and sometimes a weary mind may confuse a dream in the little day with the Spirit Path."

"It was a medicine dream, shaman," she insisted, "not a dream in the little day. It came upon me in full waking hours, all at once, and was over in a heartbeat."

This testimony drew more troubled murmuring from the others. Indeed, this was the way visions came unless they were deliberately sought.

Now Chief Gray Thunder interceded.

"Old Grandmother, I was there at Beaver Creek when your son Half Bear fell to a Pawnee battle-ax. Long now have you served the tribe and taught our young women the beadwork which makes our tribe the envy of the Plains. You are a good woman. But in the hoary years, a mind may slip its tether occasionally. Are you sure of this thing?"

"I am sure, Gray Thunder. And as penance for this violation of Hunt Law, Maiyun told me, the errant youth must set up a pole to ward off this disaster."

More talk erupted from the people. Chief Gray Thunder folded his arms until all had quieted. "Setting up a pole" was a harsh voluntary penance which could expiate a sin against the Arrows. It could not be ordered; the transgressor must agree on his own to do it. The grueling ordeal consisted of setting up a pole on a hill and hanging from it for the better part of a day by bone hooks driven through the chest muscles.

Now Arrow Keeper was deeply troubled. The Cheyenne faith in vision compulsion was deep and strong. He knew that this faith was sometimes abused—murderers had avoided banishment, for example, by claiming that Maiyun ordered them in a vision to kill.

On the other hand, the law of the Vision Way was clear: If Maiyun did truly speak to a mortal in a vision, His voice could not be ignored. The price for ignoring his command was death or insanity. And in this case, an entire tribe was being compelled to an action—failure to do as told might thus mean the destruction of the entire tribe.

Arrow Keeper was fully aware of the deceit Touch the Sky's enemies were capable of. This might well be a ruse, and the youth had already suffered greatly from the unjust whipping. But was it worth risking the entire tribe to find out if the old grandmother spoke straight-arrow?

"Fathers! Brothers!" Little Horse said. "This thing would be scanned! I too respect Calf Woman and her clan. But the frosted years are upon her, and this time I do not believe she has truth firmly by the tail!"

"You *would* speak up for your friend," Black Elk said, "no matter what the outcome for your tribe. When he left his tribe to fight for the whites, you went with him then too, though we were surrounded by enemies and needed every warrior."

Many of the Bull Whips spoke up in support of Black Elk's words.

"Like Little Horse I too am troubled by this," said Spotted Tail, leader of the Bowstrings. "Touch the Sky was soundly whipped for his misadventure with the buffalo. Why would Maiyun demand such a harsh additional punishment as this?"

Some others spoke out in favor of this. Again Gray Thunder folded his arms until it grew quiet. Honey Eater, her face tense, listened to the proceedings with her lower lip caught between her teeth. Black Elk saw this and scowled darkly.

"It is not our place to question the decisions of the Supernatural," he put in. "We mortals debate in council, and this is a good thing, But the pronouncements of Maiyun are not for debate. They are meant to be carried out. All of you here know well the price to be paid for ignoring His will."

Even Arrow Keeper had to agree Black Elk had spoken well this time. This was a terrible dilemma, pitting the welfare of the tribe against the suffering of a youth who had already been far more wronged than any other in the tribe.

Touch the Sky, for his part, had already realized everything as old Arrow Keeper had. Now, as every face in camp turned toward him—some sympathetic, some accusing, others simply confused—he realized how cleverly Wolf Who Hunts Smiling and Swift Canoe had trapped him. He could not be forced to this terrible, painful ordeal which had been known to kill a man. But if he refused, once again he would seem to put his own life ahead of the tribe's.

"Enough!" he said, his voice clear and strong. "Calf Woman claims she had a vision. Though I suspect this 'vision' was placed over her eyes by hands other than Maiyun's, I cannot call a respected old grandmother a liar. She claims I must set up a pole or our people are lost. So let all debate end and the tribe retire to their tipis. Tomorrow, I will swing from the pole!"

Earlier, Stone Mountain and Kicking Bird had slipped past the Cheyenne sentries by way of the river. The scouts pulled their frail boat, made of buffalo hides stretched across a frame of green cottonwood, up onto the sandy bank just below the enemy camp. Walking on their heels to avoid leaving footprints, they stashed it in a thicket and crept right up on the camp.

Kicking Bird had once been a prisoner of the Southern Cheyennes for several moons and understood much of their tongue. Soon he had learned of their plans for tomorrow. He Bear's Kiowa Apache had joined the combined Kiowa-Comanche band earlier. Now the attack was set.

They had learned all they needed to know. Now it was time to return to their people and report. But Kicking Bird lingered some moments longer, admiring the beautiful Cheyenne girl with the harshly cropped hair.

They must be sure to grab this one; she would fetch a good price. Even the ragged hair could not detract from her finely sculpted cheekbones, huge, almond-shaped eyes, flawless skin like wild honey. The doeskin dress clung to the sweeping curves of her hips like a second skin. She was surely much finer to look at than the venereal-tainted Mandan women he had known from many raids in the north country.

And now here was another piece of good luck. The brazen young buck who had ruined their earlier attack on the first camp would be alone and helpless while the rest were hunting.

The Comanche smiled to himself in the darkness. Soon he would no longer have to suck the tar out of his pipe; there would be plenty of tobacco once the Comancheros in Santa Fe paid for a fine group of Cheyenne slaves. And this tall brave who had stood boldly before the attack—those hooks through his breasts would seem like child's play compared to what the Red Raiders of the Plains had in store for him.

Chapter 15

Hairy Wolf used a pointed stick to draw a diagram in the dirt. Iron Eyes and He Bear, the newly arrived Kiowa Apache war leader who had led 20 seasoned braves to join this fight, crouched on both sides of him.

They were hidden in a wide apron of shade behind a mesa to the east of their enemy's camp. The warriors of all three tribes huddled behind them in small groups, checking their weapons for the final time and passing around earthen jars of *pulque* or cactus liquor. None of the warriors in this group, unlike their enemies from the Northern Plains, was worrying about counting first coup or undergoing elaborate religious rites. Southern Plains tribes did not count coup nor care as much about scalping. War was not for honor, but for goods and profit.

Neither did they harbor taboos about attacking at night. But He Bear had not arrived until well after dawn with his warriors, and their numbers without his band were not great enough against the well-armed Cheyenne—fanatical warriors who did not retreat until they or their enemy were dead. Nor would they be able to engage in their favorite attack tactic, circling in an ever-tightening pattern. The land around here would not permit it, nor the scattered line of hunters.

"South of the herd and the Cheyenne camp," Hairy Wolf said, drawing a ragged trench, "are the redrock canyons. The tribe has these canyons to its left flank, the herd dead ahead, the river on its right flank. They must ride straight into our main force, which I will lead."

"This has a good look to it," He Bear agreed. "*Me gusta*. Trapping them is a good thing, and so is attacking them like the paleface soldiers like to attack. These Cheyenne dogs, they like to flee on their ponies until the pursuers' horses tire. Then they whirl and suddenly attack. This way, they have no room for such tricks."

"Even better," Hairy Wolf said, "Iron Eyes will lead a hidden force of his Comanches on their most surefooted ponies. He knows a secret trail once used by the Navajos. It leads deep through the redrock canyons to the south. He will approach unseen through the canyons while my force attacks head-on."

"My warriors slip up from the canyons," Iron Eyes said. "They stay carefully behind the hunters as they desert the hunt and turn back to rush out past the camp and meet Hairy Wolf's force.

We can grab all the slaves we can carry, without once getting off our mounts," he added boastfully. "They will realize soon enough, but these are our fastest ponies. None of theirs will catch ours in this country we know much better than they. Once we reach the Llano, they won't have a chance."

"What about this young shaman?" He Bear said. Unlike the Kiowa, who left their long hair unrestrained, He Bear and his warriors wore red flannel bands. "You say he remained unscathed by bullets or arrows during your first attack. And the Pawnees refused to attack the Cheyenne Chief Renewal ceremony one spring after this one supposedly commanded a grizzly to attack them. I'd like to see such a big Indian."

"Before they join Iron Eyes and the rest, Red Sleeves and Standing Feather will pay him a visit while he swings from the pole, another of their superstitious practices. They will slice off his eyelids and slit his belly enough to pull some gut through for the carrion birds. He fancies himself defiant, but watching the crows eat his entrails will make him beg like the rest who defy us."

Before the hunters rode out for the kill next day, the Bull Whip soldiers took charge of Touch the Sky's punishment.

As the custom for voluntary penance required, Touch the Sky selected his own sturdy cottonwood limb and sliced it from the tree with an ax. He spiked one end, then followed Lone Bear and the rest of the Bull Whip troop to a lone hill just south of camp. From there, everyone who stayed behind could watch him swing all day. And the hunters would all see him as they filed by.

Touch the Sky held his mouth in its grim, determined slit. Again the punishment was unjust, but how could he prove he did not have the stink on him and was not frightening off the buffalo? Calf Woman's "vision" had not convinced everyone in the tribe, true. But enough were impressed by the realization that the entire tribe might be suffering because of him—and indeed, in his confused heart of hearts, Touch the Sky thought it possible that he did carry the stink.

So he never once hesitated as he secured one end of the pole into the dirt at the top of thc hill. Nor did he flinch when Lone Bear drew the curved-bone hooks out of the parfleche over his hip.

"Remember this," Lone Bear said, "I did not declare this punishment. You chose it, buck. Now it must go forward. I will see that the thing is done right."

"I see clear enough," Touch the Sky said, "that Wolf Who Hunts Smiling and Black Elk are keen for this."

"They may be, but *I* am not!" a Bull Whip said, though a stone-eyed glance from Lone Bear hushed him.

Another brave tied Touch the Sky's hands behind him with sturdy rawhide thongs looped tight over both wrists. The same tough rawhide was used for the halter arrangement which was attached to the hooks and would fit over the top of the pole. From this he would dangle, his weight held by hooks in his muscles.

Without another word, Lone Bear drove the first hook deep into the hard-sloping curve of

Touch the Sky's left pectoral muscle. There was surprisingly little blood, but the pain corded his neck and arched his entire body like a bow.

He met first Black Elk's, then Wolf Who Hunts Smiling's eyes and held them, showing them no fear or pain—only hatred and the promise of sure vengeance. Then his vision blurred when Lone Bear drove in the second finely honed hook.

But that pain was as nothing compared to the sensation when several braves picked him up and lashed the halter to the pole. His feet dangled only a short distance above the ground. But it was enough to leave all his body weight tugging on the hooks. They felt like giant rattlesnake fangs trying to pierce through to his heart.

"You will hang there until the last buffalo is killed today," Lone Bear said. "This is decreed by Hunt Law. Any who attempts to help you will hang beside you."

But Touch the Sky, deep lance-points of pain ripping through him, held his mouth slitted and refused to make a sound.

Long after the hunters had ridden out, Arrow Keeper stood beyond the last clan circle of conical tipis. He stared toward the grotesque sight on the hill above him, his heart stung with pain for the youth's suffering.

How viciously clever his enemies had been this time! There was no way out for Touch the Sky. Had he refused this penance, every bit of bad luck from now on would be blamed on him. And truly, the tribe was not short on bad luck and suffering.

All of this had been foretold in Arrow Keeper's first great vision, the same vision Touch the Sky had eventually sought for himself. The hand of the Supernatural was in this thing. But so too were many trials and sufferings for the youth once called Matthew Hanchon—a name for which he had paid dearly ever since leaving the white man's world for the red man's.

Too dearly, Arrow Keeper suddenly decided.

Watching the young buck hang out there, the skin of his breasts stretched to the point of tearing, he made up his mind to visit old Calf Woman.

The pain was too great, too intensely focused in his chest, for Touch the Sky to put it completely outside of himself. He hung semiconscious now, the morning sun growing hotter on his stinging flesh. His vision alternated between blurry awareness of his surroundings and a red film of pain as effective as a blindfold.

He had been aware, earlier, when a rumbling thunder and the angry bellowing of bulls announced that the herd had begun to stampede. It was followed by the sharp cries of the hunters as they gave pursuit, beginning to isolate sections of the herd. But he knew it would be a long time before the final kill was complete and someone returned to free him.

When he saw the two Comanche braves climb over the rim of the nearby canyon, headed straight for him, he realized his tribe's mistake in ignoring the rugged string of canyons.

One of them removed a knife from its beaded sheath. Touch the Sky could not even lash out at them with his feet as they came closer—the slightest motion sent additional fiery pain throbbing deep into his chest.

The war-painted Comanche raised the narrow-bladed knife toward Touch the Sky's left eye and brought the tip against the soft skin where the eyelid met the forehead. The Cheyenne knew he meant to remove the lids and leave his eyes to literally bake in the glaring sun.

The next moment a rifle spoke its piece, and a gout of blood and brain erupted from the knife-wielding Comanche's skull. A heartbeat later, a throwing ax split open the rib cage of the second one.

And then there was another moment of intense pain, a flash of red, filmy confusion before Touch the Sky briefly passed out. When he came to again, he was lying in mercifully cool grass. Arrow Keeper, young Two Twists, and another of the junior warriors leaned anxiously over him.

"When I found Calf Woman boiling coffee," Arrow Keeper told his young apprentice, "it was easy enough to learn from her that Wolf Who Hunts Smiling and Swift Canoe had been playing the foxes. They will pay for this, little brother. I have already sent a runner ahead to the hunt, commanding the soldiers to arrest them. I went to Gray Thunder. It was he who issued this order to free you immediately."

Wincing, but forcing himself to sit up, Touch the Sky said, "Father, do not arrest Wolf Who Hunts Smiling yet! He is too good a fighter, and warriors will be needed. Those two Comanches came up out of the canyons. I fear our enemies have used them for some graver purpose too."

* * *

When the mirror signal was flashed by one of the Comanches down in the canyon, Hairy Wolf's main band launched a direct attack on the Cheyenne camp.

Cries of "Remember Wolf Creek!" echoed through the riders as their well-trained mounts raised spiraling whirlwinds of alkali dust. As intended, they were almost immediately spotted by the Cheyenne sentries. They, in turn, flashed signals to the warriors engaged in the hunt, urgently summoning them back.

Below in the canyon, Iron Eyes had decided on the added precaution of dividing his braves into two groups. They would ride up separately and approach the camp behind the hunters from two different directions. Once the battle had begun forward of camp, they would strike quickly while the foolish Cheyenne were preoccupied in counting coup.

Touch the Sky heard the first wolf howls of alarm from the junior warriors even as he was returning to camp, Arrow Keeper and Two Twists helping him walk.

Now they could hear the attacking enemy as they approached, see the swirling dust on the horizon to the east. Soon the main body of Cheyenne hunters rode hard from the west to meet the fight before it could reach the camp.

As Little Horse flashed by, long, loose black locks streaming in the wind, Touch the Sky desperately signaled him to stop. At the same moment he stopped young Two Twists as the youth prepared to mount and join the defending force.

"We must ride back toward the herd," he shouted to his friends above the din of the riders. "I fear the slave-takers have cleverly tricked us by using the canyons! This attack to the east, it is a diversion!"

He nearly cried out at the protesting pain in his chest when he swung up onto his gray and pushed her hard to the west, toward the river valley and the now-stampeding herd. But his suspicions were soon confirmed: All three Cheyennes saw it when a score of well-armed braves streamed up out of the canyon ahead of them, heading east toward the camp.

Touch the Sky made only one fatal mistake: He assumed this was the entire force. In fact it was only half of Iron Eyes' men.

His mind was preoccupied with a greater problem: As the sounds of a fierce battle rose behind them, where the two main forces were closing for the kill, he had to decide how three Cheyennes were going to stop 20 braves from reaching the women and children.

One possible answer came to him when he saw the band maneuver itself between a sharp cliff and the last fragment of the panicked buffalo herd. Truly, the Cheyenne were too few to stop the slave-takers—but perhaps a few hundred charging buffalo could literally send them under.

He desperately signaled his companions and they nodded agreement. They fired their rifles, whistled, and shouted their shrill war cry to turn the buffalo. The furious bulls constantly tried to gore his pony as Touch the Sky recklessly, desperately pushed the gray right up tight against them.

Realizing the Comanches were about to burst out into the open, Touch the Sky made a final, dangerous effort. Linked to his pony only by a handful of mane, he swung his entire body free and lashed out hard with both feet full into the bearded face of the biggest bull.

After the hard impact, his legs flew down into the unbroken sea of shaggy fur and he felt himself trapped tight between two of the animals. Then, even as the momentarily intimidated bull veered sharply toward the cliff, Touch the Sky made a supreme effort to outwrestle death and won—he wrenched his upper body hard, and a moment later he was bouncing freely on the back of his pony.

The buffalo barely avoided the cliff as they swerved. Nearly half of Iron Eyes' band were not so lucky. The inexorable weight of the herd literally swept them, screaming, over the edge to a hard death on the flint and rock rubble below. This unnerved the others, who turned and fled back into the canyon on foot when their ponies panicked, several of them leaping over the cliff to death.

Touch the Sky, Little Horse, and Two Twists all raised high their lances in victory. But there was no time to celebrate now. As one, they let out their war cry and raced to join the main battle east of camp.

From the canyon brim, Iron Eyes and the remaining force of 20 had watched once again as the young medicine man defeated sure death and routed their companions. But clearly he was not infallible—look now how he rode to join the feint! These Northerners had a good deal to learn about the art of war as fought by those who had driven out the Spaniards.

He had just shed good Comanche blood. Now his tribe would pay dearly. Scalps were worthless things, good only for a bit of decoration in a war lodge. It was the *living* who were valuable. The Northern tribes were averse to slave-taking, but why? What more logical way to literally profit from revenge?

And the Cheyenne women, were they not the best and the cleanest on the Plains? Until marriage they wore a knotted-rope chastity belt, and any man who touched that belt would never smoke the common pipe again. With the dripping diseases so common, they brought top prices from the Comancheros who delivered them to their new owners.

Iron Eyes had heard the scouts speaking about this slender maiden with the cropped hair—how she was as proud as she was beautiful. The Comancheros would not miss a few bites off of a juicy steak. Before she was sold, the Comanche men would teach this beauty about pride.

Chapter 16

The battle turned out to be less fierce than it sounded.

At first Touch the Sky rejoiced when he saw the attackers fighting a retreating battle. Most of the gunshots he, Little Horse, and Two Twists had heard were from Comanche pistols. Though good Colt cavalry guns, ideal for close combat, they were ineffective at longer ranges. The Comanches were used to firing them just to make noise, in the same way that they again sounded their captured Bluecoat bugle. And like most Southern Plains tribes they were spendthrifts with ammunition. The next raid would always provide.

The Cheyennes, however, along with their cousins the Sioux, had learned bitter lessons from the blue-dressed palefaces about conserving ammunition and powder. They were also much better equipped this year with rifles. Many of the enemy's bullets and arrows had fallen short, and the attackers did not seem keen for combat with knives and battle-axes—though once an agile Comanche brave turned around to face a Cheyenne pursuer and managed to stun his pony with a vicious blow of his stone skull-cracker.

Despite the Comanche superiority on horseback, the Cheyennes had developed an evasive riding style which impressed their enemy. When within range of enemy bullets, they clung by their feet to the pony's neck, then tucked their body down so that the enemy saw only their feet and occasionally a face glimpsing at them from under the pony's head. They could even shoot accurately from this position, a fact which a taunting Kiowa soon discovered when he flew dead from his horse.

But overall, Touch the Sky noticed, the combined bands were content to lead their pursuers and avoid any battlefield heroics. It began to look more and more like a feint, not a battle. They were being drawn further and further east, away from camp.

Away from camp!

Trade rifles cracked from behind them, the plain but sturdy British guns favored by the Indians of Gray Thunder's tribe. Touch the Sky's eyes met Little Horse's. In that horrible moment, both braves suddenly realized their mistake.

When they whirled their ponies back toward camp, Two Twists joined them. Spotted Tail, Tangle Hair, and a few other Bowstrings had also heard the shots, and now the small band raced west in a skirmish line, the red streamers of their lances flying straight out in the wind.

More rifles cracked from the direction of camp; they could hear the shrill cries of the marauders even above the pounding of their galloping ponies. But all Touch the Sky could do was remember Honey Eater from the night of the Arrow Renewal, when she had looked so regally beautiful in her finery—so beautiful that even her stubbed hair could not mar her perfection.

Now he realized he had made a fatal mistake in judgment—that first band rising out of the canyon had not been the entire second force of warriors. He had shown further bad judgment when he led his friends in joining this sham attack instead of remaining at the camp.

This time he could not blame Black Elk or Wolf Who Hunts Smiling or any of his enemies. His carelessness had placed Honey Eater and the rest in danger too terrible to comprehend.

Desperately he dug his heels harder and harder into his pony's flanks. The shots from camp were less frequent now. But the first scream of a Cheyenne woman reached Touch the Sky's ears, and he cried out to Maiyun to *please* give them just a little more time.

Arrow Keeper too had watched the main battle turn into a rout by the Cheyenne braves. This was clearly not going to be another bloody Wolf Creek battle. But he knew better than to rejoice too early. His vision had clearly shown blood on the Arrows—not the literal blood of battle perhaps, but possibly a symbol of great suffering and loss for the tribe.

He had watched Touch the Sky fly past with the others to join the battle. Chief Gray Thunder too had ridden in the fight, though the Headmen would not let him leave the last line of riders. Arrow Keeper was accompanied by the elders, the women, and the children. Sure the tribe was momentarily safe, even the last of Two Twists' junior warriors had joined the main battle, eager for their first coup feather.

With their eyes fixed to the battle due east, those left in camp did not notice Iron Eyes and his force until they were swooping into the camp behind them and an old man shouted the alarm.

Their speed and agility were incredible. Arrow Keeper watched a Comanche brave lean far away from his pony and expertly scoop up a small child who was running toward a tipi, screaming. Another bore down on a young woman of about 16 winters and whisked her up onto the horse with him. He tapped her with his skull-cracker to subdue her fierce fighting.

Arrow Keeper lifted the .34-caliber British trade rifle he was carrying and fired, but his aim was off and his bullet flew wide. Besides, the Comanches moved so quickly it was nearly impossible to draw a good bead on them.

Instead, he gathered up two small children and broke for the cover of a tipi, tossing them inside. He rushed back out and encountered an old woman too stunned to move. The Comanches were not kidnapping elders, but already they had shot a few. She too he pushed to safety inside the tipi, ordering her to hold the children still.

Despite the lightning speed of the surprise assault, many in camp fought fiercely. One Comanche had been knocked soundly from his horse when a woman from the Eagle Clan swung on him with a wooden war club. But he leaped back on top of his spotted pony, whirled it around, and smashed the woman's skull so hard with his stone-cracker that Arrow Keeper heard the bone split like a walnut shell. A moment later the shrieking, drunk Comanche had scooped up a screaming girl.

He ripped off her clothing as he raced back toward the canyon, exulting in fierce, high-pitched cries. Arrow Keeper lunged toward a fallen elder and picked up another rifle. He hoped to at least drop the enemy's horse and give the girl a chance to escape on foot. But as he sighted on the Comanche's horse, another Comanche flew past closer at hand and kicked the old man hard in the skull with his stiff cavalry boot. Arrow Keeper dropped as if he'd been poleaxed.

Miraculously, Honey Eater had been missed in all the excitement. Now the main body of Comanche raiders was heading back for the canyon escape route, clutching captured children and young women. But Iron Eyes, still full of the scouts' report, had remained behind just to spot her. And now, despite the swirling dust, he lived up to his name, catching sight of a beautiful girl as she herded some crying children toward a tipi.

He wore spurs of Mexican silver. Now he gave sharp rowel tips to his horse, bearing down on the girl. His pistol cracked once and a boy was knocked to the ground, blood squirting in a high arc from a hole over his right ear. He fired again and a little girl screamed piteously when the slug lodged in her groin.

Honey Eater watched both children die before her eyes. She swept the others behind her and started to run, herding them like a prairie hen with chicks fleeing before a windstorm. The ground pounded behind her, and a child looked back and screamed, his eyes like huge black watermelon seeds in his fright.

Honey Eater too started to turn her head. A moment later she felt strong hands grip her under both arms and swing her up onto horseback.

Her suicide knife was already in her hand, but now it wasn't meant for her—not so long as a fight with child-killers was possible. She lashed out hard over one shoulder, slashing the Comanche war leader's face and almost breaking free of his grip.

Again she drew back her arm to cut him. A heartbeat later the steel butt of his pistol slammed into her temple, and she went slack.

The rest rode back to grim news: six elders and children had been slain, a dozen more wounded. More than 20 women and children were missing. Pursuit was out of the question—their ponies were exhausted from the double exertion of the hunt and the running battle. Nor could any strangers ever hope to outrun such excellent horsemen in their own country. One scout, River of Winds, was sent to follow them and blaze a trail.

And there could be no question what fate awaited the captives. Some would be tortured, no doubt, but not enough to mar their looks. They were intended for lives of degradation and slavery among Mexicans and palefaces.

An emergency council would be meeting even

before the butchering and skinning of the kill and the return to their permanent summer camp on the Powder. But though he would attend like all the other warriors, Touch the Sky's mind was made up.

He was on his own now.

A door deep down inside of him had closed, finally and permanently, on any hope of conciliating his enemies to avoid sullying the Arrows. Cooperation with the likes of Black Elk, Wolf Who Hunts Smiling, and Swift Canoe was impossible. Now he was *for* any one of them who dared cross him, and this new readiness to kill was clear in his eyes, which ran from no man.

His carelessness had allowed Honey Eater and the others to be taken. Little Horse and Two Twists constantly reminded him that they too had failed to look for a second band of Comanche. But Touch the Sky could not shake his sense of guilt, his sense that this time he had truly failed the tribe.

"Black Elk thunders to his troop brothers," Little Horse said as they met for the upcoming council. "He boasts that no Comanche or Kiowa dog will rut on his wife, that he will string their hides from his lodgepole the way they hang up roadrunner skins. At one time I admired him, brother. I thought he was straight-arrow, but I see now that he holds himself above the Arrows as does his cousin."

But it was Arrow Keeper who saw the situation as clearly as Touch the Sky did. He took his assistant aside before the meeting of the Headmen and warriors.

"You know," he said, "that the crisis is coming

to a head? That you will soon be forced to kill or be killed even within your own tribe?"

Touch the Sky nodded. But with Honey Eater a prisoner, her fate at this very moment unknown, revenge against his tribal enemies was a remote thought.

"You have done your best to avoid it. Now, they have beaten you, tried to kill you for an elk, and tricked you into setting up a pole. You have atoned one time too many for the fact that you were raised by palefaces."

"Truly, Father. But I'm done with apologies and shame. I no more chose my place than that red-tailed hawk there by the river chose his. And Father, we both know that in Black Elk's case it is not my past with white men which makes him keen to kill me."

It was Arrow Keeper's turn to nod. The entire right side of his face was swollen and bruised from the kick which had knocked him out during the raid.

"You have tried the peace road. Now your mind is swollen with thoughts of rescuing Honey Eater and the others. In your distraction, your enemies will move against you again. Do you see that it is time, once again, to separate yourself from the tribe? That this thing must be done yourself?"

Touch the Sky had already concluded the same thing. He would listen to the council, would show no disrespect. But from here on out, he rode alone and followed no man unless he chose to. They had marked him as an outsider, punished him as one. Then so be it. He would act like one.

His heart was in an agony of loss over Honey

Eater. But in that same heart he vowed silently that between them was a genuine love which gave *him,* not Black Elk, a husband's right and obligation.

If others would ride with him, fine. If not, he would ride alone. He belonged to no clan, no soldier society, and was said to have the stink which scared away the buffalo. But who among them could also say he feared any warrior?

Yes, he had a husband's right and a warrior's pride and strength and courage. He would track his enemies into the very heart of their stronghold. One way or another he would rescue Honey Eater and the others. And *any* man who interfered—including any Cheyenne—would be killed.